My
Ita
Holic

ALSO BY SUE ROBERTS

My Big Greek Summer

My Very Italian Holiday

SUE ROBERTS

Bookouture

Published by Bookouture in 2018

An imprint of StoryFire Ltd.

Carmelite House
50 Victoria Embankment
London EC4Y 0DZ

www.bookouture.com

ISBN: 978-1-78681-606-1
eBook ISBN: 978-1-78681-605-4

For all of my grandchildren.

Prologue

Someone once told me, 'life is what happens when you're busy making other plans'. It makes me wonder whether we should bother making plans in the first place.

The thing is, I used to be a real planner. Lists for everything adorned various notice boards around the house and I liked to give myself a deadline. 'Super organised' is how people would have described me. But these days, I don't plan so much, because if there's one thing I do know, it's that life can change in the blink of an eye. And no amount of planning can prepare you for that moment… Life has a funny way of turning out how you least expect it to.

Chapter One

It's a glorious afternoon and I stop to sit on my favourite green bench so I can take in Lake Ullswater in all its glory. Clusters of wild thyme are nestled amongst the grass near the water's edge, replacing the daffodils that grow in abundance in the spring.

There's a stillness about the water today that has a mesmerising effect if you stare at it long enough. The sun is streaming between trees that overhang the lake edge, creating an enchanting dappled shimmer. I watch a swallow dive and skitter across the water, sending ripples outwards. Adam and I often used to walk along this path in the late evening, where the only light came from the occasional beam of a car's headlight as it slowly navigated the country lanes. I still miss those evenings together, and I feel a pang of sadness as I think about them.

Late summer is the busiest time of year in the Lake District and the recent unbroken hot spell has seen visitor numbers soar. There are endless queues for the lake steamers that transport people along the water to various villages. In Windermere, the main departure point, restaurants and bars are bursting at the seams with people enjoying food and cool drinks in the beer gardens while children excitedly feed ducks near the water's edge. Tourists line up for the little ice cream kiosks with striped tarpaulin shades on the road that leads down to the lake. My guesthouse, here in Glenridding, is no exception – we're packed to the rafters. I was born and bred in the Lakes and feel so lucky to have spent my childhood in such an idyllic location.

I'm savouring the last few minutes of my break when a family walk past. A girl, who can't be much older than ten years old, lags behind and is soaked to the skin. Her arms are folded tightly across her chest and she has a thunderous-looking face for someone so small. The fair-haired boy, who looks a couple of years older, is walking in front and keeps turning around to smirk at her.

'Good afternoon.' I smile. 'Beautiful day isn't it?'

'Try telling that to these two,' says the mum, pointing at the kids and rolling her eyes. 'We went canoeing on the lake and my daughter capsized. She wasn't really expecting it,' she tells me in a low voice.

'Kids eh?' I reply, wondering not for the first time if I will ever become a mother myself.

I look down at my watch. It's time I headed back, so I get up from the green bench and follow in the same direction as the family.

'He pushed me in the water!' screams the slightly chubby-cheeked girl with the heavy blonde fringe, as she points at the boy.

'No I never, you stood up too near the edge,' the boy sniggers.

'Mum, tell him, he's laughing at me,' says the girl, stamping her foot.

The boy, presumably her brother, lifts his hand to make an L for loser sign above his head, before running off to catch up with Dad, who is walking several yards in front of the family, carrying a canoe.

'Dad, tell him!' screeches the girl.

Eventually, the dad stops in front of Helvellyn House and opens the brown wooden gate to a six-bedroomed bay-fronted guesthouse, similar to mine, but painted soft pink. He looks at the children and sighs.

'I'm telling you both, pack it in or we're not going to the cinema in Ambleside tonight.'

They both fall silent as the boy pokes his tongue out at his sister.

I pick up a magazine for later from Val's village store and arrive back at Lake View, my bed and breakfast business. What was once a grey and slightly dilapidated building is now an elegant cream Victorian residence with dark wooden window frames at the bay windows. The front garden, once sprouting nettles and wildflowers, is now a neat green lawn with a pretty cherry tree at the centre.

I pluck the deadheads from two hanging baskets filled with mixed peonies, nestled either side of a highly polished red front door. As I search in my handbag for the keys, I take a moment to admire the brass knocker I salvaged from an antiques fair in Keswick, a nearby market town. The sign in the window shows 'No Vacancies' and the sight of it makes me feel so lucky to live in such a special place and for things to be finally working out. There's no way I would ever have dreamed that I would be running a B&B in the Lake District with my younger sister Hannah.

I finally manage to locate my front door key, when Hannah sprints into view wearing her black and pink Lycra running gear, not a hair out of place on her short platinum crop as she bounces along. She comes to a halt right next to me, then bends forwards and places her hands on her knees.

'Jeez, I think I should stick to fell walking. This running lark is bad for my health,' she wheezes.

'Well maybe you should save the running for the cooler weather. I couldn't run for a bus in this heat, never mind around the lake.'

'That's 'cos you're not as fit as me. I could always beat you in a race,' she teases.

'That's because you've got more of an athlete's build than me,' I say, jokingly, running my hand down my shapely figure.

'Are you trying to say I look like a boy?'

'Alright, girls!' Paul Barlow says with a wink as he walks past. Paul thinks he's God's gift to women and today he's dressed in jeans and a short-sleeved white T-shirt that shows off his muscular, tattooed arms.

'I could help you work up a good sweat, Hannah,' leers Paul, ogling Hannah's trim figure.

'I bet you could. But I'm very choosy about who I do a horizontal workout with.'

'Ooh filthy mind, you. I was thinking more of the gym at the hotel across the road, show you some weight training.'

'No you're alright thanks, I don't want muscles. One Sylvester Stallone in the village is enough.'

'Oi, he's an old man, not a thirty-two-year-old prime specimen like me. I'll still take it as a compliment though,' laughs Paul as he sweeps back his dark hair.

Paul returned to Glenridding recently following a break-up, but when his mum passed away last year, I think his dad, Thomas, was glad to have Paul around again. Paul's a nice bloke really. Soft as putty deep down and the type that would do anything for anyone. He just peddles this muscle man persona about the village, which is only ever going to attract the wrong type of woman.

'See you later, gorgeous,' he growls, before heading off towards the pub.

'Not if I see you first,' says Hannah under her breath.

We both burst out laughing. I'm about to head back to work, when I'm interrupted by a desperate cry.

'Gina, hold up a minute,' shouts Rob, the gardener from the large hotel over the road.

He and my friend Katy, a receptionist at the hotel, are heading towards us, carrying a girl with long dark hair whose head is lolling forward.

'Gina,' says Katy breathlessly. 'We need to get Ellie to hospital.'

'Oh my God, what on earth has happened?' I ask, as I recognise the fifteen-year-old local girl who lives a few streets away.

'Well she drank this for a start,' says Katy, waving an empty vodka bottle. 'I found her staggering near the edge of the lake at the hotel when I nipped out for a smoke. I rang for an ambulance but they'll be forty-five minutes. The drive there is only twenty minutes but I can't leave the hotel reception.'

Before she can finish her plea, I've opened the door of my car so Katy and Rob can help Ellie onto the back seat.

'No worries,' I say, leaping into the front seat to turn the engine on.

'I'll take care of everything at Lake View this afternoon and inform Ellie's mum,' Hannah says reassuringly.

'Oh and I'm not sure about these,' says Katy, heading over towards the car window and handing me an empty foil paracetamol packet. 'I asked her if she'd taken any but she wasn't making any sense. She kept on muttering about someone called Mark, saying she couldn't bear to be without him. Sounds like boyfriend trouble, poor girl.'

As we make our way along the winding country lanes to Carlisle, I try to keep my focus both on the road and on Ellie. What if she vomits? I think, chucking a plastic bag from the footwell onto the seat behind me, hoping she has the sense to understand why. I start panicking and put my foot down – praying to God that Ellie will be OK.

Twenty-five minutes later we arrive at Carlisle hospital. I pull up outside the hospital entrance and try to attract the attention of anyone who'll listen. A kindly woman in her twenties, who's staring at her phone outside, comes to the rescue.

'Can you hold the door open, and then we'll need to lift her under her arms to carry her.' Ellie is limp but conscious, and as soon as the three of us enter the A&E department, we're greeted by red lights showing an approximate waiting time of two hours. Great.

'Excuse me, I know you're busy but we have a situation—' I squeal to the receptionist. But before I can finish speaking, Ellie is despatched to a cubicle, where a middle-aged nurse in a navy uniform swiftly appears. She begins to ask Ellie some questions but the girl is mumbling incoherently.

'Do you know if it's just alcohol she's consumed?' asks the nurse.

'No idea, a friend found her near the water's edge stumbling along with the empty bottle. She found this on the floor,' I say, handing her the empty foil packet.

The nurse attaches a blood pressure cuff to Ellie's arm as she begins her appraisal of her medical state. Ellie begins to mumble.

'Mark, why can't I see you over the summer?' she slurs before lapsing into silence.

'Ellie, who's Mark?' asks the nurse gently.

At that moment, a distraught woman bursts through into the A&E department, still wearing her slippers.

'Where's Ellie?' she cries.

'We're here.' I wave, recognising the hospital whirlwind as Ellie's mum, Lynn.

'Oh my baby, what's happened?'

Ellie lifts her mascara-streaked face. 'He said he won't be able to see me over the summer. Six whole weeks. I can't bear it.'

She rolls over to the side of the bed before vomiting violently all over the floor.

'That's good,' says the nurse, pulling a large sheet of blue paper from a roller on the wall, placing it over the vomit on the floor.

Once we are informed that Ellie is out of any imminent danger, we leave her with the nurse and I usher a stricken Lynn over to the café.

'I wish I knew what was going on with her. I don't even know who this Mark is. I asked her to invite him over for tea once, but she just rolled her eyes and told me not to be so embarrassing. She doesn't tell me anything much these days,' she says, with a wistful look in her eyes.

'Is it someone from school?' I ask.

'Yes it is. At least I think so,' Lynn replies, weeping into her coffee.

It's almost seven o'clock and Hannah and I are sharing a bottle of wine in our small flagged garden space outside the annexe, which is an extension of the bed and breakfast. It's a balmy evening with a pink-tinged sky overhead, bringing the promise of more sunshine tomorrow.

'Poor Ellie. I can't believe she thought someone was worth ending her life for.'

'You know what's strange, though? Lynn didn't know who Ellie's boyfriend was.'

'Really? That's odd. The only Mark I know in the village is Mark Spencer, the history teacher,' says Hannah, as she takes a handful of peanuts from a bowl.

'No, it couldn't be, could it?' I sigh, taking a large glug of white wine.

'Isn't he married?' Hannah asks.

'He is, yes. So it can't be him, surely?'

'Although he is going to France for the whole of the summer holidays, which would explain why Ellie couldn't see him…'

'Either way, Ellie's obviously unhappy. Maybe she could help out here, take her mind off things. I could do with someone to help me with the breakfasts in the morning, all I have at the moment is you.' I push Hannah on the arm and we both chuckle.

'That's a good idea, and it might be worth mentioning something to Ellie's mum. I mean, if Mark isn't in her class – it might be Mr Spencer?'

'I think it certainly needs checking out. If he's got nothing to hide, then it's fine isn't it?'

'I think so. It could just be a teenage crush, but I think Lynn still needs to know,' Hannah says reassuringly.

We've got a full guesthouse at the moment, which means an early start tomorrow, so we finish our drinks and head inside. I'll probably have to leave the windows open to get to sleep in this heat. I think of young Ellie. I hope she sleeps well tonight.

Chapter Two

The breakfast things are cleared away and it's only quarter to ten which is the best scenario for us. The residents were all early risers, sitting down to their breakfast at eight o'clock before going out for the day, making the most of the good weather. We serve breakfast up until ten but there are always those couples that stroll into the breakfast room at 9.50 looking bleary-eyed and slightly hungover, ready to hoover up the remains of the breakfast buffet.

I love the light and airy breakfast room mostly because of the views across the garden towards the beautiful peaks. We have light oak tables that match the floor and beige studded high-back chairs. The floor-length French windows that lead out to the garden are draped in light green curtains. Cream-coloured walls are adorned with black and white photographs of movie stars past and present. It took Adam and I a while to get this space just right, but now it's one of my favourite rooms in the house.

After the breakfast rush, I tidy up the guest bedrooms. As I straighten up the rooms, I set about placing fresh flowers in vases in each of the six rooms which are all named after famous poets. It's one of my favourite bits of the job, adding the finishing touches, and as I sit in the window seat of the Wordsworth room, I stare out at the verdant green peaks. Down the hall, I can hear Hannah singing along to a Beyoncé song on the radio while she's busy packing for a hen party weekend in Liverpool. Much as I like her friends from university, I live in fear that every meeting she has with them will ignite a desire in her to leave the village again. We're similar in so many ways, but Hannah has always had a sense of adventure. We both grew up around here but I can't help thinking that she has had her wings clipped. After studying English Literature at Lancaster Uni, she travelled to France and around Europe. When she returned, she spent a year or two working for a children's charity in Carlisle and was contemplating a trip to Asia, when my life fell apart. When Adam died everything stopped.

I silently admonish myself for having such selfish thoughts about Hannah leaving, when she bursts through the bedroom door.

'Slacking again, eh, sis?' she teases, as she picks up a blue and silver cushion from the bed and hurls it at me.

'Oi! I've just plumped those cushions up. Anyway, I'm not the one who's off gallivanting to Liverpool, am I?'

'Well I did ask you. Maybe you could do with a break. Dad would have helped out.'

'I'm sure Dad would have but I don't like to abuse his generosity unless it's a special occasion. Trawling the streets of Liverpool drunkenly, carrying inflatable willies, doesn't really qualify.'

'Oh and Lynn just called,' says Hannah. 'Ellie's being discharged today after she's had a chat with a nurse from the mental health team.'

'Thank God she's OK. They don't think it was attempted suicide, do they?'

'She didn't say. I think it's procedure after someone's been admitted after drinking too much. Talking of alcohol, I'm going to grab a bottle of Chardonnay from the wine rack – I'll replace it.' She grins.

She disappears downstairs and a few minutes later I pad down my thickly carpeted stairs but stop mid-way when I hear a loud crashing sound coming from the kitchen, followed by an expletive.

I tentatively walk into the kitchen and immediately notice that my white soup tureen has smashed onto the flagstone floor and my heart sinks a little. It was a wedding present from Adam's parents and even though I rarely use it, I'm saddened to see it shattered all over the kitchen floor.

'Sorry, sis,' says a sheepish Hannah. 'Although to be fair, you never use it. It's always sat on the shelf. Who uses soup tureens these days anyway apart from the queen?' she laughs.

She smiles that huge Julia Roberts smile that lights up the whole of her pretty face and I instantly forgive her.

I survey the mess on the kitchen floor. The ladle sits defiantly intact amongst the debris like a soldier that has survived a battle. Shards of ceramic are strewn everywhere.

'Don't worry about it,' I say, trying hard to hide my disappointment. 'Let's get this lot cleared away then we can go and have a coffee in the garden.'

The long garden at the B&B looks out towards Helvellyn, a soaring peak which attracts serious walkers. The lawn is dotted with several green wrought-iron table and chair sets, where we serve breakfast during the fine weather. Once I've set the place straight, there's nothing I enjoy more than having this quiet corner of the garden to myself. Well, with Hannah.

A strong sun is beating down and bathes the garden flowers in a glorious golden hue. These August days are long and sultry, and the evenings end with red skies promising yet more sunshine the following day. Families will return to us tonight with exhausted, rosy-cheeked children, carrying fishing nets on sticks. In the early evening I like to escape to my favourite green bench, overlooking the river, to watch the red kites and swallows circle overhead ready to swoop in search of fish.

I pour us both some coffee from a cafetière and we share a home-baked chocolate brownie as Hannah peruses the bookings in a ledger.

'I'm sorry about the soup tureen, sis. It must seem like a little bit of Adam has disappeared.'

'It doesn't matter,' I say, sipping my coffee. 'They're only possessions, aren't they? When someone you love dies, it makes you realise that material things don't matter at all.'

'I think Adam would be so proud of you,' says Hannah, reaching across the table and grabbing my hand. 'You're doing a great job here, as you can see from all the glowing TripAdvisor reviews.'

'*We're* doing a great job. I couldn't do it without you.'

'No that's true,' laughs Hannah, never one for false modesty.

'Anyway, back to business,' I say.

'Ever the professional! There's a Marco Gallardo from South America arriving around lunchtime. He's coming alone,' Hannah says, scanning the bookings and frowning slightly.

When Hannah first arrived here, she thought that any lone male guest was a serial killer and kept reminding me to lock my bedroom door at night. It took me a while to convince Hannah that actually, lots of blokes hike alone. They meet up with other walkers in pubs, exchanging notes over a pint of real ale, barren landscapes being the perfect antidote to stressful day jobs.

We currently have two families staying, two couples and one middle-aged guy in the single room. Marco will be arriving later this afternoon to take the remaining single room. Six bedrooms in total and, luckily enough, they are almost always booked out.

Hannah closes the booking ledger and stands up to leave. 'Right, I'd better get on. See you later,' she says before heading across to the annexe where we live. It's an extension which is accessed by a door at the side of the guesthouse. It's a beautiful space, flooded with natural light, thanks to the floor-length windows along one wall.

'Good morning, Dominika,' I say brightly as our cleaner arrives. 'Lovely morning, isn't it?'

Dominika started working here a couple of years ago when I was struggling to run the place, after Adam died. She's one of the family now who can turn her hand to anything. I can totally rely on her in any situation and although I love my sister to bits, the same can't always be said of Hannah.

'Good morning, yes, it is a beautiful day.' She smiles.

She doesn't often smile. With her high cheekbones, pale skin and soft blue eyes, Dominika has an alluring beauty. I thought she was very serious when I first encountered her and although she has a very cool presence, I was soon to learn that she has a wicked sense of humour.

'Oh, I almost forgot, Dad's coming around in an hour to fix a broken shelf in the kitchen. Will you let Hannah know?'

My dad does the DIY around here and I'm so grateful that he can help us with odd jobs. I never had to ask for his help in the past, as Adam was a builder. We'd painstakingly restored this crumbling old grey stone building, spending evenings and weekends stripping, plastering and painting walls. We'd work in our paint-splattered overalls, and end the night sitting on the floor eating fish and chips straight from the paper. This was the home that we planned to fill with children. I'm grateful that we got to spend three glorious summers together in the home that became our bed and breakfast business, before that fateful day. Those memories will live with me forever.

'Of course. Have a nice morning,' Dominika replies, no doubt wondering if Hannah had anything to do with the broken shelf.

'Right then I'm off,' I say, picking up my car keys from the hook on the wall in the kitchen. 'I'll be back before our new guest arrives and there's no one checking out this morning.'

One of the small inconveniences of living in a small Lakeland village is that you have to travel for things like a hairdresser, or fashionable clothes shops. But it's not all bad, as it's a scenic twenty-minute drive along winding lanes flanked by lakes and trees with green leaves that are already streaked with yellow, signalling autumn.

As I jump into the car, I think about how much I'm looking forward to having my thick red hair washed and my scalp slowly massaged. It's the one time I feel really relaxed and carefree. Even if it is only for a short while.

Chapter Three

When I arrive back at the guesthouse just before two o'clock, our new guest is being checked in by Hannah.

Marco Gallardo is tall, dark-skinned and slim. He's not drop dead gorgeous, although he has a definite sex appeal.

'So, we've put you in room two at the top of the stairs to the right.' Hannah beams. 'Can we tempt you to tea and scones at three o'clock? The scones are homemade by yours truly.'

'I will have the tea, but I don't eat scones,' he says in a South American accent. 'I like to take care of my body'. He strokes his flat, toned stomach.

Hannah and I exchange a knowing glance at one another, before he turns to us both and hovers in the hallway.

'So you don't recognise me?' he asks in surprise.

Hannah and I exchange puzzled glances.

'Sorry, no, you haven't stayed here before have you? I'm sure we would have remembered,' I say, searching the recesses of my brain for some sort of clue.

'You don't watch *Come Dance With Me*?' he asks, looking slightly crestfallen.

'No, we're more *X Factor* girls on a Saturday night. Or girlie movies.' Hannah shrugs.

Suddenly the penny drops.

'Oh, are you a dancer on *Come Dance With Me*?'

'Yes,' he says, puffing his chest out. 'The best dancer on the show, although that Damon Day thinks he is the best. He looks good because he gets the best partners,' he sniffs in his heavy accent, 'whereas I get the old women. This year I have an actress who says she is fifty-seven years old. When I meet her, she looks older than my mother. She must be at least seventy. I am stuck with someone who drags their feet along the floor like a seal's arse.'

I stifle a giggle and avoid looking at Hannah, who would undoubtedly make me erupt with laughter.

'Well I'm sure she'll soon be up to scratch with an expert like you,' she says, which makes him positively preen. 'What are you doing in these parts, anyway?'

'I have been in Blackpool for the show and I think maybe I will relax for a while. Everyone tells me I should visit the Lake District before I go home.'

'Home?'

'Mazatlan. It's a seaside resort in the south west of Mexico. I will go home after the finals in London, if I make it that far.'

He's quite uptight but it might be fun having a bit of glamour around for a few days. Hannah is just about to show Marco to his room when the front door swings open and in walks our friend Katy from the Hotel on the Water across the road.

'Hi, girls. Do you mind if I pinch a couple of your Ullswater steamer leaflets?' she asks, already picking a few from a shelf on the wall. 'We've run out. It will save me walking down to the tourist information centre. I will replace them I…'

She turns around in the hallway and stops dead in her tracks, as if she's seen a ghost.

'Oh my God, it's you! It is you, isn't it?' she says, her cheeks flushing. 'Are you Marco from *Come Dance With Me*?'

Marco flashes a smile and strides towards her before lightly taking the back of her hand and kissing it.

'I am Marco Gallardo, yes,' he states proudly.

'I knew it!' Katy says, excitedly. 'You're my favourite dancer!'

Marco is strutting like a peacock. Thank God someone recognised him; I didn't fancy dealing with a dancer with a deflated ego for three days.

'I'm so pleased to meet you!' Katy gushes. 'Are you staying here?'

'For a while days, yes. I am… how you say, *recharging my batteries*.'

'Wait till I tell my mum that one of the *Come Dance With Me* dancers is in town. She loves you all, although I think Damon Day might be her favourite.'

The temperature in the room has just plummeted to zero as Marco flares his nostrils, turns on his heels and heads up the stairs with his suitcase.

'Was it something I said?' a bemused Katy asks.

'I think you just mentioned his arch rival. It would seem these dancers have huge egos.'

'Whoops. Oh well, I'm sure he'll get over it. Right, I'll catch you later, I'd better get back with these timetables.'

Katy always manages to put her foot in it, but it's never intentional. She has the biggest heart of anyone I know, even if she also has the biggest mouth. When I lost Adam, she proved what a truly wonderful friend she was, giving me little inspirational cards and gifts and texting me every single evening to say good night. I don't know how I would have survived without her.

'Ooh by the way, have you heard from Lynn? I hope everything is OK with Ellie?' asks Katy.

'Yes, hopefully she's being discharged today after she's had a bit of a chat with someone from the medical team.'

'Good to hear. Right, see you later.'

I walk in to the kitchen to find our dad Don closing up his large black toolbox, having fixed the kitchen shelf. We bought him the toolbox with its little compartments that hold every nut, screw and bolt imaginable as a Christmas gift one year.

'Oh hello, love. I've fixed the shelf; the bracket had come loose. Maybe that big dish was too heavy for it.' As he smiles, it lights up his soft grey eyes.

I think of the soup tureen, now consigned to the rubbish bin.

'Never mind, lesson's learnt. Thanks for fixing it, Dad. I don't know what I'd do without you,' I say, planting a kiss on his cheek.

Dad lives alone in a row of stone terraced cottages nearby, which is the house I grew up in. We've always been incredibly close, especially since my mum buggered off with a dance teacher from Penrith. That was almost four years ago now. She left Dad broken-hearted, and I'm incredibly protective over him. I don't think I've ever fully forgiven her really. One day, a year after her departure, she reappeared in the village begging forgiveness after the relationship had broken down. My dad, rightly, was having none of it. She'd hurt him so much that he couldn't risk it happening again. Mum was always a vibrant, attractive woman who, over the years, had grown bored of village life and yearned for something more. Now she's living with someone ten years her junior in an apartment in Manchester. I hardly see her these days, although she has maintained some contact with Hannah.

Dad picks up his mug and drains his tea. 'Right, love, I'll be off now. I need to brush up on my geography for the quiz night at the Black Bull later, it's my one weak spot. This week there's a hundred quid up for grabs.'

'A hundred quid? I might pop over there myself, I'm pretty good at geography.'

'You should. It's about time you started getting out a bit more, love.'

I can't remember the last time I'd joined the girls on a proper night out. We used to have regular evenings out at an Italian restaurant a few miles away in Pooley Bridge, enjoying the attention from the sexy waiters.

Maybe it's time I thought about moving forward a little? A few glasses of Chianti with the girls suddenly seems like a good idea. I'll ring Katy later to arrange something.

Chapter Four

It's been a godsend having young Ellie here part-time. Her jovial nature is a big hit with the guests, and she is a different girl to the one I rushed to the hospital three weeks ago. The smile seems to have returned to her large green eyes this last week, due in no small part, I'm sure, to the presence of a hunky sixteen-year-old boy who is staying here with his family. He's providing a perfect distraction from whoever that Mark character was. Plus, I think Hannah's rather pleased with the extra pair of hands, as she skulked back from her hen party weekend sporting sunglasses and the headache from hell.

It's Monday morning now and Ellie and I are in the breakfast room. 'I wasn't trying to kill myself, you know,' Ellie tells me as she helps me set up the breakfast buffet. 'I don't want you thinking I'm a nutter or anything.'

'I wouldn't have thought anything of the sort. Everyone reacts to heartache in a different way, I suppose.' I think back to the days of my bedridden grief.

'Yeah but he wasn't even a real boyfriend, I just *really* loved him. I feel such an idiot now,' she says, placing some Danish pastries into a basket.

'No one thinks you're an idiot. I once had a massive crush on Duncan from Blue. I was convinced once he set eyes on me, that would be it. We'd set up home together and live happily ever after. I waited for him at a stage door exit for hours once, half frozen to death. When he finally emerged, he didn't even make eye contact with anyone. Security ushered him to a nearby waiting car that sped off. Talk about disappointed. Anyway, good things often come out of a bad situation.'

'I'm still waiting for that to happen.' She shrugs.

'Erm excuse me, what about working here? I'll have you know hordes of teenagers around here would give their right arm for your job.'

'I know,' she says, suddenly crushing me in an embrace. 'I'm really grateful that you've given me this job, Gina. You're so kind.'

'Oh don't worry, you're not a charity case. I need you here so I can sneak off for a few more hours here and there. Like now, for example. I'll be back in a bit. You can give Dominika a hand doing the bedrooms later.'

'But Dominika always moans at me and tells me I'm not making the beds properly,' says Ellie, pouting as she polishes some cutlery. 'She's a right fussy one.'

'*Perfectionist* is the word I think you're looking for, which is no bad thing in our business. OK, you finish up here and then you can water the plants in the garden. We've had no rain for over a week.'

'Deal!' She smiles.

Ellie looks so small and childlike with her slim frame and long brown hair, which she is wearing in plaits today. I don't think her fragile body could have taken a mixture of alcohol and tablets, so it was a relief to discover there had been only two paracetamol in the foil.

I leave the guesthouse, heading off to the graveyard to place some flowers on Adam's grave.

It's quiet when I arrive with a huge bunch of sunflowers. There's something healing about these gorgeous flowers – I love how they gravitate towards the sun, nourished and strengthened by the light. The gentle creak of the gate distracts me from my thoughts, as Old Tom walks into the graveyard. He's carrying a large bunch of freesias and lifts his hand to wave as he sees me. Tom is Paul's dad, who lost his wife Betty last year. They'd celebrated their fortieth wedding anniversary a few months earlier at the Black Bull. I wonder how anyone could bear to be parted from someone they have spent their entire life with? I think of the crushing grief I experienced when I lost Adam even after seven years.

'I was just waving to Old Tom,' I whisper to the grave. 'Did I tell you Paul Barlow is back in the village? I think Tom's really happy to have his son around again since Betty died.'

It's people that give us the strength to carry on, I think to myself as I place the sunflowers onto Adam's grave.

I arrive home around five o'clock, just as the family with the little girl return from the Peter Rabbit exhibition. It's almost September now and the evenings are starting to become a little cooler.

'I've seen Mrs Tiggy-Winkle's laundry,' exclaims Poppy, her large blue eyes sparkling. Her little hands are carrying a jute bag with a picture of Jemima Puddle-Duck on the front. The ear of a chocolate Peter Rabbit is poking out of the top.

'Have you been to Beatrix Potter's house up at Far Sawrey?' I ask her mum, Jane, as she forbids Poppy from eating any more chocolate before dinner. 'It's well worth a visit. She lived there for many years.

The vegetable patch with the little picket fence is what inspired the Peter Rabbit story, apparently. It's owned by the National Trust now, who keep it immaculate.'

'It's on our to-do list.' Jane smiles. 'This little trip is all about Poppy to be honest. We thought we were going to lose her last year,' she almost whispers, on the verge of tears, as Poppy spots Simba, our tabby cat, who has just darted in through the front door with a returning guest.

'Leukaemia. We were lucky to find a bone marrow donor and she had a transplant. She seems as right as rain now, although she obviously has to have regular check-ups.'

I can only imagine what they must have been through. But then I can't envisage ever having a child of my own. That dream died the day Adam passed away. Suddenly I have an idea.

'It's so nice taking Poppy to all these lovely places but do you ever get any time to yourself?' I ask the couple in front of me, who, despite their loving stares, look completely drained.

They glance at each other.

'To be perfectly honest, no, not really,' replies Jane. 'Phil's parents have both passed away and my mum lives forty miles away from us. She does come to stay occasionally, but she's not in the best of health and Poppy is a bit of a livewire.'

I glance at Poppy, who is now scooting along the polished floor in the hallway with open arms chasing a disinterested Simba.

'Well I can highly recommend the food at the White Lion,' I say. 'If you fancy having an evening alone I could babysit. I could cook Poppy some pasta here. I think she would be happy playing with Simba.'

I look over at our grey tabby, who has finally succumbed and is lying on her back having her tummy tickled, as Poppy giggles. Ellie walks past with some fresh towels for the guest bedrooms and smiles.

'I was looking at the menu for that place this afternoon.' Phil grins. 'If I'm honest I think it's a great idea. I could murder a good steak and a couple of glasses of red.' He looks hopefully at his wife.

'Are you sure it wouldn't be too much of an imposition?' Jane asks in surprise.

'No, not at all, it will be lovely. And you'll only be across the road. Go and spend a couple of hours together on your own.'

'Oh thank you. That's if Poppy will stay, of course. She can be a little clingy sometimes, having spent so much time in hospital.'

Poppy didn't need much convincing after I told her she could watch *The Little Mermaid* on DVD and snuggle under a mermaid blanket with a sparkly tail.

Jane and Phil dropped Poppy off at the annexe in her pyjamas and dressing gown before setting off. Simba welcomed Poppy by rubbing herself against her legs purring, much to her delight.

'Didn't know we'd started a babysitting service.' Hannah smiles as she enteres the lounge, having topped up the breakfast cereals and jams for the breakfast buffet. I told her all about the conversation with Poppy's parents and what a precious little girl Poppy is.

'Ah how awful. Thank goodness she's OK now. I can't imagine what her parents must have gone through.'

'I know, and it doesn't sound as though they get much time together on their own. That's why I offered to watch Poppy for a few hours.'

I glance at the little girl, who is twirling her feet around in the sparkly tail of the mermaid blanket and humming along to 'Under the Sea', a small bowl of strawberries on her lap, as she watches *The Little Mermaid*. I swallow a lump in my throat.

It's just after ten o'clock when Poppy's parents return from the pub to find their daughter asleep on the couch. They look relaxed and happy and I can't help but notice them untwining their hands as they walked in.

'I'll carry her up to the room.' Phil smiles. 'Once she's asleep she's out for the night. Well hopefully, anyway,' he says, casting a loving glance at his wife.

'Thank you so much,' Jane says, gently squeezing my arm. 'That was just what we needed. Good night, Hannah; thanks again, Gina.'

When they leave, Hannah pours us a large glass of Merlot each and we have just settled down to watch an episode of *Suits* on Netflix when there's a tap on the door. We glance at each other in surprise. The residents have their own key to the front door so nobody knocks at the door of the annexe after 9 p.m. unless there's a problem.

'Good evening, I am so sorry to bother you ladies.' It's Marco, looking a little sheepish. 'I have lost my key to the front door. Could you let me in?'

'Come in,' says Hannah. 'Do you fancy a nightcap?'

'A nightcap?' He frowns.

'A drink.'

'No thank you, I must not. Tomorrow I climb a mountain.'

He's been out all evening basking in the attention of the locals and looks slightly the worse for wear. The loss of keys invariably involves alcohol, and this is the third key that's gone missing this month. Maybe I should start charging for them, if this is set to be a trend.

'A mountain?' Hannah enquires. 'Really?'

"Yes, why not? I have to keep in shape,' he says, stroking his blue linen shirt, that's no doubt covering a six pack, whilst admiring himself in the mirror over the fireplace.

'Well I would check the weather first,' advises Hannah sensibly. 'I think it's meant to be quite misty in the morning and people have got into real difficulties on Helvellyn.'

'I am climbing Scafell Pike,' he says casually.

'Really?' I ask, genuinely surprised. 'Now that is a mountain. In fact, the only real mountain as all the others in the Lakes are peaks. It's only serious climbers that usually tackle it though. You do know it's over an hour's drive away from here?' I never even noticed any climbing gear; he only arrived with a holdall. 'Well good luck with that but be careful. Anyway, come on, let's get you inside,' I say, grabbing the master key from a hook and ushering him out. As he heads upstairs, tiredness suddenly takes over. I decide I'll finish my wine and go to bed, ready for whatever tomorrow throws at me.

Chapter Five

Valerie Smyth, known to everyone as Val, is standing behind the counter of Glenridding village store reading the newspaper. She's dressed in her usual attire of a polo neck sweater under a gilet and blue jeans. Val seems to have a different colour polo neck for every day of the week. Today's pale blue sweater lights up her blue eyes and emphasises her neat dark blonde bob.

The shop still has an old-fashioned bell on the front door to alert Val to customers when she nips into the back room for some stock. It's amazing how many goods fit into the long narrow aisles; every essential item you could possibly need is displayed along the shelves and in various baskets around the shop. There is even a selection of children's toys including kites, footballs and colouring books, which save the sanity of parents in the self-catering cottages. Some families arrive with teenagers imagining bonding weekends mucking about on the water all *Swallows and Amazons*, but unless children are introduced to the great outdoors from an early age, they often become bored.

'Morning, love, how are you?' asks Val, putting her newspaper down as I enter the shop.

'I'm OK thanks, bit of a headache. It's a bit cooler out there this morning. Have you heard from Daphne lately, it's her birthday coming up, isn't it?'

Daphne is Val's daughter who moved to Leeds and who I know Val misses every single day. Not that she'd let on.

'I spoke to her a few days ago. She's fine,' Val replies, not pursuing the conversation.

'Will you be visiting her around her birthday, or shall I pop her card in the post?'

I was good friends with Daphne when we were growing up. Val had named Daphne after a character in *Neighbours* and she had to endure taunts about her name all the way through school – although I imagine Val was blissfully unaware of Daphne's misfortune.

'I probably won't be visiting her on her actual birthday as that drive is a bit much for me really. She's visiting me at the end of the week though, while Ben is away on a business trip.'

Daphne left the village four years ago with Ben, a hotshot salesman who had passed through. She's now living with him in a swanky apartment.

Val can't contain her smile over Daphne's visit. Since Val's husband left the two of them have become a close team.

'Right, well I'll put the card in the post tomorrow, then. It will be nice to see Daphne again when she visits. It's good timing actually as we're having a girls' night out at the weekend, so she might like to join us.'

'That will be nice,' Val says, although the expression on her face says something entirely different. Maybe she wants her daughter all to herself at the weekend, although Daphne will make her own mind up.

We're interrupted by the doorbell tinkling and in walks Hannah with Marco. Val's hand flies to her mouth as she recognises him.

'Oh my goodness. You're that dancer from *Come Dance With Me,* aren't you?'

Marco smiles and puffs his chest out. 'Yes, I am Marco.'

He charms Val at the counter while Hannah selects some bottled water from the fridge.

'Are you going for a walk?' Val enquires.

'I am climbing the mountain,' Marco states proudly.

'Scafell? I'm not sure you should do that today.' Val frowns. 'The weather isn't looking too good. Even Malcolm Von Trapp wouldn't go up the mountains in this weather.'

'Who is Malcolm Von Trapp?' asks Marco.

'Well, it's not his real name. He's called Malcolm Evans really. He climbs the fells for charity and bursts into songs from *The Sound of Music*. He attracts quite a following, a bit like Forrest Gump. Sometimes he actually wears a nun's outfit. He's raised thousands for children's charities.'

'He sounds like a crazy man,' laughs Marco.

Not as crazy as you, I think to myself when I consider how Marco is dressed.

He's wearing jeans, a woollen jumper and a hooded jacket that looks a little flimsy. The expensive-looking brown leather boots on his feet seem solid but they're not climbing footwear.

'Marco seems to think he will sprint up Scafell,' whispers Hannah to Val. 'I'm joining him, and I can assure you we're going nowhere near it. I'll take him to one of the smaller fells, he'll never know.' She winks.

We'd seen it all before, out of towners looking at the fells and thinking it would be a breeze to reach the summit. I've lost count of the number of times mountain rescue has been out to save some ill-equipped walker, wearing the wrong gear or ignoring maps and not walking along the correct paths.

'Right,' says Val, holding the door open as we leave and turning the shop sign to closed. 'Today I'm taking a lunch break and I'll see if I can book a lovely afternoon tea for me and Daphne in Carlisle. It will be a nice birthday surprise, I'm sure Daphne will love it.'

Chapter Six

The following morning, I head up to one of the family bedrooms after breakfast has been cleared away. I tend to move a few board games between the rooms and leave some children's books in a pine bookshelf on the landing. It's the little extras like this that the families always comment on, and that then lead to repeat bookings.

Plus, I just love it when children stay. I once worked as a secretary at the local primary school and I loved it when the children popped into the office returning the class registers or running errands for their teachers. We have two bedrooms in the annexe and there was a time when we considered adding another room if me and Adam ever had children. But that will never happen now.

As I glance out of the window at a distant fell, I think of the day I finally got out of my own bed following my husband's death. I think I might have just stayed there forever had my sister not physically evacuated me from it. It was a cold morning three weeks after the tragic event, when Hannah appeared in my bedroom brandishing a white towel and a bottle of shower gel.

'Get up and have a shower,' she ordered.

I attempted to drag the duvet over my head but she persisted.

'I mean it,' she'd said, gently but firmly. 'I'm not going to hang around here and watch you rot. I know it's horrible, Gina, but life has to go on. For all of us.'

We went for a short walk the day Hannah forced me out of bed. I remember taking lungfuls of fresh air, hoping the misery would be expelled from my body as I exhaled. Each day she forced me to walk a little further until one day we'd completed several miles. Some days, Emmy, a slightly eccentric tea shop owner in the village who has a penchant for odd socks, would spot us as we walked past. She would usher us inside her café and silently appear with tea and cake. Emmy makes the most unusual cakes with flavours such as raspberry and ricotta, although I could have been eating cardboard, my senses dulled by grief.

My dad came around every morning in the days following Adam's death. Later, he was the one who would come to the grave and just sit with me, after he'd done a shift on the Ullswater steamers taking tourists out on the lake. I hazily recall a day when Dad took me by the arm and guided me back home, as I'd been at the graveside for hours, while daylight gently turned to dusk.

I've always been close to my dad. When I was a child we would go fishing together or for long walks. He taught me the names of the all the flora and fauna in the local area. We often did things as a whole family too, but I treasured my special times with Dad.

My mother came to Adam's funeral bright-eyed after a recent brow lift and stayed all of two hours before making her excuses to leave. She touched me lightly on the arm before leaving, saying, 'Let me know if there's anything I can do,' but we both knew they were empty words. I'm not convinced she even came of her own volition, more likely Hannah or Dad had told her it would be the right thing to do. But that's Mum all over.

Chapter Seven

It's Saturday evening in early September and I stare at the pile of clothing I've yanked out of my wardrobe. After much deliberation, I select a knee-length black dress and some high-heeled strappy shoes for my girls' night out. For the first time in years, to my surprise, I feel a jolt of excitement.

Hannah has a nineties CD blasting out as she sculpts her hair with some gel. She stops for a sip of prosecco every now and then, before belting out the words to the next track.

I love seeing Hannah so happy and carefree. Seeing her like this reminds me of when she was a teenager, getting ready to go out on a date with her first love, James Royle. She'd expected their love to last forever, but when she went away to university, his attention wandered as he found it difficult to cope with the separation. She hasn't been serious about anyone else since.

I'm putting the finishing touches to my make-up when Hannah tries to refill my glass but I stop her, putting my hand over it.

'I'll be legless before we even get to the restaurant if I carry on.' I smile.

'Alright then but we're having champagne at La Trattoria, or maybe prosecco. Champagne's a bit pricey isn't it?' She giggles. 'And do you know what? I do actually prefer prosecco,' she says, quaffing the remains of her glass.

The doorbell chimes and I rush along the corridor in my heels. As I open the door, I'm greeted by a vision of loveliness; Katy's wearing a sparkling silver top and skinny jeans while Daphne looks effortlessly chic, as ever, in a black off-the-shoulder jumpsuit.

'It's so good to catch up with you ladies,' Daphne squeaks as Katy beams behind her. There are hugs all around as the girls step inside.

'Have we got time for a quick drink?' pleads Katy, grabbing the remains of the bottle of prosecco and swigging it, while the taxi hoots its horn outside.

'Oh, cheers.' Daphne smiles. 'I didn't want any anyway.'

'Thanks again, Dad, you are so kind!' I call out as I run past him on reception, which he's manning in my absence, ushering the others out of the door.

Ten minutes later we pull up outside the restaurant, its sign illuminated with a soft red light. There are two large ferns in silver pots outside with white fairy lights strung through them.

We step inside to a gentle waft of garlic and all at once I feel as though I am in the middle of Rome. I gaze at the pillars, the white stuccoed arches and the sepia-coloured mural of the Coliseum. Right in the middle of the restaurant there is a fountain with pink flowers gently swirling around the base. We pass a chef who is spinning a pizza base at an open kitchen as we are shown to our table by our handsome waiter.

'Ladies, welcome. Gina, it has been too long,' says our waiter Vincenzo, pulling my chair out for me. He's tall, dark and drop dead gorgeous. I must remember to book a table here more often.

'I have missed you ladies. How beautiful you all look tonight,' he purrs as he hands us each a menu. We order two bottles of prosecco and some bottled water as we peruse the food menu.

'Ooh I don't know what to have, it all sounds divine,' I say, drooling over the dishes.

There are veal dishes with ratatouille, chicken parmigiana and a whole array of tempting delights, as well as the usual pasta and pizzas. A passing waiter is delivering a pizza to a nearby table and a waft of oregano hits my nostrils.

'I'm not having a starter,' declares Hannah. 'I'm saving myself for some gelato, or maybe tiramisu. Maybe even both. I'm absolutely ravenous.' She laughs. 'Marco is as fit as a fiddle, isn't he? I thought I was in good shape but he wore me out.'

'Oh aye?' says Katy, with a mischievous look. 'You kept that quiet!'

'I'm talking about climbing the fells,' replies Hannah with a grin. 'I didn't think he'd manage Scafell so I took him to Place Fell. Watching him practically sprint to the summit I really think he could have done Scafell after all, even without the right walking shoes. He barely paused for breath.'

'They're super fit, those dancers. I bet they've got tons of stamina.' Katy raises an eyebrow suggestively.

We fill our glasses with prosecco and I propose a toast, as Vincenzo returns to the table with some complimentary breadsticks and olives.

'Here's to friendship!' I say, as we chink our long-stemmed glasses together.

'And to moving on,' says Katy, glancing in my direction. As she finishes her glass it becomes obvious that she must have been drinking earlier tonight. Her voice is becoming increasingly loud and her flirting with the waiters is bordering on crude.

Our meals arrive after we've picked over the olives and breadsticks, and the aroma of my lasagne makes my stomach rumble. Despite having tried just about every dish here over the years, the lasagne is the one I always return to because it's simply divine. Hannah has gone for a creamy veal tagliatelle and Daphne and Katy have both opted for meatballs with linguine. The food is so delicious we barely say a word during our meal, apart from muttering the occasional groan of pleasure. We're perusing the dessert menu when Katy suddenly bangs her hands down onto the table.

'Right then. Who's for cocktails?'

I'm really in the mood for a one but I'm hoping it won't send Katy over the edge.

We beckon Vincenzo over to order our cocktails.

'So,' says Katy mischievously, 'if you were going to name cocktails after us lot what would they be called?'

'Let me give that a minute's thought,' he replies, scanning us all with his dark brown eyes.

'For you? A pocket rocket,' he tells Katy, which is fitting, given her small stature and bubbly personality. She squeals with laughter.

'And you…' He turns to Hannah. 'A golden goddess.'

She rolls her eyes.

He looks at Daphne. 'I think you have a drink named after you already – a Black Russian. Tall, dark and slender.'

'And finally, you,' he says turning to me and holding my gaze. 'A chandelier.'

'A chandelier?'

'Yes, because you light up the whole room.'

'Ooh you're as cheesy as a block of parmesan,' I say with a laugh, as he disappears to fetch our drinks. We give him a round of applause and he stops and gives a little bow, before heading off.

'Right, who's for a nightcap back at the guesthouse?' asks Hannah after we've finished our cocktails and paid the bill.

'OK,' Daphne agrees. 'But just the one, I'm going for afternoon tea with my mum tomorrow and I don't want to be hungover.'

'I'm OK, I'm on an afternoon shift,' says Katy. 'Have you got any vodka?'

I shoot Hannah a look that says *don't show her the full bottle* – we have a kind of unspoken language that only the two of us understand.

Back at the annexe Hannah cranks the music up a little and Katy stands up to dance, a little unsteady on her feet. Daphne has bid us all a good night after a small single malt whisky, so there's just the three of us.

'Ooh what I wouldn't do for a night with one of those hunks at the restaurant,' says Katy. 'Our waiter didn't even bloody notice me, though. He only had eyes for Gina.' She waves her glass in my direction.

'Hardly, he flirts with everyone. It's all part of the Italian restaurant experience.'

'Well he didn't flirt with me. I even slipped my phone number into his hand and I saw him drop it into a bin,' she huffs.

Katy's not averse to one-night stands, which is of course entirely her own business, but she always regrets it the next morning.

'You could have had your pick of the men in that restaurant,' she continues, 'but you never seem to notice. Don't you have any *needs*, Gina?'

'No, Katy, they died along with my husband,' I say a little sharply.

Hannah jumps up, trying to diffuse the tension. 'I'll make some coffee.'

'Well I couldn't manage without it for so long,' Katy witters on, completely oblivious to my feelings.

'Well maybe you've never really been in love.'

'What is love anyway? And why doesn't this house have any more booze?'

Katy stumbles up to leave when she realises there's no more alcohol left. Hannah and I escort her back to her live-in accommodation at the hotel, a few minutes' walk away.

'Well it's been lovely,' she says with a slur, squashing us in a hug as she puts the key in her front door. 'I can't wait for our next night out. Good night, Hannah. Good night, Saint Gina.'

Chapter Eight

It takes me ages to get to sleep after I've gone to bed. Saint Gina? What the bloody hell did Katy mean by that? I hope that's not the impression people have of me. I mean I do like to help people out whenever I can, but I'm no saint. Far from it. Maybe Katy's feeling a bit dissatisfied with her own life, who knows? I don't know why I'm even thinking about it really. Katy was clearly drunk and I'll never forget her kindness in the months following Adam's death. She's a lifelong friend, despite her sarcastic comment.

I lift the silver-framed photo from the dark wooden chest of drawers and smile. It's a picture of Adam and me wearing bobble hats, looking all red faced and happy. We'd just been on a circular walk around the lake. I remember it clear as day. It was around this time of year when the leaves began to change from green to gold.

Our home, which was to become Lake View Bed and Breakfast, came to us quite unexpectedly, just as we were considering renting somewhere. A widow called Iris had lived at the house for many years and the place had run into disrepair. The front garden had become overrun with nettles and some of the local children believed that a witch lived there. It didn't help that on the odd occasion that she did venture out she was dressed entirely in black. As I started to notice her less and less around the village, I called on her one day and offered to do some shopping.

The interior of the house was dark and depressing with a faint smell of damp and Iris all but lived in the front room of the house to save on heating bills. The room had a green patterned carpet, two battered old oxblood leather chesterfield sofas with throws over them and a large bookcase along one wall lined with dozens of novels. A slate fireplace lay redundant as it became too difficult for Iris to stoke up the fire with the heavy logs, a small two-bar electric heater providing warmth instead.

I began to visit her regularly, doing a little shopping and house-work and even occasionally bringing some logs and making up a roaring fire. It was sad watching Iris become frail and practically housebound. I remembered her as a formidable post mistress at Glenridding General Store before Val owned it. Over the years, she had changed so much.

Iris once told me that she liked Adam and felt that we were a perfect match. 'I can usually sense these things,' she'd assured me. 'I'm so pleased for you, Gina. You deserve to be happy.'

One bright spring morning Iris came out carrying a tea tray as Adam and I were tidying her garden.

'Now then you two, sit down,' she commanded. 'Have you seen any houses you want to buy around here?'

'Plenty,' said Adam. 'But none that we can afford without a lottery win.' He shrugged.

'Do you like this house?

'Yes, it's beautiful. Who wouldn't?'

'Well that's what I thought,' said Iris as she lifted the teapot with her papery hands and poured the tea. 'And being young, you would have the energy to update the place. I can't imagine the current décor is to your taste.' She smiled.

Adam and I glanced at each other.

'What are you saying?' I asked tentatively.

'Well, why don't you have this place? I haven't got long left in this world and it sickens me that young people can't afford a home in the village they grew up in.' Iris and her deceased husband Bob had never been blessed with children and she was the last surviving member of her own family, so there was nobody to inherit Lake View Cottage.

'You mean buy it from you?' I asked, suddenly feeling an excitement in the pit of my stomach.

'Well I might as well just let you have it. All I ask is that I have one room to live in. I won't be any bother.'

There was no way we would have taken the house from Iris, but we did agree on a generously discounted price as the house needed updating. We gutted the whole place over the year that followed, Iris growing ever frailer as she watched our progress with a constant smile. It was almost as if she had waited until the last set of curtains were hung before she passed away peacefully in her favourite chair.

Adam's building skills had turned four large bedrooms into six and saw an extension built on the side of the house as the idea of a guesthouse began to take hold. I remember the day it was completed, standing outside admiring all of our hard work, my head resting on Adam's shoulder as I dreamt of our future together. We managed to agree on the front door being a shiny red colour, which was my idea, rather than Adam's suggestion of blue. It amused me that our ideas for décor were always completely opposite, yet in every other way we got along so well. We did agree on one thing though. Lake View Bed and Breakfast looked absolutely stunning. We opened its doors in the late summer and were almost solidly booked from day one. If only we could have stayed in that happy bubble forever.

Chapter Nine

It's just after twelve and I'm tidying up in the lounge when Dominika is about to leave. Hannah seems to have gone AWOL.

'Have you seen Hannah?' I ask Dominika.

'Yes, she is in the garden, dancing. At least I think that's what you call it,' she says, without expression. 'See you tomorrow.'

I walk outside to find Marco standing with his hand on his hip shaking his head. 'No, no, no! You have to keep the upper body still. Move the bottom half of your body only.'

'Oh, I get it, like the River Dance? Well you should have said.'

They spin around the patio, Marco tutting then finally cursing as Hannah steps on his toes and he loses his balance, landing squarely in one of the garden chairs. I emerge from my hiding place and burst out laughing.

'Your sister will never make a dancer,' he tuts. 'Perhaps I can teach you a few steps before I leave?'

'I'm sorry, I'm afraid it runs in the family, Marco. Two left feet, both of us.'

Marco shakes his head and disappears upstairs to collect his bags. He's checking out shortly and we'll be sorry to see him go. Since he's been with us, he's shared all kinds of gossip about the stars of

Come Dance With Me that we have sworn we will take to the grave. Although I'm not sure all of it's true. I still find it hard to believe that Damon Day takes the female dancer's sequinned dresses home and parades around in them in secret…

We wave Marco goodbye as his hire car disappears out of view. It always feels bittersweet when a guest leaves but we've promised to tune in to every show from now on, on a Saturday evening.

As I turn back inside, I'm debating what to do this afternoon when a text pings through from Katy:

R U free this afternoon? Fancy meeting at the Cabin at 1?
K. Xxx

The Cabin is the Helvellyn café at the foot of the peak. It's a log cabin that sells huge cooked breakfasts to sustain the walkers as well as an assortment of homemade cakes and scones. It's been a while since I've been there and indulged in a caramel chocolate brownie and it beats making my way through the never-ending to-do lists at the guesthouse.

As I set off to meet Katy I bump into Jean, the landlady of the Traveller's Inn, who tells me they will be hosting a karaoke evening the following Friday.

'Spread the word.' The bubbly Jean, who's wearing her blonde hair piled up loosely on her head, smiles. She's goton jeans and a rock band T-shirt that gives her the appearance of someone far younger than her sixty years.

I arrive at the Cabin just before Katy, who I watch from the window as she walks along the gravel path towards the café, with her head down and hands stuffed into the pockets of her green parka. Her hair is tied back today and she isn't wearing make-up which is unusual. She acknowledges me at the corner table before going straight to the counter and ordering two lattes and a caramel brownie.

'These are on me,' she says as she places the tray down on the table.

'Aren't you having a cake?' I ask.

'No, I feel a bit hungover,' she says quietly. 'I just wanted to say sorry for last night. I was a bit of a cow, wasn't I?'

'A bit thoughtless maybe.' I stir my coffee. 'And do you remember calling me Saint Gina?'

'Oh bloody hell, did I? I'm sorry, Gina. Maybe I just wish I was a bit more like you.'

'What, bereaved?'

There is a silence for a second then we both burst out laughing.

'Oh I'm sorry,' says Katy, reaching across the table to give me a hug. 'Anyway, you know what I mean. Even with all the things that have happened to you, your mum leaving, then Adam dying, you just seem so together. My life's a mess. I'm nearly thirty and living in staff accommodation in a hotel and I can't seem to meet anyone to settle down with. Not how I imagined how my life would be.' She sighs.

'Hmm, well maybe you should get to know blokes before you sleep with them.' I am honest with her, as only a best friend can be. 'Give yourself a chance to get to know someone first, before getting carried away.'

'I know what you say is true and I always feel bad the next morning, but it's nice to feel that closeness to someone. I often think that maybe it could be the start of something, but it never is.'

'That's because you meet them at the hotel. They're only there for five minutes before moving on. You need to meet someone in the real world,' I say, before taking a mouthful of my utterly delicious, gooey caramel chocolate brownie.

'Oh sure, around here?' She gestures to the rolling hills and peaks outside. 'It's not exactly the throbbing metropolis of the North, is it?'

'Have you thought about trying an online dating site?'

'No thanks. One of the hotel guests put me right off that. She met this bloke who seemed perfectly OK in the beginning but she decided he wasn't for her when she realised he was obsessed with *The Lord of the Rings*. His whole two-bedroomed house was an exact replica of the Hobbit house. When she broke things off he stalked her for two months until he was issued with a restraining order.'

'Oh no. I'm sure there are many success stories though. In fact, I know so. My cousin in Liverpool met her husband on the Internet. They've just celebrated their tenth wedding anniversary.'

'Well whatever, it doesn't appeal to me. I'm thinking maybe I need a change. I've done all my exams in hospitality now, so I might start to look for a job in a big city. Or maybe even the cruise ships, as that's a way to see the world, isn't it?'

'Working on the cruise ships sounds good, although didn't you get seasick on the local steamers when you were little? I seem to remember you throwing up into some woman's handbag.' I laugh.

'Oh God I did, didn't I? I think I was about seven years old. Thank goodness I've grown out of that now; besides I've heard that you don't really feel the motion of the sea on those huge cruise liners. Anyway, let's wait and see. Things in life can suddenly change, can't they? As you well know,' she says gently.

'I know. Anyway, talking of change, would you believe Jean has talked Ted into having a karaoke night next Friday at the Traveller's. Are you up for that?'

'Karaoke, really? Too right I am. Good old Jean. Ted swore he would never go in for that stuff. He's all about real ales and conversation. He'll be selling porn star Martinis next!'

'I know, I doubt it will be a regular occurrence. It might depend on how it affects his profits though,' I say, laughing.

As I smile at Katy, I realise I'm actually beginning to enjoy my life again. I'll never stop missing Adam but I think I've accepted his death now. I consider how healing the Lake District has been for me. And who knows what tomorrow may bring?

Chapter Ten

It's late September and the weather feels a bit strange today. The sky is a curious mixture of orange and grey with solemn black clouds hovering in the distance. I hope it doesn't rain too much as the water levels are already pretty high. You can predict the weather when you live in the countryside as your whole body becomes like a human barometer. I get slightly stiff joints when it's about to rain and a thudding headache before a thunderstorm. Plus, the air smells different. There is an earthy pungent smell as the rain clouds drift overhead.

It's just before lunchtime and I've popped to the Traveller's Inn over the road to borrow another shovel from the landlord, Ted. Leaves are steadily dropping from the leaves in our garden as autumn approaches and I think it's about time Hannah gave me a hand clearing them.

The Inn is a whitewashed eighteenth-century building, all horse-brass and oak beams with red velour bar stools. Usually the most exciting thing that happens here is the occasional live band, the weekly quiz night, or if the quiz machine actually pays out, as it did to a passing tourist last week – much to the rage of the locals.

'Hi, do you have a shovel I can borrow, please?' I ask Ted, who is bringing a crate of mixers up from the cellar.

I notice he has some new flavour crisps behind the bar, including sea salt, balsamic vinegar and crushed black pepper. Seems he's going all out for this karaoke night.

'Hello, Gina love, yes there's one at the side of the pub near the recycling bin, you can grab it on your way out. Are you stopping for a drink?'

'No thanks, it's a bit early for me, I'm saving myself for tonight. I'm looking forward to the karaoke.'

'I'm not sure I am,' grumbles Ted. 'It was all Jean's idea.'

'I'm sure it will be a huge success. Anyway, see you later. Thanks for the loan of the shovel.'

'Not a problem. See you tonight. Ta-ra, love.'

As predicted, the heavens opened just after lunch and there's been a steady downpouring of rain throughout the day. The weather has forced me to stay indoors and catch up on some paperwork, as well as order some new pillows online. All in all, it's been quite a productive day.

It's almost seven thirty in the evening now, as I hurry along to the pub, which is surprisingly full considering the filthy weather outside. A stage has been erected in a corner of the lounge bar, where the karaoke machine stands and disco lights silently flash beams across the original oak wooden floor.

I shake out my umbrella and place it in a stand near the front door. The pub is only a two-minute walk from the B&B but it's still pouring down outside. Daphne raises an arm as she sees me and pats an empty seat beside her.

'Great, thanks for getting a table. I didn't expect it to be this busy if I'm honest,' I say, removing my wax jacket and placing it over the back of my chair.

'Me neither,' replies Daphne. 'Is Hannah not coming over?'

'In a little while. She's on the phone to my mother, no doubt listening to her latest drama. Anyway, I'm getting a drink, anyone need one?' I say even though I notice their glasses are over half full.

'We're alright, love,' says Val, who has made a bit of an effort this evening. She looks attractive in black trousers and a pretty grey top that matches her eyes. I honestly can't remember the last time I've seen her in anything other than roll neck jumpers and jeans, apart from at my wedding when she wore a striking turquoise two piece.

I order a glass of cider at the bar and I notice a bloke with fully tattooed arms and wearing a black hat, staring at me.

'DJ Steve,' he says, holding his hand out. 'Can I buy you that?' He gestures to the amber-coloured liquid Ted has just placed on the bar.

'No thanks,' I say brightly.

'Not a problem,' he replies, removing his sunglasses and looking me up and down. 'Maybe later, eh?'

Maybe not, I think to myself. And who the hell wears sunglasses indoors? In the Lake District. In the middle of a storm.

'Attracting attention already, eh, Gina?' teases Daphne when I sit down at the table.

'Oh yeah, from DJ Steve the sleaze? Lucky me!' I laugh. 'How was your trip to Carlisle?' I ask Daphne.

'It was really nice actually. It was good to spend some time with Mum. I probably bought a load of things I don't even need.'

'Even though you have all those shops in Leeds?'

'I know. They're all a bit soulless though. You might be able to buy a designer dress in a fancy place like Harvey Nicks, but none of them have the heart of the shops around here.' She sighs. 'I never thought I'd miss this place so much.'

Katy arrives a few minutes later, having just finished her shift, and heads straight for the bar. She's wearing denim shorts over black tights and DJ Steve wastes no time in chatting her up. Paul is sat at the opposite end of the bar nursing a pint of lager and he gives Katy the once-over as she walks past. If my memory serves me right, I think she may have once had a bit of a fling with Paul. Katy accepts Steve's offer of a drink and jumps up onto an adjacent barstool. She lifts her hand and waves at us, but I get the feeling we won't be seeing very much of her this evening.

Half an hour later Hannah arrives, just as someone is murdering 'My Way' on the karaoke.

'Jesus, has Ted got any earplugs?' laughs Hannah as she returns from the bar and takes a sip of Mountain Runner, a local honey-coloured real ale.

A stern-faced middle-aged woman on the next table taps Hannah on the shoulder.

'Excuse me, love, that's my husband up there. He's only having a bit of fun.'

'Fun for who?' mumbles Hannah into her beer, but audible enough for the wife to hear. Hannah's right though, he sounds like a dog being strangled.

'Who do you think you are? He enjoys a good singsong, does my Kevin. Where's the harm in that?'

'No harm at all,' agrees Hannah. 'I just don't know why he has to inflict it on the rest of us.'

Uh oh.

'Well you're a bloody laugh a minute, aren't you?' The woman is now on her feet hovering over our table with her hands on her hips. Karaoke Kev is attempting a high note, unaware of the unfolding drama.

'Look, I don't mean to be nasty but karaoke is just so bloody self- indulgent. If you have a half decent voice, that's fine. In fact it's great, it's entertaining. If you're tone deaf you should stick to singing in the shower. I mean, I like watercolour painting but I don't expect people to hang my pictures on their living room wall.' Hannah laughs, rolling her eyes.

A bloke at the bar almost spits his beer out. He's been watching us the whole time, a smile spreading across his face.

'Miserable bloody cow,' replies the wife, retreating to her table as her husband strides towards her with a satisfied grin on his face. She obviously tells him what Hannah has said as they both turn, giving us filthy looks.

Val and Daphne nip to the toilets as the good-looking, fair-haired bloke from the bar strolls over and sits on one of the empty stools next to Hannah.

'I could do with someone like you working for me,' he says, smiling. 'My supervisor wouldn't say boo to a goose. The shop floor staff are getting away with murder. Greg Marsh.' He extends a hand to Hannah. 'Pleased to meet you.'

'Hi,' says Hannah, who seems to have flushed a little pink. Or maybe it's the glow of the red flashing disco light.

'I'm Hannah and this is my big sister Gina.'

Val and Daphne reappear once the introductions are over, and Greg pulls an empty stool over from another table and settles in.

'So, ladies, can I buy you all a drink?' he offers, standing up to go to the bar.

He returns to the table with a tray of drinks, just as the karaoke is taking a break and DJ Steve is playing a Kylie Minogue song.

'So,' says Hannah. 'What brings you around these parts?'

'My cousin's wedding at the Hotel on the Water. The beer at the bar is shocking and overpriced so I've sneaked out for a pint of real ale. I've been there all day so I'm sure they won't miss me. I left as a load of sugar-hyped kids were zooming around the dance floor to the "Superman" song. It should be safe to go back soon. Are you ladies local?' he asks, making eye contact with everyone.

'All of us live across the road,' I say. 'The B&B is run by me and Hannah and the shop is owned by Val.'

'I'm local too.' Daphne smiles. 'Although I've defected to Leeds.'

'Ah, seduced by the big city, eh?' he says, before taking a sip of Wainwright's bitter.

'Something like that.' Daphne sips her Chardonnay.

'What about you, do you live in the Lakes?' asks Hannah.

'Ulverston. I work at the Derwent pencil factory as a production manager. And before you say it, I know, it doesn't sound like the most exciting job in the world but it actually is pretty interesting.'

Hannah raises an eyebrow.

'No, really,' says Greg. 'For example, did you know that the humble Derwent pencil assisted the RAF during World War Two? A tiny compass and a map of Germany were embedded in the pencil, only revealed when it was broken in half. They were manufactured in secret. Could have meant the difference between life and death.'

'We went on a school trip to the pencil museum once' recalls Hannah. 'It was nearly as exciting as the lawnmower museum.'

'Everyone in the lake district has been to the pencil museum on a school trip, I think' laughs Greg. 'And did you just say that there's a lawnmower museum'?

'Yeah in Southport. Dad took us there when we went on holiday one year. Mum stayed at the hotel bar, chatting to a load of blokes in pastel coloured jumpers who were on a golf weekend, whilst dad fantasised about owning a solar powered flymo.'

Hannah and Greg seem captivated with each other, so we leave them to discuss the finer points of rubbish museums.

Val is perusing the karaoke songbook when we hear the sound of clapping and a 'whoop whoop' from DJ Steve, Paul and a few other blokes from the bar area as Katy makes her way towards the karaoke.

She starts to belt out a ballad about hunky men and by the time she has reached the chorus of 'My Kind of Guy' we are all on our feet joining in. Katy is raising the roof with her fabulous singing voice. I howl at her choice of song and she points to the group of men at the bar every time she sings the chorus, enjoying every single minute.

'She's bloody brilliant, isn't she?' Jean says, as she collects some glasses from our table. 'She's wasted around here. She should go on *X Factor*.'

Katy exits the small stage to thunderous applause and resumes her place at the bar surrounded by her adoring male fan club.

During another break from the karaoke, Katy comes over and joins us at the table for a drink.

'Hi, ladies, are you all having a good time?' She beams.

'Yeah it's great isn't it? And wow! Katy, I knew you could hold a tune, but you were brilliant up there,' I say.

'Ooh you were, love, just like a real pop star,' says Val. 'I was considering getting up and doing a number myself, but I couldn't have topped you.'

'Thank goodness for that,' Daphne whispers to Katy.

'You were amazing,' I tell her.

'I'm just having a bit of a laugh. Makes a change seeing some different faces in here tonight. I don't fancy any of them though.' She laughs. 'Actually, DJ Steve was telling me that he used to work on the cruise ships. I told him I'd love to do that myself. He said there's a mass recruitment day coming up soon at the Adelphi hotel in Liverpool. I might have a look into that.'

After the last stint of karaoke, which is by now warbling drunkards singing the wrong song lyrics, DJ Steve plays a Jennifer Lopez number that has everyone heading for the dance floor. Daphne grabs Val by the hand.

'Come on, Mum, let's have a boogie.' She smiles, shaking her sleek dark hair over her shoulder. I decide to join them on the dance floor, leaving Hannah and Greg alone.

I wink at Hannah across the table and she flushes slightly. And this time I'm pretty sure it's not the glow of the disco light.

Chapter Eleven

We arrive back at the B&B just before eleven o'clock and Hannah adds a pod to the coffee machine to make us a latte.

'Well that was a good night,' I say, opening the cupboard in search of some crisps.

We move into the living room with our karaoke recovery kit of warm drinks and gossip to pick over. We're just settled on the sofa with our drinks when a text pings through on Hannah's phone. A huge grin spreads across her face.

'Do tell,' I say with a smile.

'It's from Greg. He says the slow dances have started at the wedding and he wishes I was there to dance with him.'

'Ooh I think he was quite taken with you. Although judging by the look on your face, the feeling is mutual,' I tease.

'He was nice though, wasn't he?' Hannah curls up on the sofa, having thrown her boots off.

'He seems like a really genuine guy and he wasted no time in texting you either. I'd say you made quite an impression on him.'

'I hope so, I really liked him. I felt as though I'd known him for ages.'

I look at my generous, wise younger sister and feel overcome; I really hope it's like this forever. We're sat hugging on the appropriately named 'snuggle' chair when the telephone rings. We both glance at each other as one does when there's a late-night call on the landline. It's Aldo, the owner of La Trattoria.

Hannah casts a quizzical glance.

'Oh no, are you alright? Yes, yes I do have a room actually. No, we're fine down here, sounds like you've taken the brunt of it. OK, no problem, we'll see him tomorrow.'

'What was that about?' asks Hannah, uncurling herself from the chair with an anxious look on her face.

"That was Aldo from the restaurant. Pooley Bridge has been flooded out including Aldo's house and his nephew is arriving from Italy in the morning so he's asked if he can stay here. Emergency services have been there for the last two hours. I'd drive over but I'm over the limit.'

'Me too, I don't think they'd want more people arriving anyway if the roads are blocked. We'll see what we can do tomorrow.'

We flick the television on and the extent of the flood damage becomes clear. The main road looks like an extension of the river, with several abandoned cars floating by.

'Oh no!' says Hannah as she takes in the scene. Emergency crews are taking people to a community centre a couple of miles away on higher ground that is unaffected. Listening to the reporter, it seems nobody is unaccounted for, which is a blessing.

We've had our fair share of floods over the years when the river that flows through the village has spilled over following prolonged rainfall. The community spirit really comes alive at times like that, making me feel a part of something that the anonymity of a big city could never offer.

It's strange to think we had all been dancing away in the pub unaware of the drama unfolding just a few miles away.

'Right, come on, let's get to bed,' I say, switching off the television. 'We've still got guests to think of in the morning who will expect business as usual, not a pair of bleary-eyed hosts. We've got our Italian guest arriving just after lunchtime too.'

'Oh yeah.' Hannah grins. 'I wonder what he's like?'

'Who knows? Anyway, good night. We've got a busy day ahead of us tomorrow.'

'I know. Night, sis. Sweet dreams.'

Chapter Twelve

The following morning one of our guest families, the Hunters, are sitting in the dining room perusing the breakfast menu. The wife orders scrambled eggs on toast, along with the young daughter, while the dad orders a full English breakfast, 'with extra bacon'. Meanwhile the son, who is a mini version of the dad, asks for pancakes. 'With Nutella,' he demands.

I don't have any Nutella but I'll quietly despatch Hannah to Val's in search of some. Dominika makes the best pancakes, so I steer her into the kitchen.

'The chubby child has no manners. I never heard a please or thanks. Maybe I should add a little tabasco sauce to the pancake mix.'

'Can I trust you to just make them while I get on with the cooked breakfasts?'

'Yes, Gina, I only have a joke with you.' She smiles, but I'm watching her.

Once the empty breakfast dishes are brought into the kitchen, I notice the jar of Nutella is empty.

'God, what a greedy kid,' says Hannah. 'A whole bloody jar of Nutella. He was slathering it on everything – not just the pancakes.'

'Really?'

'Yep. Buns, croissants, pastries, you name it.'

We're just giving the kitchen a final wipe down when the Hunter family eventually emerge from the dining room. The dad had read his newspaper from cover to cover, consuming endless cups of tea whilst his bored wife looked on. The boy looks deathly white.

'I feel sick,' he suddenly announces, clutching his stomach.

No surprise there then. He makes a strange belching sound before clutching his stomach again. Oh no.

'There's a toilet just here,' I say, steering him towards one that's just off the entrance hall. He seems to be turning greener with every step we take.

'I'm not sure I can make it,' he says. 'Mum, I'm going to be sick—'

He barely gets the word out of his mouth before he projectile vomits a pool of mud-coloured slush all over the parquet floor. I want to puke too. God knows what he must have eaten the day before but it smells like a dead rat.

'Good God,' says Dominika. 'That looks as if it has come out of his arse.'

'Dominika, you're not helping. Please go and get the blue cleaning roll and some disinfectant.'

'Well there must have been something wrong with the food,' grumbles Mr Hunter. 'We should put in a claim if it's made the lad ill.'

'Don't you bloody dare,' says Mrs Hunter, rounding on him. 'There was absolutely nothing wrong with the food, it was delicious. You never stop him when he eats too much and when I try to interrupt him you tell me *he's a growing lad.* Some role model you are, Douglas.' She pokes her husband's paunch.

Douglas is standing there with his mouth open.

'And you can stay here and look after him. Come on, Lexie, we're going out,' she says, grabbing the young daughter by the hand and heading for the door. She pushes the front door open with Douglas shouting after her, asking her when she will be back.

'I don't bloody know!' she screams across the hall as she holds the door open and smiles at a tall, dark and handsome stranger.

'I believe I have a reservation here. I hope I haven't come at a bad time. My name is Fabio Garcia,' says the guest before flaring his nostrils and asking, 'I don't wish to be rude but what on earth is that disgusting smell?'

Fabio is ushered into the lounge, with Hannah offering him some coffee and walnut cake.

'I don't think I should be sitting around eating cake,' he says a little tersely. 'I must go and see if my uncle is alright. I would be grateful if you could please just show me to my room.'

'No problem,' I say brightly. 'Follow me, you'll find tea and coffee making facilities in your room anyway.'

Fabio is booked into a single room which overlooks the fells. It has a dark wood writing desk and fitted wardrobes along one wall, with black and white prints of the lakes hanging on the nutmeg-coloured walls. It feels sophisticated, yet charming, and I hope it will suit Fabio perfectly.

After Fabio is checked in, I trundle back downstairs and find Hannah placing the cake underneath a cake dome, making sure to cut a gigantic wedge off first. 'I don't think I'll offer these fit blokes any more of my cake. They're all far too body conscious. They don't know what they're missing though,' she says, taking a bite of the cake, making appreciative noises. I don't know how she stays so slim, although she never seems to sit still for long and she does enjoy strenuous fell walks I suppose.

'I think he's just keen to see Aldo. I might offer him a lift with us in the 4x4 when we head over to assess the flood damage later. That small hire car will never make it through any flood waters.'

'Ooh is he going to sit in the front with you, Gina?' Hannah laughs, nudging me. 'Don't pretend you haven't noticed how hunky he is. Better not let Katy clap eyes on him.'

'Hunky, really? I hadn't noticed.'

'Yeah, right…'

Fabio is about to leave the B&B without a word when I intercept him in the hall and offer to take him to Pooley Bridge in the car with us. He seems a little reluctant to accept the offer until I tell him he might do some damage to the hire car.

'OK, you know best.' He shrugs, folding a map of the local area and putting it into the pocket of his expensive-looking leather jacket.

We drive the few miles in virtual silence as Fabio stares out of the window. I'm not sure whether he is just admiring the stunning scenery or wishing he was somewhere else. I suspect the latter.

'So,' says Hannah in an attempt to engage our guest in conversation. 'Did you have a good journey here?' She cranes as far as her seatbelt will allow in his direction.

'Uneventful,' replies Fabio, briefly turning around before staring out of the window again. I notice his deep blue eyes, which look unusual against his tanned skin and dark hair. It's a striking combination.

'Well, uneventful is good.' She smiles. 'Last time I got on a plane from France a man had a heart attack and we had to be diverted to Orly airport instead of Charles de Gaulle.'

Fabio grunts slightly.

'Oh and remember when I got stopped at customs because I had a pair of scissors in my bag,' I recall.

'It wasn't just a pair of scissors, Gina. You had scissors, a Stanley knife, a roll of Sellotape and a huge tub of green glitter.'

Fabio looks puzzled.

'I used to work in a school,' I explain. 'I was working on a project for the entrance hall and had forgotten they were in that bag, which was huge. Customs staff seemed a little uncertain about my explanation though. I mean what did they think I was going to do with all that stuff? Tape someone to a chair and threaten them with a knife before turning them into a Christmas tree?'

In the rear-view mirror, I notice a smile at the corners of Fabio's mouth.

We arrive in Pooley Bridge a few minutes later and park the car at the end of the high street. Most of the water has thankfully subsided as it often does with a flash flood and furniture is standing outside of people's front doors as they mop the debris from inside.

Dad is outside La Trattoria with Aldo and raises his hand to wave us over as soon as he spots us.

Fabio and Aldo greet each other with a real Italian welcome as they kiss each other on the cheek and embrace.

'You are looking so well,' Aldo says, smiling at his nephew. 'I am sorry to divert you to Gina's guesthouse but my house is flooded. Luckily the restaurant hasn't been hit too hard, just an inch or two of water inside but we've managed to clear it out. I'm hoping that we won't be out of action for any longer than a day or two.'

The restaurant is at the top of a street, which has a slight incline so luckily much of the water has passed through and settled down at the bottom of the valley.

'And now,' says Aldo, patting Fabio on the back, 'I will take you for a late lunch. Just a short drive into Ambleside. I know a fine restaurant.'

'As good as yours?' Fabio smiles.

'There is no comparison as it is not Italian,' laughs Aldo.

'Would you like us to put a camp bed in Fabio's room, Aldo?' I call over, assuming he'll want to spend some more time with his nephew.

'Gina, you are an angel but there is no need. I will manage in the upstairs of my house for now; it's just that it's no place for a guest.' He smiles. 'But thank you.'

I remember when Aldo first opened his restaurant in the village over twenty years ago, causing great excitement amongst the locals. We went there as a family when I was a young girl and I can still remember the thrill of eating the most delicious pizza I had ever tasted, followed by tutti frutti ice cream. As the years went by

I recall Aldo standing in the doorway of the restaurant before opening times, wearing a blood-red waistcoat over a white shirt, puffing on a large cigar and looking like a film star. He had brown curly hair and a strong, manly face with smiling brown eyes. He is still an attractive man although his face is now craggy and his hair completely grey.

Hannah and I stay on with Dad in the village to check that all the other local businesses are OK. We're there in a heartbeat to help Dad out in any situation, just as he has been for us over the years.

Fabio arrives back at the B&B just after seven that evening as Hannah heads to the annexe to get ready for a night out with Greg. He's driving over from Ulverston and has booked a room at the White Lion, where he is taking Hannah for dinner. I ask Hannah if she will be coming home tonight and she looks slightly affronted.

'Gina, this is a first date! I'm not going to be spending the night with him. He's only staying over because he's hoping to enjoy a few beers.' She grins.

'We'll see. You're a grown woman you can do what you like, see how things go.'

Fabio smiles at me as he walks through the hall.

'Did you have a nice afternoon?' I ask cheerfully.

'Yes thank you. It was lovely spending time with my uncle.' His demeanour is so much more relaxed now.

'Do you fancy a drink?' I ask, gesturing to the lounge that has a small bar area in the corner. Fabio hesitates for a moment before nodding his head and following me. There are no other guests about and to be honest, there often aren't as all the bedrooms have televisions.

'Nice room,' says Fabio, casting an eye around the large bay windowed space, furnished in hues of grey with splashes of orange. There are two large comfortable sofas and a huge stone-coloured rug on the polished wooden floor. We have a wood burner along the main cream-coloured wall and there are several displays of wooden twigs and holly, artfully crafted by Hannah, as well as vibrant cushion covers made by Daphne.

'Thanks. It took a while to get it just right. My husband and I could never agree on colour schemes.'

'I am sorry to hear about your husband, my uncle told me,' says Fabio sincerely.

'Thanks. For a long time, it all seemed a little surreal.'

'What happened? Or is something you don't like to talk about?'

'I don't mind. In fact, I quite like talking about Adam, I don't want him to be forgotten. He just went out one day for a walk on the fells with a friend and never came home. It had been raining and he lost his footing on a slippery ridge and fell forty feet to his death. I've come to terms with it now, largely thanks to the huge support I've been shown from family and friends.'

'Heartbreak is a terrible thing. Especially if you weren't expecting it.' Fabio sighs and I wonder if he has also experienced the loss of a loved one.

I retrieve a bottle from a drinks cabinet and pour us each a single malt whisky, before sitting opposite him on one of the large grey fabric sofas, a slate coffee table between us.

'So is this just a social visit to see your uncle, if you don't mind me asking?'

'If only it were as simple as that.' He exhales deeply and sinks back into the squashy sofa. 'I am here to run some ideas by my uncle Aldo. My grandmother has died recently and left me a guesthouse in Italy. It's a bit of a mess at the moment. Two of the rooms haven't been used for a while as there's a problem with the plumbing. I think Grandmother let things slide a little as she got older. The place needs a lot of updating and I know nothing about running a hotel,' he explains as he sips his Scotch and visibly relaxes.

'I'm sorry to hear about your grandmother. Is the hotel still open?'

'Yes, mainly for students and walkers who are passing through and exploring the mountains. It's not the place for couples seeking a romantic weekend away, I'm afraid. At least not at the moment.'

'What is it you do for a living?' I ask.

'I'm an accountant. Running the business side of the hotel would be no problem but that's about it. I know nothing about hospitality and soft furnishings,' he says as he swirls his drink about the glass.

'Don't you have any family that could help?'

'I have a sister in Milan but she has no interest in the hotel whatsoever. Last time she visited our grandmother at the hotel she turned her nose up at everything. I was surprised she even walked on the old carpet in her shiny new Louboutins.' He grins.

'Who's looking after it at the moment?'

'A lovely couple called Luca and Maria. They do the breakfasts and the bookkeeping and a young girl called Giorgia does the cleaning. Business is ticking over, but it could be so much more,' Fabio says, sipping his Scotch thoughtfully.

'Whereabouts is the hotel?' I ask.

'It is where I believe to be the most beautiful place in Italy.' He smiles broadly. 'Lake Como. I was toying with the idea of changing it into a high-end restaurant with rooms. The view from the breakfast room looks out over the lake. I think it would make an incredible restaurant. I was asking Uncle Aldo's advice about it all. He told me that getting the right chef is everything.'

'Sounds amazing,' I say. 'And of course Aldo's right about the chef.'

"I know. I wish I could persuade my uncle to come to Lake Como and work in the restaurant but his life is here now. If my idea of a restaurant works out he did say he would fly over and help me hire the right staff, though.'

'Don't you be trying to take Aldo away from us. The Lakes wouldn't be the same without him. I suppose it's OK if he visits you though.'

Hannah, dressed for dinner in a pretty green linen dress, suddenly comes bursting into the lounge and flicks the television on.

'Sorry,' she says, turning to Fabio. 'It's just that one of our previous guests is on the telly.'

She turns the television on to *Come Dance With Me*, to the sight of Marco twirling a well-preserved sixty-something (at least) around the dance floor. I refill our glasses and we settle in to watch.

'He was here?' Fabio asks.

'Yes, a few weeks ago. He was complaining about his dance partner then, although they look pretty amazing, don't they?'

'He's a bloody good teacher,' says Hannah. 'Although I think he gave up on trying to teach me anything.' She laughs.

I recall the day in the garden when Marco ended up falling into the wrought-iron chair in the garden and let out a laugh.

We watch them twirl around the dance floor, straight-backed and intense-looking as they dance an Argentine tango. The acting ability of his partner, soap veteran Louise Lewis, is evident as she pouts her painted red lips and stomps her feet whilst swirling her black and red dress like a matador's cape. When the dance finishes the crowd are on their feet.

'He's very good,' says Fabio, casting a glance at me. 'And he's certainly got your undivided attention.'

After the dance is wrapped up, Hannah goes to answer the front door to a smiling Greg, who is clutching a huge bunch of flowers. He comes in to the lounge to say hello, before whisking Hannah away to dinner.

'Do you like dancing?' asks Fabio, once they've left.

'I prefer to watch it if I'm honest. I do enjoy dancing but usually to a CD when no one's watching. Two left feet, I'm afraid. What about you?'

'Not great. I'm OK at the slow numbers though.' He grins.

I feel a little flutter of something as I imagine being in Fabio's arms, swaying gently to a smoochy number.

We chat easily for a while longer before Fabio yawns and announces it's time for bed.

'Tiredness has taken over a little,' he says, getting to his feet. 'Maybe it's because I had an early start this morning. I'll see you tomorrow, thank you for the drink. Buona notte, Gina.'

Something about the way he says my name, and wishes me good night in Italian, gives me a warm feeling. Or maybe it's just the effect of the whisky.

Chapter Thirteen

I wake from a light sleep just before midnight as I hear Hannah return home. My bedside light is on, which Hannah takes as a cue to come in for a de-brief on her date.

'Five to twelve,' I say, eyeing the clock on the bedside table. 'Do you turn into a pumpkin after midnight?'

Hannah laughs. 'I've had such a wonderful evening,' she says, sitting on the edge of the bed. 'The hours just flew by, we've got so much in common. We both love old movies and fell walking, not to mention food. I think I might have found a bloke who will actually eat my cake. And would you believe his parents used to have a guesthouse?'

'Really?' I say, sitting up to take a sip of water.

'Yeah, in Appleby. They retired recently and decided to sell up. They now live in a bungalow in Ulverston just a few minutes away from Greg's apartment.'

She has a glow about her that I haven't seen in a long time and it makes me so happy.

'So when are you seeing him again?'

'Tomorrow, actually.' She smiles. 'When we've finished up here after breakfast, we're going to go for a walk up to Easedale Tarn. He's going to head back late afternoon after a spot of lunch.'

'Sounds lovely, the weather forecast is good tomorrow.'

'I know. Oh, Gina, I really like him. It just feels so natural being with him.' She beams as she heads off to her bedroom to change into her pink striped pyjamas. She returns to my room and plonks herself down on the edge of the bed as she removes her make-up with a cleansing wipe.

'Did you have a nice evening with Fabio?'

'Well, he was pleasant enough company.'

'So are you going to admit how gorgeous he is now?'

It's true, I find Fabio both handsome and intriguing but I don't want to give too much away.

'He's good-looking without a doubt but he's not going to be here for that long.' I smile. 'No one ever is.'

'Well, maybe he will return soon? I'm sure you have made quite an impression on him. And if you haven't, you need to do a bit of flirting.'

'I'm not sure I'd even know how,' I laugh. 'I haven't been out with anyone since Adam. Besides, I don't think romance is on his mind. It's more of a business trip. He's thinking of turning his grandmother's B&B, or villa as they're called in Italy, into a restaurant.'

'Sound exciting. Whereabouts in Italy?'

'Lake Como.'

'Ooh, really? I'd love to go there. Maybe we should take a little holiday together when he's done the place up.'

'Maybe. I just loved visiting Naples on my honeymoon and I fell in love with Italy. We stayed near the beach which was breathtaking but we also explored the city itself, which takes you by surprise. One day we were walking through a street of bars, restaurants and food vendors when we spotted a museum. It was pretty unassuming from the outside, and you could easily have missed it. The entrance was across a little Italianate courtyard dotted with olive trees. Once inside I was totally stunned to come face to face with Caravaggio's *Seven Acts of Mercy* which covered a complete wall. I mean, it's one of the world's most glorious paintings and there it was in a small museum down a gritty little street in Naples.'

'You always were the culture vulture.'

'Ooh, I know. I just love the history and there was something special about Italy. It cast a spell over me.'

'You're sure it's just Italy that's cast a spell over you?' Hannah prods.

Talking to Hannah about my honeymoon reminds me that it's been years since I took a holiday. In fact, it was four years ago when Adam and I took a city break to Barcelona for a few days and Dad – dutiful as ever – stepped in to help out. We had the most wonderful time soaking up the atmosphere of the markets and admiring the stunning architecture. We always vowed to return and spend a little longer there but it wasn't to be. We actually had our first and only argument on that holiday that we both blamed on tiredness. Looking back, it was entirely my fault because I had insisted on booking a particular hotel for its location that turned out to be a fleapit. We traipsed around for hours before we finally found alternate accommodation as it was during the Spanish holidays. Adam was annoyed with me because he had originally chosen a hotel that I had dismissed because of its location, on the outskirts of the city.

'It was luxurious, though,' he'd moaned. 'I thought you deserved it. I wish I'd just bloody gone ahead and booked it now.'

I spent the evening apologising and I recall the making up being so much fun.

As I look at Hannah, I hope Greg could be the one for her. She really deserves to be happy. She has convinced me that there is nowhere she would rather be living than the Lakes but I worry that she's doing it out of a sense of sisterly duty towards me. I think that falling in love here would give her a genuine desire to stay, making her life complete.

Chapter Fourteen

It's a cold, crisp morning with a bright sun against a pale blue sky with wisps of cloud when Greg rings the doorbell. It's early October now and the weather can be a little changeable but today Hannah has been blessed with perfect walking conditions.

'Two minutes,' Hannah says to Greg as she wipes her hands on a tea towel and disappears into a cloakroom at the back of the kitchen. She emerges wearing a thick waterproof bubble jacket, woollen hat and a chunky knitted scarf that she snuggles her chin into.

'Bloody hell, are we climbing Mount Everest?' Greg laughs.

'Don't be fooled by that sun. The higher we climb the colder it will get. Are you sure you'll be warm enough?' she asks, eyeing Greg's waterproof jacket. He isn't wearing a hat or gloves.

'I'll be fine,' he says. 'I've layered up, best thing to do.' He lifts his jacket to reveal a chunky jumper with a thermal vest underneath. He fishes some gloves out of his pocket. 'I'll put these on later. But I never wear a hat. Once I start walking my head gets really sweaty,' he laughs.

Fabio appears from the lounge where he has been reading the morning paper over a coffee.

'Good morning,' chirps Hannah.

'Buongiorno,' Fabio utters with a perfect smile.

'What you up to today then?' Hannah beams. 'Do you fancy coming for a walk with us? Gina's coming.'

'Am I? I don't remember agreeing to that. In fact I'm not sure you even asked me.'

Hannah has a mischievous twinkle in her eye.

'My uncle's restaurant is opening for business again tomorrow,' Fabio says. 'I will be going along later today to have a look at the kitchen set-up and chat to my uncle. This morning I have no plans.'

'Well, that's settled then. Come along with us and see some of the real beauty of the lakes. Four hours round trip so you'll be back in plenty of time.'

Fabio glances at this watch. 'OK. Maybe I will come along for a little walk and take in some fresh air.'

'Anyway, sorry to disappoint you, Hannah, but I was planning to do some bookkeeping this afternoon,' I say.

'It does seem a shame to be indoors on such a beautiful day,' says Fabio. 'Tomorrow it may rain.'

'Well there's every chance of that.' I smile. 'Well, OK then. Maybe I will, it's been a while since I've been on a decent walk.'

We're about to head off when Paul Barlow knocks at the door, asking if I have a spare laptop he can borrow for a couple of hours. I return with an old one that still works perfectly well.

'Cheers, Gina. I need it to look for a job. I've set up as a courier, but I can't get any decent jobs with a car. I need to save up for a van.'

'No worries. Keep hold of it for as long as you like.'

Five minutes later we start our walk, leaving the village behind as we begin the ascent towards the tarn. The country road is dotted with grey and white pebble-dashed holiday cottages with green wooden frames around the multi-paned windows. There's a couple of workshops selling wooden stools and small coffee tables, near an old granite church. Before long, all we can see before us is a long path flanked by wild flowers and bracken.

We turn a corner and approach a stile that leads into a part of the route that passes through a forest. I turn to the right and notice a hotel sign that directs walkers through the grounds as a shortcut to the ascent of Helm Crag and my heart stops. Helm Crag is where Adam lost his life, and its presence, shrouded in mist, looms menacingly in the background. I breathe deeply.

'Are you alright?' asks Fabio, stopping for a moment.

I could avoid his question but I decide to answer him honestly.

'I just haven't been over this way for some time. I'm taking it all in,' I say, realising I'm shaking slightly.

'Are you sure you are OK?' he repeats, gently.

'It was just seeing that peak in the distance. I'd forgotten it was so visible from here. But really, I'm enjoying the fresh air, let's carry on.'

We continue walking for around an hour, passing a landscape that changes from rust-coloured heathers to large oaks and fields dotted with sheep, the low hum of a tractor in the background. We pass a young couple sitting on a tartan blanket enjoying a picnic, even in this slightly cooler weather, with flasks of tea replacing summery cordials. They smile and say hello.

A long gravel path leads us to a stunning waterfall where I sit myself down on a large flat rock and realise that I am slightly out of breath.

'God, I'm unfit. I'm not sure I can even be bothered carrying on to the tarn,' I say, taking a long glug of water.

'What exactly is the tarn?' Fabio asks. 'Is it something I should make the effort to see?'

'It's a lake at the top of the mountain.'

'Ah, a lake. It makes me think of Lake Como, back home.'

'Well, it's nothing like that. More like a reservoir. Though I'd love to see Lake Como one day.'

'You should. So there is a lake. That's it?'

''Fraid so.'

'What else is there?'

'Nothing, really.'

'No bar for an Aperol spritz stop, after all this walking?'

'Nothing at all, I'm afraid.'

'That's a shame. There is a coffee shop or gelato kiosk with the best ice cream at the end of almost every footpath back home. So shall we turn back?' he suggests.

Hannah and Greg are way ahead and I have to cup my hands around my mouth and holler to them until Hannah turns around.

'We're going back,' I say gesturing to the path that leads down to the village. She stops for a second then gives a thumbs-up before pressing on with Greg.

We are ambling down the footpath leading towards the village when I suddenly stumble over a protruding rock. Fabio is at my side at once, grabbing my elbow and steadying me. As I feel the strength of his body and the musky scent of his aftershave, I can barely put one foot in front of the other to carry on.

When we arrive back at the village, I'm rather glad that we didn't make it up to the tarn. I really am unfit, and I let out a contented sigh as I see Lake View.

'I think that maybe now that we are back in one piece, I am indebted to your excellent guiding up the mountain. I noticed a little café on the river,' Fabio says. 'Shall we grab a coffee'?

'So you just wanted to get me alone, it wasn't that you couldn't handle the perilous hike?' I tease.

'Am I that obvious? Actually, tomorrow evening I am dining at Aldo's restaurant. I would love it if you could join me.' He moves closer and fixes me with a long stare of those intoxicating blue eyes.

Is it the fresh air or is my heart beating a little faster?

I turn around as I hear the sound of a familiar voice calling my name.

'Hi, Gina!' bellows Katy as she walks out of the post office.

'Hi, Katy,' I say, trying to compose myself. 'This is Fabio, Aldo's nephew, he's over from Italy.'

'Aldo from the restaurant? Wow, so pleased to meet you,' she says, grabbing his hand and shaking it warmly. 'All the way from Italy, huh? I bet the weather's a bit different there.' She grins, looking him over with a flirtatious look in her eyes. I'm not sure if it's my imagination but Fabio seems to be giving her the same appreciative looks. Maybe he makes a habit of hiking with widows and then inviting every woman he meets out for dinner. Suddenly all the exhilaration I felt from the walk seems to have evaporated.

'It can get quite cold in the winter but not as cold as here, I imagine. I really prefer things a little hot,' he says in return.

Is he flirting with her?

I'm thankful when Katy makes her excuses and heads off to finish her shopping. We arrive at a little café alongside the river and find a table on the outdoor terrace. Within two minutes a text has pinged through on my phone.

Oh my God, how long is the Italian stallion staying?
K. xxx

'So, would you like to invite your friend to join us for dinner tomorrow?' Fabio asks as we sip our coffee. 'And also Hannah. I would like to know why local people think the restaurant is so good.'

'Why not? I'm sure they'd both like that.' I smile.

Especially Katy, I think to myself. I'm sure Katy would like that very much.

Chapter Fifteen

I can't believe I thought Fabio was asking me out to dinner alone. I suddenly feel more than a little foolish as I select something to wear for the restaurant, disregarding the slinky red dress I was considering earlier. I fling some clothes onto the bed and finally opt for a crisp white shirt and a pair of black trousers.

Hannah taps on my bedroom door before entering.

'Since when did you knock on the door?' I laugh as she plops herself down onto my huge, king-sized bed, eyeing the pile of clothes.

'I dunno, that's what real grown-ups do, isn't it? Actually, sis, do you mind if I give tonight a miss? I've not long been home as Greg and I went for a long lunch. He's going to set off shortly then all I want to do is curl up with a good book.'

'And text each other all night.' I grin.

'Besides, I thought it might be nice for you and Fabio to be alone,' she teases.

'Hmm, except we won't be.'

'How come?'

'He asked me to invite Katy. We bumped into her in the village on the way back from the walk,' I say, hanging the red dress up. 'This is all business to Fabio.'

'Stop right there,' says Hannah, lifting the dress back out of the wardrobe and laying it on the bed.

'Whatever the reasons, you dress up, show up and have fun. Oh, and borrow my red Chanel lipstick too. Why should you shrink into the background while Katy will probably be wearing a see-through dress or some similar slutty ensemble?'

'Hannah!'

'What? I'm not being horrible – it's true, that's just Katy. You know I love her. And what if it is purely business? You don't go out that often. I'll be here if there are any problems so go and enjoy yourself,' she orders as she heads for the bedroom door.

I'm still not sure about the red dress. It's a little over the top for a Monday night out but maybe the black trousers are a little too formal. I think I'll wear my new jeans and a pretty blouse. I'll still borrow Hannah's red lipstick though.

When I've put the clothes away I lie down on my huge bed and sink into its deep mattress. I close my eyes for a minute, exhaling deeply as I consider the thoughts that are swirling around in my head. I've been so devoid of any feeling following Adam's death that it's reassuring that at least I am able to feel some sort of emotions, albeit conflicting ones. Is it a betrayal of my husband's memory if I am attracted to another man? It's coming up for two years since Adam died but it feels like no time at all. I sometimes feel as though I don't know where my life is heading, although I suppose that's only natural when everything you took for granted is ripped apart.

I head downstairs and tell myself to stop being so ridiculous. Fabio is here to take some advice from his uncle about transforming an old-fashioned Italian bed and breakfast into a modern hotel with a top-class restaurant, end of story. If there's one thing I do know about it's my guesthouse, so I can offer him some business tips. Plus, I do love eating the divine food at La Trattoria.

When I enter the lounge, Hannah and Greg break free from a kiss and then sheepishly jump up before Hannah leads him towards the front door. They look so good together. Greg is tall and broad-shouldered, whilst Hannah is petite and small-boned. It's like looking at a handsome prince and princess, albeit a princess with a pixie haircut.

'Bye, Greg,' I say, giving him a kiss on the cheek. 'Hope to see you again soon. I might even complete a whole walk next time.'

'You probably made the right choice.' He grins. 'It got pretty cold up at the top. Even my head felt a bit cold.'

'Well, I did tell you to wear a hat. You lose most of the heat through the top of your head,' says Hannah.

'Not true actually, that's a myth. You only lose around seven per cent.'

'Been reading the back of the cereal packets again?' teases Hannah.

I head back upstairs for a shower and as I glance across the hallway Greg is giving Hannah one last lingering kiss in the doorway. On the one hand, I'm so happy for them but a nagging concern about Greg pulling me apart from Hannah kicks in. And I wonder where Hannah's future will lie now?

Chapter Sixteen

It's business as usual after the flood and everything seems as it always does at La Trattoria, apart from a very faint damp smell that nobody mentions. The restaurant is surprisingly full for a Monday evening, Aldo's special meal deals being popular with tourists and locals alike. Fabio walks in behind me, and we arrive to find Katy already seated in the small bar area nursing a glass of white wine.

'Hi,' she says, jumping off her stool and greeting us both with a kiss. She's wearing tight white jeans and a red ruffle-fronted blouse.

'Ooh, you smell nice,' she gushes at Fabio, making no comment to me, despite the generous waft of Dior emanating from my skin.

We grab a drink and then take a seat at a wooden table with a good view of the open kitchen, which Fabio observes with interest.

'What do you both think of open kitchens?' he asks as he takes a sip of Merlot.

'I think they're brilliant,' says Katy. 'I think they really add to the atmosphere of the restaurant.' She pours herself another glass of white wine from a bottle.

'I think it depends on what kind of mood you want to create,' I say, spearing an olive with a cocktail stick.

'What do you mean?' Fabio asks curiously.

'Well, I think if it's a relaxed dining environment like this, then it's fine. I'm not sure it would work in a more formal dining room. Diners like their food to magically appear with a waiter in places like that.'

'Interesting,' says Fabio. 'I'd never really thought about it like that.'

'I heard you were thinking of turning a guesthouse into a swanky restaurant,' Katy says. 'Aldo was telling me about it earlier. Don't forget if you need any experienced staff, I'm your woman. I've passed all my exams in hospitality and I'm ready for a change.' She holds his gaze with her big brown eyes.

'I'll bear that in mind,' he says with a smile. 'Although I actually want to keep it as a guesthouse, or a villa as we say back home. I'm just considering opening the breakfast room as a restaurant in the evenings. Excuse me for a moment, ladies.' He stands up, taking his mobile phone with him. He begins to take photographs of various areas of the restaurant and even persuades a table of four women to let him photograph their food, as he charms them all with a free bottle of wine which is very well received.

'Oh my God, Gina, he's just gorgeous,' gushes Katy. 'It's a pity you're not looking for a romance, what with him staying in your guesthouse too. If I were you, I'd be right in there.' She winks.

'Well, he's not here long – isn't it always the way? In a couple of days, he'll be back in Italy and as I've said before, it's hard to get to know someone when they're just passing through.'

'Doesn't mean you can't have a bit of fun though, does it?' says Katy with a twinkle in her eyes.

My heart sinks a little; clearly our heart to heart in the cabin the other day is a distant memory.

Fabio returns and photographs the menu on his phone.

'I'm sure Aldo would send you some menu ideas,' I laugh. 'Although any decent chef would surely create their own menus, wouldn't they?'

'Yes, of course,' he agrees. 'I just like to have some ideas to hand on my phone. I really like it here, it has a good vibe. It would be wonderful to create something like this back home,' he muses.

'Surely you're halfway there with the location and you have the benefit of the beautiful weather.'

'Ah, the weather. Yes, the sunshine dances across the lake during the daylight and the moon shimmers in the evening, illuminating the boats that take the tourists back to their hotels.'

'You paint a beautiful picture, Fabio,' Katy drawls, leaning in closer. 'Bet you can't wait to get back home.'

'It's true I am looking forward to returning home, although the Lake District does have its attractions.' He grins as his gaze follows an attractive woman in a tight black dress from the table next to us.

'You aren't wrong there,' laughs Katy as our food arrives.

We inhale the aromas of the appetising bowls of creamy carbonara and plates of tomato-and-basil-covered gnocchi and say very little for the next few minutes as we savour the delicious food.

'Can I ask you ladies; how do you prefer the waiters to behave? Purely professional, or with a little, what is the word you use here, "banter"?'

'There's nothing wrong with a bit of flirting. In fact, it's the law in Italian restaurants, right?' Katy laughs, taking a glug of her wine.

'Some people would find it offensive to be openly flirted with. But a little oozing of charm is perfect,' I suggest.

'I take your point. I suppose it's all down to the training of the staff,' says Fabio.

Throughout the evening, Fabio periodically disappears to the bar area to chat to locals and to watch the chefs in the kitchen. As we're eating the final spoonfuls of silky tiramisu, soon enough a very pleasant evening is almost over. Aldo heads over with some coffees and biscotti, smelling of cigar smoke, having just returned from outside.

'So,' he says to Fabio, 'I hope you have enjoyed this evening. I trust you have seen lots of happy customers. You could have the very same thing. It's all down to customer service and fantastic food.' He smiles.

'You make it sound so simple, Uncle. If only I could persuade you to come with me.'

'Twenty years ago, yes, I would have considered it, but my life is here now. I have great friends and the Lake District needs a touch of Italy! Besides I am too old,' he laughs, taking a sip of strong Italian coffee.

'You have more energy than half the men I know. But of course I know your life is here, I am teasing. I do expect a visit in the not too distant future though,' Fabio says, before Aldo heads back to the kitchen and our talk turns to work.

'How long have you worked at the Hotel on the Water?' Fabio asks Katy, with keen interest.

'Six years. Before that I worked at a hotel in Grasmere.'

'Grasmere. Famous for the poet William Wordsworth and a famous gingerbread shop, I believe?'

'Correct.'

Katy makes him laugh as she tells him some stories from the hotel, as I sit there feeling increasingly uncomfortable.

'We get all sorts turning up at reception, you know. A couple of weeks ago we had these two couples dressed as tarts and vicars asking for the *special* room. I just looked at them blankly. "Do you mean the bridal suite?" I asked, a little confused. They went on about it being a party room with a video recorder. The *vicar* kept winking at me and nodding his head upstairs, I thought he had some sort of nervous twitch. Eventually the penny dropped. They thought we were a bloody swingers' hotel.' She howls as she drains her glass. Fabio is laughing heartily, revealing a row of even white teeth. 'Then the buxom fifty-something wearing a French maid's outfit says, "This is the Hotel on the Lake, isn't it?" When I told her that we were the Hotel on the Water and the Hotel on the Lake was a mile away in a forest, they couldn't get away quick enough. Fancy that, aye, the Hotel on the Lake having swingers' nights.'

The owner of that hotel is a sixty-something genteel grey-haired lady called Lucy. You never can judge a book by its cover. I remember being shocked by that one myself when Katy first told me.

'Well, it's time I headed back,' Katy says, standing up. 'I'm on an early shift in the morning and it's after ten.'

'We'll walk you back,' says Fabio, getting to his feet.

I'm surprised that Katy is heading off; this is not how I thought this evening would pan out. Maybe her outrageous flirting is nothing more than a little fun. Besides, I'm sure she'd never show any interest in a man I was interested in, as she's never done anything like that in the past. Not that she knows that I'm interested in him, mind you.

'Right then, this is me,' she says as we drop her at her door. She gives us both a kiss on the cheek before heading inside.

Back at the guesthouse I offer Fabio a whisky in the dining room of the main house.

'Don't you trust me in your own part of the house?' He grins.

'I don't want to disturb Hannah, that's all.' I laugh, thinking it a slightly arrogant thing to say. 'Besides, the best quality Scotch is locked in this cupboard.' I smile, opening it up and retrieving a forty-year-old single malt.

'Katy's a hoot, isn't she?' I say as I flop down onto one of the sofas, keen to gauge his reaction.

Fabio nods and takes a sip of his Scotch. 'Mm, this really is very good, you must give me the name of your supplier for my hotel.' He comes and sits beside me on the sofa, rather than on the one opposite. 'Yes, I like Katy, she's quite the character but she's not really my type,' he says as he inches closer.

'Really? What is your type?' I ask, as the fiery Scotch burns the back of my throat, setting my senses on fire.

'You talk too much,' says Fabio, as he takes the glass from my hand and places it on the table before kissing me softly on the lips.

Chapter Seventeen

It's the day before Fabio is due to fly back to Italy and he has gone to spend the day with his uncle in Pooley Bridge.

I'm in the breakfast room, finding myself daydreaming about last night. Fabio was courteous over breakfast but it was almost as if that magic moment we shared on the sofa last night never took place. Was it just the effect of the alcohol? He had consumed quite a few glasses of wine at the restaurant, finished off with the whisky. I remember how he looked at the woman in the black dress at the restaurant and chatted so easily with Katy. Maybe he's a player who charms and seduces women with ease, never really committing to anybody. Besides, do I even want somebody who is looking for commitment? Am I even ready for that?

As I'm carrying a tray of dishes into the kitchen, I hear a tap on the kitchen door.

'Hi, Dad,' I say in surprise. 'Aren't you working on the lake this morning?'

'I'm heading over to Lake Coniston,' he says, an excited note in his voice. 'The *Top Gear* team are on the lake filming with amphibious cars, trying to break some sort of speed record. Gerry from the Black Bull told me the production team need some extra hands and he put a word in. Young Mick's covering for me as long as I get him Jeremy Clarkson's autograph.' He grins.

'Oh, nice one, Dad. Try and get a selfie too, although I prefer James May. I didn't realise they were filming in Coniston, they kept that quiet.'

'They probably would have been overrun with fans if they made it public knowledge. Anyway, see you later, love.' He helps himself to a croissant from the table on the way out. 'You might even see me on the telly when the show's aired.' He winks.

I don't think I've seen Dad as excited by anything in a long time. He has a predictable but content life. In the evening he can usually be found at the Black Bull playing dominoes with his friends or attending quiz nights. He's become quite the cook too, expanding his repertoire from traditional English food to risottos and curries. It would be nice if he had someone to share his cooking with but he doesn't seem keen to find anyone. I do wonder how he'll cope with being all alone when he retires. The weather can get quite cold on the lake in the winter months so I don't suppose he can do that job forever, and then what will he do?

As I cross the hall I am surprised to see someone at the front reception asking Hannah about checking in.

'I'm afraid your room won't be ready until at least midday,' Hannah informs the tall man with long legs, wearing a long green jumper. 'Usual check-in time is two o'clock, but we could probably be ready around twelve. You can leave your bag here if you like.' She gestures to the large grey holdall.

'Hmm, OK,' he says, thoughtfully scratching his chin. 'I could do with a coffee. I'll go out and find somewhere.'

'Go into the lounge, I'll bring you some through if you like,' I say cheerfully. 'I think there's some cake left too.'

It's just after eleven and I'm in the lounge chatting to our new visitor when I receive a text message from Fabio asking me if I am free this afternoon. My heartbeat quickens a little as I tap out a reply, agreeing to meet him for dinner at the White Lion later.

'This cake really is delicious; your sister should enter *Britain's Best Baker*,' our guest says.

'I'm always telling her that but she reckons she's only good at cakes. She doesn't think she's any good at pastries or biscuits but I disagree.'

As I leave the lounge, I pass Hannah in the hallway, who has a huge grin on her face.

'What's tickled your fancy? Or should I say *who*?' I ask.

'Greg, if you must know.' She beams. 'He's invited me over to his flat for a meal next Saturday. I might even stay over.'

'You'd better bin those Bridget Jones knickers then and get yourself some new ones,' I tease.

'I do not have Bridget Jones knickers! I own one pair of Spanx that I needed for a slinky dress last New Year after I'd indulged too much over Christmas. Although you're probably right. Some of my knickers are nearly as old as me,' she laughs.

'I'm not quite sure that's true but even so you might want to do some shopping online and get a next day delivery.'

'Good idea, sis,' she says, placing her mobile phone into the back pocket of her jeans. 'No time like the present, I'll go and have a browse on the Internet now. Oh, and Dominika says the new guest's room will be ready in fifteen minutes.'

'By the way, our new guest has just eaten a piece of your cake. He said it was amazing.'

'Really? A man ate my cake?!'

'Yep. He suggested you go on *Britain's Best Baker*.'

'Well that's nice of him to say, but I don't think I'm in the same league as those bakers. They can whip up a confectionery Taj Mahal with a dozen eggs and a length of ready-to-roll icing,' she laughs as she scoots off to shop online.

While I couldn't be happier for Hannah and Greg taking things to the next level of their relationship, it sparks the need to speak to Adam at his grave. Then a pang of guilt tears through me as I remember that I'm meeting Fabio later and I decide to postpone visiting the grave until tomorrow. It will be the day before Bonfire Night then. Adam always loved Bonfire Night.

Chapter Eighteen

Fabio returns from seeing Aldo, telling me he has booked a table for six o'clock at the White Lion. He leaves this evening and I still feel completely confused by our situation, if indeed there is a situation. His flight to Milan leaves Manchester at midnight, so I would imagine he will be leaving around nine.

It's fairly busy in the pub when we arrive; a few families are enjoying an early dinner and several regulars are chatting over a pint at the bar. The restaurant area is modern but cosy with light wooden tables and chairs that have tartan-patterned seats of red and beige that match the heavy curtains. There's a roaring log fire along one wall, with a huge stag's head above it giving it a Highland feel.

'It's a shame you're going home just before Bonfire Night as its quite fun in the village,' I say, in between mouthfuls of mushroom risotto.

'There wasn't a great amount of availability with the flights. Although to be honest I need to get back home, I have so many ideas buzzing around my head. I really think I can make a success of my grandmother's hotel so I need to start putting some plans into motion.'

'Tell me more about your ambitious plans?'

Fabio exhales deeply. 'A lot of it will be cosmetic, as the hotel is already full of really beautiful Italian furniture and marble flooring. But it needs a refurbishment, especially the dining room if it is to be the modern restaurant I visualise. And of course, the plumbing needs to be sorted in the two unused rooms.'

Fabio eyes the plate of food that has been placed in front of him.

'I will miss many things about the Lake District,' he says, looking at me intently.

'Such as?'

'I will miss this delicious beer.' He smiles. 'Although the food not so much.' He giggles.

'English food has come a long way in recent years, I'll have you know,' I say patriotically.

'I know, I know, I am just joking. Aldo took me to a restaurant in Ambleside for lunch today and the food was fantastic.'

'When I was a child it was all pans of stew and fish and chips,' I tell him. 'Actually, it was mainly fish and chips unless my dad was cooking as Mum wasn't great in the kitchen. There was a little chippy next to the ice-cream shop on the high street that was family-owned for generations. I still remember the blue and white striped tarpaulin outside and the huge blue fish painted on the window. They sold the tastiest battered onion rings I have ever tasted to this day.'

Fabio pulls a face. 'Battered onion rings?'

'Don't be such a food snob,' I tease. 'Here, taste this.' I offer him a forkful of my risotto. He chews it thoughtfully.

'Hmm, not bad, although you have never tasted a mushroom until you have tried a porcini mushroom from Italy. Sautéed in a little olive oil and garlic with some bruschetta they are simply delicious.'

'If all Italian food tastes like the food Aldo serves in his restaurant, I can see why you're so passionate about it. Do you like to cook yourself?'

'Yes, it's a great passion of mine. Working in finance can be quite a, how you say, conservative job, some might even say a little boring. I began cooking several years ago and I think I'm pretty good at it.'

'I adore Italian food. Could you see ever see yourself helping out in the restaurant?' I ask as I fork the last of the risotto into my mouth.

'Who knows? I never say never about anything in life. What will be will be, or *quel che sarà sarà*.'

I plump for sticky toffee pudding for dessert which is utterly delicious and even Fabio agrees. It's made in a little bakery in Cartmel several miles away, which is world famous. I considered the ice cream too but would no doubt have had to listen to Fabio compare it to the gelato from Italy.

We pass the rest of the evening chatting pleasantly until it is time for Fabio to leave for the airport. It's a cold night with an inky sky that is illuminated by alarmingly bright stars. We walk across the road to the B&B chatting easily before stopping to look at the sky, where Fabio points out several constellations including Orion the hunter.

'Very impressive. You seem to know a lot about stargazing,' I say, wishing that this evening would never end.

'As a child my grandmother bought me a telescope and I would spend hours staring at the night sky. On a clear evening the skies are so beautiful over Lake Como. Sometimes you feel as though you can almost touch the moon.'

'You are very poetic.' I smile. 'Or maybe it's an Italian thing. I mean you manage to make pizzas sound like the food of the gods when it's basically cheese on toast with different toppings.'

Fabio looks aghast, so I quickly turn the conversation back to the moon.

'I think I read somewhere that the brightness of the moon is something to do with the water. I suppose we're both very lucky to live in such beautiful places.' I smile.

Fabio looks so handsome in the moonlight in a grey woollen coat with a striped scarf tucked inside.

'Gina, it has been such a delight getting to know you this past week,' he breathes, stepping closer so that I can smell his expensive aftershave. 'I hope I can count on your advice for the décor in the hotel, you have very good taste – judging by the work you've undertaken at Lake View.'

'Why thank you. And I'd be happy to help.'

He moves in closer and slips his arms around my waist.

'Maybe one day you can come and see the villa for yourself,' he says as he presses his lips against mine, softly at first but quickly deepening. Time seems to stand still as the stars silently weave their way across the universe. It's been so long since I have lingered in a man's arms that I want the moment to last forever. I feel so warm and secure, I have an urge to ask Fabio to cancel his flight and lead him inside to my bedroom, then shake myself for even considering it. After all, I hardly know him and he certainly hasn't made any promises. But this feeling I have is like nothing I have experienced in a long time. I feel such a strong sense of attraction that maybe my heart is ruling my head.

When we finally break apart and Fabio's car has disappeared around the corner, I stay outside the B&B for just a few minutes longer. I think the stars were burning unusually bright tonight. It's almost as if they were showing me how small we are. We must keep moving forward to be happy. And as I put the key into the door of the annexe I suddenly feel full of renewed hope and optimism.

Chapter Nineteen

As I enter the lounge I find Katy, Va and Hannah are huddled around the television in the lounge to watch Marco, who has somehow managed to make it to the final of *Come Dance With Me*.

There are plates of savoury dips, crisps and peanuts and Hannah has just popped open a bottle of prosecco.

'Hi Gina, thought you might appreciate a little company after Fabio leaving. I've recorded the final.'

'Perfect', I say, proffering my glass for some prosecco.

'I can't think of a nicer way to spend an evening.' Val smiles as she sips a glass of cherry brandy, which she'd been given as a birthday present in the summer. Apparently, it's the one she saves for 'special occasions'. She obviously feels this evening is one such occasion.

The intro music to the show starts up and we all hum along. The dancers swathed in glittery sequinned gowns make their way down the curved staircase onto the wooden dance floor. Marco is dressed in a striking turquoise shirt and a pair of black trousers, while his partner Louise Lewis is resplendent in a pink satin dress with a lightly feathered hem.

We watch the other dancers do their thing around the dance floor and soon enough it is the turn of Marco and Louise.

'Ooh, go on, Marco!' says Val, raising her glass to the television.

Right on cue, Marco flashes a smile at the camera, almost as if he has heard her.

It is obvious that Louise Lewis has had more work done on her face as she almost looks younger than Marco. She has the large, open eyes of a twenty-five-year-old and the lips of Angelina Jolie.

'Holy moly,' says Katy. 'If she has any more lifts she'll be shaving her pubic hair off her chin.'

Val almost chokes on her cherry brandy.

Their first dance is a waltz and they glide along the floor effortlessly, straight-backed and elegant.

'It's like watching Fred Astaire and Ginger Rogers in one of those old movies,' sighs Hannah.

'They really are brilliant, aren't they? I think you were right, Hannah, Marco must be a really good teacher.'

We top our glasses up and graze on corn chips and smokey paprika dips, eagerly awaiting Marco's second dance.

'I think this cherry brandy has gone to my head,' says a slightly flushed-looking Val, giggling as she reaches for some peanuts.

'Do you want some water?' I ask, jumping up.

'Not a chance,' laughs Val. 'I don't get out very often, although maybe I'll add some lemonade to my next drink if you have some.'

There's a break in the show while the votes are collated and the adverts are showing hotel offers.

'These summer holiday adverts are on television earlier and earlier. We haven't even had Christmas yet,' says Val.

'Are you OK?' whispers Hannah, gently squeezing my arm.

'I'm fine, really,' I reassure her.

'Where would you go on holiday if you had the chance, Val?' asks Hannah.

'Oooh, well, I've always fancied Paris. It just looks so romantic with all those gorgeous buildings and little French bistros. John never was the romantic type, he was more the practical type. You can imagine how shocked I was when I discovered he had cheated on me. I never thought he had the imagination for that.' She takes a slug of her drink. Then she throws her head back and laughs. Hannah and I glance at each other, wondering whether we should laugh awkwardly with her, when thankfully the ad breaks are over and the show resumes.

'I'd definitely go back to Italy,' I say, recalling the wonderful streets of Naples. 'Fabio painted such a wonderful picture of Lake Como that it's definitely on my list.'

'I think Gina has had her head turned by a certain Italian,' says Hannah before bursting into 'That's Amore'.

The next thing Katy and Val are linking arms, swaying from side to side as they join in the chorus.

'Behave, you lot!' I laugh. 'Anyway, be quiet, the results are in.'

A hush descends over the audience as the glamorous presenter with the long blonde hair announces that voting is now closed.

'Ladies and gentlemen. The winners of this year's *Come Dance With Me* are…'

The pause seems to go on forever. Almost to the point of irritation.

'Come on,' slurs Val. 'Get on with it'.

'Marco and Louise!' She beams as a flurry of coloured confetti cascades from the ceiling.

We all leap up from our chairs and onto our feet, cheering. Marco looks momentarily stunned until it sinks in that he has actually won and he lifts Louise off the ground and twirls her around. He sheds tears of emotion when he lifts the glitterball trophy but it is hard to gauge any expression on Louise's face as it's botoxed to death.

'Well, this calls for a celebratory drink,' says Val, standing up, before promptly falling down again.

'Coffee, anyone?' asks Hannah, jumping to her feet.

'Coffees all around I think,' I say, glancing at Val, who is firmly sat back in her chair, struggling to keep her eyes open.

Chapter Twenty

It's just after ten o'clock the next morning and there's something in the air today – I find there's always something about November 5th. It was my mum who gave Hannah and me our absolute love of fireworks day. We would toast marshmallows over a fire pit in the garden while Dad lit a huge box of fireworks. Rockets of silver, purple and green would burst into the sky and I don't think I had ever seen anything more magical. Mum would scream as firecrackers zigzagged along the ground and Catherine wheels spat from the garden fence, and Hannah and I would write our names in the air with sparklers. Afterwards we would be bundled into the car, Mum giggling and promising us fish and chips on the way home for supper after we had driven around local villages, stopping to look at the bonfires. Sometimes we never even got out of the car, viewing them from the cosy haven of the back seat.

The breakfast things have been cleared away as all the guests have filled up and left for the day. This evening there's a bonfire and firework display at the Traveller's Inn and the whole village will probably attend. Traditionally, the guy is usually dressed as a Disney villain, and this year it's Captain Hook. Hannah said it looks like our old headmaster Mr Percival who was known as Mr Pervert, but that's a whole other story.

I'm in the kitchen, putting the toffee apples on some trays near a window that is slightly open so they will set quickly, before giving the surfaces final wipe down. There is a lingering smell of ginger from Hannah's baking, the finished cakes stacked in a trio of red baking tins with white hearts dotted on them.

It's bitterly cold today, although rain isn't forecast which is good news for the bonfire later.

Bonfire night has always been a real event in the village with everybody contributing to the evening in some way. The tables are set up around the grounds selling glo-sticks, sweets and drinks for children as well as a hot chocolate stall. The children make huge colourful banners that are Sellotaped to their stalls advertising their wares, such as cakes and glow in the dark play dough, with proceeds going towards their school fund. There's also a carousel ride which generates great excitement from the children.

Ted's gone all out and booked a hog roast this year as he says he can't be doing with the clearing up. He's become quite the event organiser lately, what with the karaoke night and now this. In previous years the bonfire display was set up on a field a few minutes' walk away, so it's really nice that it's being hosted at the pub. I think Ted's going a bit soft in his advancing years. He often wears a serious expression on his large, ruddy-complexioned face, but it belies an affectionate nature. He leaves lollipops at the bar for children these days too, although he insists it's Jean's idea.

After I've put the finishing touches to the sweet treats for this evening, and admired Hannah's gingerbread parkin, I get ready to visit Adam's grave. I pull on a thick padded coat and some gloves, heading along the road to the churchyard.

Nowadays, I don't go to church so much. After I lost Adam, it shook my faith in God and all that I believed in. I'd always thought that I was a good person and couldn't understand why I was being subjected to so much suffering. Strangely enough it was a visiting vicar who helped me enormously by pointing out a scripture from the bible when he found me alone in church one day. It read: *Accident and unforeseen circumstance befall us all.*

It made me realise that losing Adam was an unfortunate, heart-wrenching tragedy. An accident. It was no one's fault and there was no grand plan. But I still find it hard to believe that the church we married in a six years earlier is now the resting place of my beloved husband. Maybe it's something I'll never be able to come to terms with.

There's a bench close to Adam's black marble gravestone, where I take a seat and begin to tell him about my morning. It feels quite natural to do this and I can manage it without crying these days. It's almost as if I'm sending someone a long email, knowing I will never receive a reply. I know he can't talk to me but that shouldn't stop me talking to him. I am still living my life so I have something to say, and I know he'd love to hear it.

I sit and chat for several minutes, zipping my coat to the very top of my chin as an icy wind bites. As I was lying in bed this morning, staring at my phone, I googled the weather in Lake Como and although not warm, it's quite a few degrees warmer than the north of England.

I tell Adam all about Hannah and her blossoming romance with Greg but I say nothing about meeting Fabio, swallowing my guilt. I talk for a few minutes more when I get the distinct feeling that someone is watching me. There's an eerie figure in a black coat standing near a tree next to the wrought-iron gates of the church. As I stand, my breath quickens. Slowly the figure walks slowly towards me until I can make out a female form.

I can't believe it. 'Mum!' I say in surprise. 'What are you doing here?'

'Hello, Gina, how are you?'

'I'm alright,' I say, slightly coldly. 'How did you know I was here? That is, assuming you were looking for me.'

'Yes, I was looking for you, Gina. Can we sit down?' She gestures to the bench. I shrug and sit down next to her.

'I had a feeling you'd be here. I know Adam loved Bonfire Night just as much as you did.' She smiles.

'Don't you dare, you barely knew him. You were too busy gallivanting off with every Tom, Dick and Harry to make a concerted effort to get to know what was going on in our lives.'

'I just wanted to see you, Gina. You never call.'

'Well you never call me,' I retort.

'You know that's not true, Gina. I have tried, many times, but you never return my calls. Hannah rings me. It's a shame that I have to find out how you are through her.'

'I just don't think there's much to talk about,' I respond, hardly recognising the cold-hearted person I become when my mum's around.

'You never could forgive me, could you?' she replies gently.

'What, for ripping our lives apart? Dad's never settled with anyone else, you know. I just hope you think it was all worth it.'

Mum puts her head down and her shoulders begin to shake gently. I realise with shock that she is crying. I don't think I can ever remember seeing my mum cry. She looks so small now, despite being a statuesque woman. I'm not quite sure what to do next but I find the humility to offer her a clean tissue. She lifts her mascara-streaked face and thanks me.

'I can't blame you for hating me, Gina. I made a mess of everything and I was a useless mother,' she says, blowing her nose loudly.

I never thought she was a useless mother. I remember a childhood touched with magic, having indoor picnics in the lounge when it rained outside. Some days, Dad would return home from work to a kitchen full of paper and glitter and nothing more than a plate of jam tarts for dinner. I remember how he would smile at us good-naturedly, despite the chaos.

'I don't hate you, Mother, I just hate what you did to us.'

'But my relationship with your father wasn't really about you, it's not as if I walked out when you were a small child.'

'See, that's where you're wrong, Mum. You *made* it about me. I was the one who had to pick up the pieces when Dad fell apart. And as for Hannah, well she had only just returned from travelling the world and wanted to think about her future. She could have used some motherly guidance. You couldn't have picked a worse time to swan off.'

'Hannah's done alright. Very well in fact. And it wasn't as if I abandoned her. We've managed to stay in touch. She forgave me.'

I can feel tears threatening to spill over.

'You just don't get it, do you? There was so much going on in my life at the time and you weren't there. I was exhausted after getting the guesthouse up and running. It would have been nice if you were around a bit more. Then I had to find the strength to watch out for Dad and Hannah. It wasn't bloody fair, Mum,' I say as the pent-up tears come cascading down my face.

'Oh, Gina, I'm so sorry.'

I stare at Mum for a few seconds, seeing genuine sadness in her eyes. She edges towards me, apologising over and over and I'm not sure how to respond.

Suddenly she leans over and embraces me. I can smell the familiar scent of her perfume that takes me back to my childhood, a mixture of familiarity and resentment simmering silently inside of me.

'So, when are you heading back to Manchester?' I ask when we break apart.

'I'm not.'

I have a vision of her trying to wrangle her way back in with Dad and my guard goes up immediately.

'Has your latest bloke dumped you, then?'

'No, Gina, I ended it,' she says with a deep sigh. 'We were never meant to last. He offered me a place to stay when I broke up with Gerald.'

The mere mention of Gerald's name makes me angry. Hannah and I called him Gerald the Jaffa Cake due to his dark brown hair and patchy orange spray tan, although I realise we were probably just bitter at the time.

'I haven't come here to upset anyone. I just want to build bridges with you and Hannah. Mainly you,' she says quietly.

I'm unsure how I feel about this, although I suppose she is my mother after all. And if I'm honest I have missed her. Maybe I owe it to myself to try and rebuild our relationship. But it's not going to happen overnight.

Chapter Twenty-One

Hannah slaps Greg's hand as he lifts the lid from a cake tin and sneaks a piece of parkin. He's driven over for the evening for the firework display but will be heading back home later.

'Mmm… it was worth the slap on the hand,' he says, his mouth full of gooey gingery cake. 'And anyway, I'm sure you'd want a taste tester. Imagine if they were inedible and you fed them to half the village.'

He ducks as Hannah flings a rolled-up ball of tin foil at him, missing his head by inches.

'Inedible? As if my cakes would ever be inedible,' she huffs.

'Well you never know, accidents happen,' says Greg. 'Our next-door neighbour made a cake for my parents' anniversary once. It was a carrot cake and instead of adding cinnamon they added coriander by mistake. It was awful. She dashed around mortified as soon as she realised what she'd done but Dad just laughed. He said he'd tried carrot and coriander soup but never thought that carrot and coriander cake would catch on.'

'Keep your hands off our Gina's toffee apples too,' warns Hannah.

Greg bursts out laughing and turns to me. 'I promise, Gina, I'd never manhandle your toffee apples.' He scurries away from Hannah, who is chasing him around the kitchen with a rolled-up newspaper.

Greg and Hannah are always laughing together and I am beginning to think they are made for each other. They head off to the pub for a drink before the firework display and I agree to meet them in an hour or so.

In my bedroom at the annexe I flick my laptop on and discover that I have an email from Fabio, and I frantically click to open it. I am pleased to hear that he has arrived safely and that he will always remember our kiss beneath the stars. Fabio informs me that he has decided to close the hotel for two weeks in early January for refurbishment as there are few visitors to Varenna at that time of year. I tap out a reply and tell him about the bonfire party at the Traveller's Inn. We message each other for a little while before he signs off with *Ciao Gina, speak soon*

There's no kiss at the end of the message despite Fabio recalling our starlit kiss with affection. It is so hard to read what he is feeling. Maybe he thinks there is too much of a distance between us and if I'm honest I probably feel the same. Chatting to Fabio has just brightened my day a whole lot more but as I close the laptop, seeing an old photo of Adam on the dressing table, I feel like I'm betraying him even thinking about a new romance.

The grounds of the Traveller's Inn are a hive of excitement as children chatter away excitedly waving their glo sticks around and buzzing about devouring treacle toffee. There's a fizz in the air as we await the firework display at seven o'clock. I've joined Greg and Hannah at the bar inside, where we're enjoying a glass of cider when Dad walks in. I wave him over.

'You look very smart, Dad,' I say, eyeing up his light blue checked shirt and navy blazer. Hannah gives a mock wolf whistle.

'Is there something you're not telling us, Dad? Have you got a date?'

We all laugh while Dad clears his throat.

'Well actually, yes I have,' he replies, looking slightly embarrassed.

I don't think my dad has been out with anybody since my mum left four years ago. Our mouths are gaping open in shock.

'Really? Ooh, who's the lucky lady then, Dad?' Hannah asks.

'Her name is Sheila. I met her when I was at Coniston the other week. She works in the café near the waterfront and makes the best sausage sandwiches I've had in a long time. No offence, girls.' He laughs, looking at our raised eyebrows.

'I've booked a table at the Star Inn in Coniston and I'll be leaving shortly, but I just thought I'd pop in and say hello. It is bonfire night after all, and I don't think we've ever spent it apart.'

'You're not staying for the fireworks?' Hannah sounds somewhat deflated, as Dad glances down at his watch.

'I'd better not, love, don't want to be late. I'll be off after I've had this apple juice.'

It feels strange knowing that Dad has a date. On the one hand, I really hope he has a good time with Sheila but I can't help wondering how he will feel when he knows Mum is back on the scene. Mum was the love of his life and she broke him in two when she left.

Ted makes an announcement at the bar for the customers to make their way outside as the bonfire is lit and the firework display will start shortly. The crowd of around fifty people, including young children, finish up their drinks and make their way outside. Excited kids run to the sweet stalls manned by the teachers and some of the pupils from the primary school. There's a smell of simmering charcoal in the air as the fire takes hold, creating colourful, crackling flames.

'Right then, I'm off,' says Dad as he drains his drink. He starts driving, disappearing around the corner just as another car makes its way into the car park. I recognise the blue Peugeot immediately. It's the same one that parked up when I went to visit Adam's grave.

Chapter Twenty-Two

'Mum!' exclaims Hannah, squeezing her in an embrace as soon as she spots her.

'Hello, love, well I always enjoyed Bonfire Night and I hoped that you'd be in here.' She smiles. 'I don't know if Gina told you but I'm staying in Ambleside for a while.'

'Yes, she did mention it. I was going to give you a ring tomorrow.'

Introductions are made to Greg and we all stroll outside to watch the bonfire being lit. It soon takes hold and young children squeal in delight as they wave their sparklers around in circles. Flames of red and orange leap into the air, licking their way towards the guy at the top who is dressed in a white shirt and a pair of black trousers. The local children have made a mask and a curly handlebar moustache in the image of Captain Hook from *Peter Pan*. The fire crackles loudly as thick smoke spirals upwards, leaving a pungent smell in the air.

Soon the fireworks are lit and the sky is momentarily illuminated with pink and green and purple fountains. Rockets zip across the navy sky, before exploding into a waterfall of silver. It reminds me of the last time the stars shone so brightly in the night sky. My body tingles as I remember Fabio's kiss, so gentle and tender.

Mum and Greg are getting along like a house on fire and I can't understand what they find so amusing. In fact, just having her here makes me feel uncomfortable – what's her agenda? The person I really care about is luckily away from here, and I wonder how my dad's date with Sheila is going. Not for the first time, I look over to my mum and wonder why she ever broke up with my dad. He adored her and would never have looked at another woman, but as Hannah once said, is loyalty in a relationship enough? Does passion fade over time or are there those that maintain it for a lifetime? Could Mum not have fulfilled her lust for life in a different way instead of breaking Dad's heart? The thoughts race through my head.

All too soon the bonfire party is winding down and the stall holders pack away their things. The dying embers of the fire smoulder gently as yawning children are escorted home, their parents conscious of not being out too late on a school night.

'Well it's been lovely meeting you, Greg.' Mum smiles in the car park, before whispering to Hannah, 'He's a keeper.'

I wish Mum could have thought the same about Dad, but I bite my tongue.

Greg gives Hannah a lingering kiss before he drives off home, and as we wave him goodbye the occasional firework goes off in the distance. Mum leaves a few minutes later and Hannah and I fall into step beside each other, heading back to Lake View.

'What a wonderful, if strange, evening,' I say, linking my arm through Hannah's.

'I know, it was strange, but it felt so natural having Greg and Mum meet one another.'

I realise that Hannah is right, perhaps it's better having our mum in our lives? Perhaps it's time to put the past behind us?

We arrive home and turn the television on as an episode of *Murder She Wrote* is about to start.

'Perfect,' says Hannah. 'I'll put the kettle on.'

'Right, OK,' I say absentmindedly, as I find myself checking the list of upcoming bookings in January. It's very quiet after Christmas, with only a few die-hard walkers checking in as the weather often freezes. Perhaps I could take some time off and head somewhere a little different? Maybe somewhere like Lake Como?

Chapter Twenty-Three

Autumn has silently disappeared as the bare trees herald the beginning of winter. It's hard to believe that another year is almost at an end as the preparations for Christmas begin in the village. The water has a calmness about it at this time of year as the boating activity on the lake is less frequent. The air is cold and fresh but the fell walkers continue their activity, wrapped up in thickly padded coats.

It's been a bitterly cold day, with a bright sun in a blue sky that turned to black just before five o'clock.

There's a palpable excitement in the air with just ten days to go until Christmas Day. I'm out for my morning walk through the village main street which has three pubs, a small shop selling souvenirs and ice cream and Val's large general store. It also has a shop selling hiking gear and three cafés including Emmy's tea shop.

As I head back towards the guesthouse, my thoughts turn to the Christmas card I received this morning in a red envelope. It was from Fabio. He wished me a merry Christmas and said he hoped all my dreams would come true in the new year. I find myself wondering whether that had any hidden meaning? I'm surprised at how much I miss him, despite him not being here for very long.

I spot Dad up ahead and I jog to catch him up, falling into step with him.

'Hi, Dad. How's things with Sheila?'

'I think that was a bit of a non-starter, love.' He shrugs.

'How come? I thought you liked her?'

'I think I was just seduced by her sausage sandwiches,' he laughs. 'We went out a couple of times but I don't think she was really my type. Don't get me wrong, she's a lovely lady but I can't see myself settling with her, and I got the impression that was what she wanted.'

'Never mind. Maybe it's best that you didn't string her along if she was looking for something more permanent.'

'That's exactly what I thought, love. It wouldn't have been fair.'

And even though I agree, I can't help wondering whether Dad will ever give his heart to someone else.

I arrive back home from my winter walk to find Hannah and Greg curled up on the sofa watching *It's a Wonderful Life*.

'Hi, sis,' says Hannah jumping to her feet. 'Fancy a glass of mulled wine? Oh, and I've made some mince pies.'

I can never resist Hannah's mince pies; they are far nicer than anything you can buy in the supermarkets.

'Go on then,' I say, shrugging off my coat. 'Just the one though or I'll be wearing a kaftan at Christmas. Do you know, I don't think I've ever watched this film? I think I started watching it once and fell asleep.' I plonk myself in an armchair before taking a bite of the utterly delicious mince pie.

'You've never watched *It's a Wonderful Life*?' asks Hannah in surprise. 'It's my favourite Christmas film ever. We're having a bit of a black and white movie day. *Roman Holiday*'s up next if you fancy it.'

'Thanks for the offer but I've got stuff to do. I'm going to have a bit of a clear out of some of my clothes. I think I'll drive into Penrith tomorrow and take them to a charity shop.'

'Ooh actually I'll have a look through my stuff too. I must have about fifteen coats in that wardrobe and I only ever wear a few of them. You can pick up some charity Christmas cards while you're there,' suggests Hannah.

The mention of *Roman Holiday* makes me dream of visiting Rome. The whole city is so romantic with its ancient monuments and I can picture the Vespas twisting along the narrow streets. Thinking of Italy, it's not long before my mind strays to Fabio. He has been consulting me on various stages of the refurbishment of the villa in Lake Como. One message included a wonderful photograph of Varenna dusted in a coating of snow. The harbour front was strung with lights that illuminated the lake and the cobbled streets. It all looked so magical. There was a huge fir tree that took pride of place in the village square and Fabio told me that as well as the usual fairy lights and baubles, the village children decorate the tree with salt dough Santas and candy canes. We have agreed to FaceTime to discuss the hotel refurbishment, and I hope he'll tell me more about Italian festive traditions.

On Saturday a Christmas tree will be erected here in Glenridding at the foot of the small high street outside St Patrick's Church. The tree is decorated by children from the local school, who cover it with hand-made baubles. Last year the tree had a 'wish upon a star' theme, with people writing their hopes and dreams onto foil stars that were handed out by the children. The school nativity takes place in the church. It's a beautiful service. Part of the production is usually outside in the church grounds where a donkey parades around carrying a weary Mary, and children sing 'Little Donkey'. Last year's donkey had an identity crisis when it decided it was a racehorse and careered through the grounds knocking the mince pie and mulled wine stall crashing to the ground and almost giving the vicar's wife a heart attack. All credit to a plucky Mary who hung onto the donkey for dear life before being pulled to safety by a teacher. This year they are taking no chances and have decided to put two children inside a costume like a pantomime horse.

I think of the little foil stars suspended from last year's Christmas tree and recall my own wish, which was for the pain in my heart to heal a little. A year certainly has made a difference. I can feel the joy in my surroundings again and somehow the colour has returned to the wondrous landscape. For a while, nature's palette had seemed like a muted shade of grey. Now I am beginning to see things in glorious technicolour once more.

The Christmas routine never changes in the village; the church Christmas fete, followed by 'Breakfast with Santa' at the community centre several days later for the children. Midnight Mass on Christmas Eve and pre-dinner drinks at the Traveller's Inn on Christmas Day. It's all so comforting yet predictable. And for the first time ever, I wonder if I want more?

Chapter Twenty-Four

Only four of the bedrooms at the B&B are occupied this week, two of them with people attending a winter wedding at the Hotel on the Water. The grounds of the hotel look beautiful as trees are threaded with white lights and ice blue lanterns illuminate the driveway. The other two rooms at the B&B are occupied by seasoned fell walkers who turn out in all weathers.

Not having a full house has given me a bit of time to have another clothes clear-out as I didn't seem to get very far last time. This time I've included the remainder of Adam's things that I hadn't previously been ready to part with. Everything's gone now. All trace of him, apart from photographs. It seems harsh but really, what was the point in keeping his clothes in the wardrobe? Nobody in the family would ever have worn them so they should go to a good home. Someone else can make use of them now. Photographs are enough for me, because they're all the happy memories, aren't they? Nobody ever takes a photo of a terrible time.

When I finish packing Adam's things into a bag, I open a drawer and find the small photo album of my family. A smiling, happy family. In one photo we're standing at the top of a peak, hands thrust in the air triumphantly. I remember Dad saying he was taking us for a walk up the biggest mountain in the Lakes, rumoured to have a giant living beneath it. If you heard his roar or felt a rumble, he said, you would have to run downhill as fast as you could.

As a child it felt like the most gigantic mountain in the world, but of course years later I recognised it as a small peak called Little Mell Fell, in a nearby village called Watermillock.

As I head to the charity shop, driving along the winter roads, dark trees silhouetted against a pale grey sky, I can see Little Mell Fell in the distance. I have so many happy memories of my family from when I was young. And just maybe there are more happy memories to be made in the future.

I arrive home just after four o'clock with a cute vintage clock that I found in the charity shop for a few pounds. That's the trouble with visiting those stores. I donate all my old unwanted possessions, then invariably come home with someone else's.

I'm speaking to Fabio on a FaceTime call this evening and for some reason, I feel inexplicably nervous.

I do a quick sweep of the front path at the B&B, brushing away some winter berries that have fallen from a nearby tree, before I head back inside shivering slightly.

Soon enough it's almost time for Fabio's call. I peer into my dressing table mirror and pull the rollers out of my red hair before brushing it into soft curls. A slick of red lipstick finishes my look. Not bad, even if I do say so myself. I still feel a little nervous about talking to Fabio so I pour myself a small malt whisky to steady myself. I check my watch; five minutes to go. He said he'd call me at six o'clock. I wonder if he is the punctual type? Then I suddenly wonder if he meant English time or Italian? Surely he would have meant the time in the UK? Next I start to worry that I've made too much effort. Would Fabio expect me to look natural with my hair tied back at the end of a busy day, rather than fully made-up?

I can't believe I feel like a teenager. Bang on the stroke of six o'clock the phone rings. It takes a few seconds for the image to come into focus but soon I am staring into the mesmerising blue eyes of Fabio.

'Ciao, Gina. How are you?'

He's wearing a bright blue polo shirt that matches his eyes.

'Hi, Fabio. I'm well, thanks. How are you?'

'I'm good. A little tired maybe, it's been a busy day, although I feel invigorated just looking at you.' He smiles. 'You look beautiful. *Bella signorina.* Are you going somewhere special?'

'Not really. I'm going to the church nativity, followed by drinks in the pub later. It's all rock 'n' roll here.'

'I'm so sad I am not there. I would love to be enjoying a drink with you later this evening. It breaks my heart I won't be there,' he says, turning the corners of his mouth down and placing his hand on his heart.

'Where are you?' I ask, my heart fluttering. 'It looks amazing.'

'I'm at the hotel, would you like a tour?'

He stands and pans the camera around the room, walking across a striking blue mosaic floor. The slightly jaded pink walls are decorated with paintings of bowls of fruit in gilt frames. In the background I notice a curved mahogany bannister. A huge chandelier in the hallway overlooks it all. I think it looks a little tired, but still beautiful.

'I thought you said the hotel looked a bit old-fashioned. It's stunning,' I tell him. 'Very Italian. I'm sure any visitor would find it charming.'

'Ah yes, the hallway is good now that the carpet has come up. It was dreadful. I can't believe Grandmother was covering up this wonderful floor. The dining room and the bedrooms definitely need updating though. And I need to get a plumber in to check the pipes in the two rooms that are unused. I'm having the electrics checked. I pray the place doesn't need a full rewiring. We do need additional sockets in the guest rooms though.' He sighs. 'But never mind about that,' he says, breaking into a smile. 'I knew it would be a lot of work. Would you like to see outside?'

He holds his laptop up, stepping outside onto a long stone veranda.

'Not a bad view,' he says, as he turns the screen to take in the scene of the inky lake. It's mesmerising. Just as he described, a boat is weaving its way across the water, the light from its deck creating silver ripples on the water. There's a large full moon in the sky that seems only a touch away.

'Can you see the island in the distance? That is Bellagio. That's where the boat is heading. The boats are only every couple of hours in the winter. There are a couple of restaurants there that are well worth the journey.'

'Is it quiet there at this time of year?'

'Largely, yes. The bigger hotels that provide entertainment remain reasonably busy but the town tends to wind down over the winter.'

'It looks so beautiful,' I sigh, wishing I was there.

We chat for a while longer before I realise it's time for me to leave for the nativity.

'Gina, before we know it, Christmas will be over. I am busy with some work for clients and of course here, over the next week or two but I am looking forward to the new year. I have a feeling next year will be special. I hope you can come and see me soon,' he says, smiling.

'Maybe. Perhaps I could help you with those soft furnishings you say you know nothing about. It would make the refurbishment suggestions easier if I was with you in person. I'm not afraid of mucking in with some decorating either,' I say, recalling the effort I put into the guesthouse. I try to sound casual but underneath my heart is beating like mad. I really could visit Lake Como; after all it's quiet here in January too.

'Gina, do you mean it? It would be wonderful to see you again soon. Plus, it would be nice to cuddle up with someone on these cold winter nights,' he says, pretending to shiver.

'So that's all you want me for? Have you ever thought about an electric blanket?' I laugh.

We finish our chat with Fabio blowing me a kiss and I feel as though I am walking on air.

Suddenly I'm really looking forward to Christmas in the village, because there'll be something exciting awaiting me in the new year. I grab my coat just as Hannah and Greg arrive to walk with me to the church. I don't think I will be joining them in the pub afterwards, though – I've got to look on the internet for some flights!

Chapter Twenty-Five

The heavy wooden door of the church creaks open to a latecomer in a red woollen coat. I realise it's Mum, who quickly takes a seat near the back, whispering, 'Sorry'.

Dad is sitting near the front with us but didn't turn around when he heard the door open. He knows that Mum is staying nearby in Ambleside but has had very little to say about it.

We're halfway through the Christmas story as told by the vicar and school children of the parish.

'Behold! We must follow that star,' says a small boy who is dressed as a shepherd.

The children burst into song, singing 'We simply have to follow that star' as they descend the altar steps and make their way around the church following a giant star suspended from the ceiling. The production is being held inside this year as they are not using a real donkey, and this year's donkey is two children in a costume, with Mary walking alongside.

After they've followed the star to the strains of 'Little Donkey' they are back on the stage knocking at the door of an inn.

'Sorry, you can't stay here. There's no room,' says a small boy with a huge voice.

'Sorry, there's no room here!' shouts the second innkeeper.

Suddenly a head pops out from the front of the donkey and turns to the teacher at the side of the stage.

'Miss, I need a wee.' The audience erupts with laughter.

'Can't you wait a bit longer?' the teacher whispers, although the acoustics in the church make her voice audible to all.

'No, Miss,' comes the small voice.

She tuts before helping him out of his costume, taking him to the toilet in the vestry. The donkey looks a sorry sight. Its neck and head are slumped on the floor as the boy at the back end remains resolutely upright.

The three kings appear at the scene of Jesus's birth bearing gifts. They look so small, with their long robes dragging along the floor behind them.

'I bring you gold,' says the first child, who has a slight lisp.

'I bring you Frank in tents,' shouts the second child at the top of his voice, and I stifle a giggle.

'I bring you myrrh,' says the last tiny child with the blonde hair and round glasses.

The show finishes with a rousing rendition of 'We Wish You a Merry Christmas' and the children receive a standing ovation.

'Oh, I love the nativity,' says Hannah, clapping her hands together like an excited child.

She's dressed in a short black faux fur jacket and a pair of tight red jeans that only she could get away with wearing.

'It's the one thing that makes me feel really Christmassy,' she continues. 'Reminds us what Christmas is all about.'

'I agree,' I say, as I fasten my grey woollen coat and slip on my black leather gloves, ready to go outside.

We are waiting at the exit for Dad, who is helping the vicar put some of the props away from the stage, when Mum spots us.

'Hi, girls.' She beams. 'Fancy some mulled wine? It might warm me up a bit. I think it's warmer out here than it was in that church, the vicar must be skimping on the electricity to pay for the church roof.' She laughs.

There's a marquee set up in the church grounds offering refreshments for a donation towards the church roof fund.

Mum returns from the tent with a tray of mulled wine and a plate of shortbread just as Dad is leaving the church.

'Hello, Don,' she says as she offers him a glass of mulled wine.

Dad takes the drink from her hand and takes a sip.

'Hello, Julia,' he says in return. 'How are you?'

'Oh, I'm alright, you know me, I'm a survivor,' she says, taking a glug of her drink. 'How about you?'

'I'm alright thanks. I'm looking forward to spending Christmas with the girls.'

Mum looks down at her shoes.

'I'd like to call in at some point and drop some gifts off,' she says, glancing at me and Hannah. 'That's if it's OK.'

'That's fine, Mum,' replies Hannah.

We finish our drinks and I make my excuses as the others head off towards the pub. Mum is driving back to Ambleside.

'Bye, Julia,' says Dad as he heads off. 'Maybe I'll run into you over Christmas.'

'Bye, Don. That would be nice.' She smiles, before starting the engine of her car and disappearing into the night.

Chapter Twenty-Six

It's just after nine thirty when I pour myself a glass of wine and fire up my laptop to search for flights to Italy.

It's the 2nd January and only two rooms are occupied in the guesthouse, so it's a perfect time to get away. I was feeling a little guilty leaving Hannah in charge again, although she reassured me that there is nowhere she would rather be in winter. After a busy day, she likes nothing more than cosying up to Greg in the evening, drinking hot chocolate and watching old films.

I had a very quiet New Year's Eve here in the village, returning home from the Traveller's Inn just after midnight after I'd wished everyone a happy new year. There'd been a band and some fireworks at the pub, yet I hadn't really felt in the mood. Fabio rang me the second it had turned midnight here and my spirits soared.

I notice to my relief that the flights to Milan are pretty frequent from Manchester, even at this time of year. From there, the trains from Milan Centrale to Varenna Esino are roughly every hour. It only takes just over an hour by train and I'm hoping Fabio will collect me from the station.

I think of the lake in Varenna and consider the similarities with Ullswater just across the road. The moon seemed so bright over Lake Como, unlike here where it's often obscured by cloud.

﹏❀

I'm travelling to Italy in two days' time. Dad was more than happy to step in and help with the breakfasts as I imagined he would be. Hannah hinted that Mum might come over and give a hand but I don't want her presence upsetting Dad. Young Ellie is still a great help but only works at weekends during school term time. Perhaps she could do a couple of hours after school to earn a little extra money. She's spending more and more money on make-up and practises her skills on anyone who'll agree to it. It's nice that she has something she is so passionate about. It turns out that Ellie's teacher, Mr Spencer, was nothing more than a crush on Ellie's part, so thankfully her make-up obsession is a healthy distraction. Although judging by how she is currently all doe-eyed over eighteen-year-old apprentice gardener Jake from the Hotel on the Water, I think she had moved on anyway.

I'm so looking forward to seeing Fabio. Ever since he sent me that Christmas card, I've really started to believe that there was something in the kiss we shared. But what if he's inviting women to the hotel all the time? What if I am just one of many? This will be the first time I've ever travelled alone and even though I'm excited, I'm also a little scared about what will happen at the other end. Every journey in my life has either been with family or as part of a couple, and I feel a pang as I think about Adam.

Even though I'm only going away for a week, I decide to pack an outfit for every weather eventuality. Varenna is never less than twelve degrees during the daytime, I'm told, but the temperature drops severely in the evening with mist and ground frost. It all sounds rather magical to me and I envisage romantic evenings spent in little restaurants on cobbled streets with windows illuminated by red shaded lamps. I'm just squeezing a thick red woollen jumper into my case when Hannah walks in.

'Hi, sis, how's the packing going?'

'Pretty good, I think. I'm not sure whether to pack anything formal.'

'Pack a nice little black dress just in case. Maybe a couple of shift dresses too, that you can dress up with jewellery if need be,' suggests Hannah. 'And why are you packing this old stuff?' she asks, lifting up a couple of old shirts and pairs of leggings.

'Because I want to be hands-on with the refurbishment. I enjoy rolling my sleeves up and getting stuck in.'

'Suppose so. It's not my idea of a relaxing holiday, though,' she laughs.

'Do you think I should pack my fleecy pyjamas? I'm lost without those in the winter.'

'Not unless you want to stay single forever. Take that grey satin nightdress and slip.'

'That's a bit presumptuous. Fabio and I still getting to know each other. Anyway, he might have a guest room set up for me.'

'How would you feel if he did?'

'Well, I suppose I would think he was the perfect gentleman.'

'I'd love to have a weekend away with Greg when the weather's warmer,' says Hannah dreamily. 'Maybe around April. I've always fancied Amsterdam in the spring, actually. I'd like to hire a bicycle and explore the city.'

'You should do, you deserve it. We can manage nicely here now, especially now that we have Ellie over the weekends.'

'I love Ellie. She's a hoot, isn't she? She's always giving me make-up tips. She says she's thinking of giving tutorials on YouTube. Apparently, my eyebrows need to be brought up-to-date,' laughs Hannah, stroking her brow.

'At least her teacher crush has passed. I caught her smiling at Jake the gardener from over the road as he walked past yesterday.'

'Oh no, you don't suppose she's going to develop a crush on him too, do you?'

'I doubt it. It was a sixteen-year-old at the guesthouse a couple of months ago. She's a fickle youth.' I smile.

'I suppose so. She's a good kid though, really hard-working.'

I'm so happy things are running well at Lake View as it makes it easier for me to go away on a little break. I realise how blessed I am with a wonderful family. I just hope Mum doesn't have any surprises in store.

Chapter Twenty-Seven

It's just after noon on the 4th January and Dad has arrived to drive me to Manchester airport. My stomach feels a little knotted as I deliberate for the umpteenth time over clothes. Have I taken too many? I'm only going for a week. I suddenly wonder if my clothes are stylish enough? Even in the depths of winter, Italian women probably exude style. I imagine them walking around in expensive, brightly coloured woollen coats and expensive Italian leather boots. My tan Chelsea boots were a great buy and they do look very chic so I really shouldn't fret. I glance at my reflection in the mirror, wondering whether I should have had my hair trimmed?

Dad eyes my huge grey Samsonite suitcase and laughs as he lifts it to put in the boot of his car.

'What have you got in here then, a dead body?'

'Just something for every occasion. Apparently the weather is a bit changeable at the moment.'

We travel along the village roads until we join the motorway that heads for the airport. It's reasonably quiet apart from the odd lorry spraying water on Dad's car.

'Thanks for agreeing to help around the B&B, Dad, it gives Hannah a little bit of free time.'

'No worries, love, you know I'm always happy to help. It's about time you had a little break. Your mother has also said she'll pop over and help if we need an extra pair of hands.'

'Mum?' I say in surprise. 'I didn't realise you were in contact with each other.'

Maybe I should be happy that my parents are on speaking terms, but I've become rather protective of Dad over the years. I don't want him to let Mum into his life again just for her to swan off again when she gets bored.

'Well, we're not exactly in each other's lives. She just rang me the other evening to ask how I was.'

'Why would she do that?' I ask, somewhat startled.

Dad exhales slowly.

'Nothing to worry about, love, but I had a bit of a funny turn in the pub.'

'What? Why didn't somebody tell me?'

'Because it was nothing to worry about. I think I just got a bit overheated. I'd been on the boat all afternoon and it was really nippy out there. I walked in the pub and it was like a furnace. I was half an hour into a game of dominoes when I nipped to the toilet. Next thing I was looking up at a couple of blokes. I'd passed out, apparently, although only for a few seconds.'

'Oh, Dad, you should have told me.'

'There was no need to worry anyone. I had the doctor check me over. He made me wear an ECG machine overnight just to be sure, but it turns out my heart is in fine fettle. I'm in pretty good shape all round as it happens. Hannah spotted me coming out of the doctor's surgery so I told her what had happened. She obviously told your mother.'

'So why didn't you tell me?' I ask, feeling slightly stung by all the secrecy.

'Because, young lady, there's nothing wrong with me. The doctor said it was the sudden change in temperature that caused the faint. A sudden drop in blood pressure. Can you honestly say you would have booked those flights if you suspected I was ill?'

I think about this and realise he's probably right.

'I suppose not. And one good thing to come out of it is you've had a good health check. I can't remember the last time you went to the doctor.'

'I can, it was 1998. I slipped on the boat and caught my leg on the corner of one of the seats. I needed six stitches in my leg and even that was because your mother was going on about it. I'd have stuck a plaster on it.'

I notice he's smiling broadly.

'How do you feel about Mum being back in the Lakes?' I ask.

'It's quite nice that we can be civil to each other and that's about it.'

'I suppose so. It was quite nice seeing her over Christmas.'

After she appeared at the church nativity, Mum called around to the guesthouse a few days later with some Christmas gifts for Hannah and me. Dad happened to be there and she stayed with us for a glass of sherry and a sandwich. I'm still wary of her motives but I can't deny that having her with us was very pleasant.

An hour later we arrive at the airport and Dad heaves my suitcase from the boot at the drop-off point for departures. There are taxi doors slamming as passengers excitedly wheel their cases towards the glass doors of the airport terminal.

'Right, well thanks, Dad, you take care,' I say, giving him a hug.

'Have a nice time, love, you deserve it. Give us a text when you arrive,' he says before climbing into his silver car and driving off.

Thankfully it's not too busy in the departure hall and the queues for check-in seem to be moving along pretty quickly. I'm at a check-in desk adjacent to a family of four, with twin girls who look around four or five years of age. Mum and the girls are wearing similar grey tracksuits with a pink stripe down the side. Dad is wearing jeans and a thick navy jumper. We seem to be moving along to our check-in desks simultaneously.

'Are you going on holiday?' asks one of the little girls, with brown pigtails, who is sitting on a green and blue Trunki suitcase.

'Yes, I am.' I smile.

'Where are you going?'

'Maisie, don't be so nosy,' says her mum.

'Don't worry, it's fine. I'm going to Italy,' I tell the little girl.

'Is that in Tenerife? 'Cos we're going to Tenerife.'

'No, it isn't. I think it's going to be sunnier where you're going.'

'That's why we're going,' says the mum. 'A little injection of sunshine. The girls don't start school until September so we thought we'd have a little sunshine holiday abroad – might just save my sanity as well as yours, eh, love?' She glances at her husband, who nods and smiles.

There are almost two hours before boarding so once I've checked my bag in I have a wander around the airport shops. My senses are assaulted by the perfumes all competing for air space in the duty-free section. An overly made-up assistant who has her brunette hair in a tight bun sprays the latest Gucci fragrance onto a sample stick and wafts it under my nose. It's a heady mix of jasmine and musk and not at all like the floral perfumes I prefer. Adam bought me my first bottle of Daisy by Marc Jacobs when we first started dating. I wore it for years but have been unable to wear it again since his death.

My eye is drawn to the aftershaves and I wonder whether I should take Fabio a gift. I remember he smelled of expensive fragrance but it wasn't familiar to me. I decide against it. Men can have a very particular taste in aftershave so I decide to buy him a bottle of single malt whisky instead, as I recall him enjoying a glass of one or two of those in the lounge of the bed and breakfast. I wander around several more shops before enjoying a coffee and a smoked salmon and cream cheese bagel, and soon enough the board shows my departure gate. I head towards the plane, a mixture of emotions swirling around my head. Am I being foolish? Did I have a brief holiday romance that should have been left at that? Am I getting my hopes up? I can't deny that a part of me is excited. But another part of me wonders: what on earth am I doing?

Chapter Twenty-Eight

To my surprise the plane is half-empty, and I find that I have a whole row of seats to myself so I open my book and settle in for the flight which takes just over two hours.

Greg is going to spend the weekend at the B&B with Hannah, which I know she is really looking forward to. When they are together there is always laughter and I reflect that it's so important to find that person to laugh along with for a lifetime.

'Would you like a drink?' asks the pretty blonde air stewardess, twenty minutes later, as she wheels the trolley bar towards me. I ask for a whisky and soda. She despatches my drink along with a small dish of peanuts before moving on, leaving a cloud of Thierry Mugler Alien perfume in her wake.

As we're mid-flight, I play over the conversation in the car with Dad. Was he telling me the truth about his health? Was it simply the change in temperature that caused him to faint at the pub? And why was Mum ringing him? Perhaps they have been communicating more than he was willing to tell me. His relationship with Sheila never got off the ground and I find myself wondering if that had anything to do with Mum being back in the Lakes. The timing seems a little bit too coincidental. Maybe I should feel happy that my parents are at least being civilised to each other, after years apart.

A short while later the stewardess reappears. 'Would you like something to eat, free of charge? We have quite a lot of food on board and, as you can see, a half empty plane.'

'No thanks, I had something at the airport. It is usually this quiet? I imagined Milan would be busy all year round.'

'Actually, it is a little quieter than usual, yes, although it often is in January as people are recovering financially from Christmas.' She smiles. 'We have full flights for the sunny destinations such as the Canary Islands pretty much all year round.'

I think of the family at the airport heading to Tenerife and wonder how they're getting on. Then I think about the long, sultry summer days spent in Naples on my honeymoon. I remember eating the best pizza I have ever tasted in a rustic restaurant down a side street and the long days spent on the beach eating gelato and sipping Peroni. I'm so excited to experience Italy again.

The blonde stewardess returns for a final lap of the plane offering duty-free purchases, which I decline. I settle in with a couple more chapters of my book and soon enough the pilot is announcing the descent and advising passengers that the current temperature in Milan is eleven degrees. He asks the cabin crew to take their seats and we have a perfect landing onto the tarmac of Milan airport. The weather outside actually looks quite bright, with a blue sky above and all the pent-up anticipation settles in. I'm actually here.

Chapter Twenty-Nine

I take a blue taxi from the airport to Milan Centrale, the charming shaven-headed driver chatting easily and informing me about a few nightspots in Milan, should I get bored in Varenna. Little does he know that I have zero intention of visiting a night spot; the closest I get to one is La Trattoria with the girls. He hands me his business card, in case I need to book him for the return journey, before saying '*Ciao*' with a wink.

As I enter the vast station, I'm greeted by a cacophony of sights and sounds. It's a stunning grey building that has a blend of various styles including art deco. It has to be one of the most beautiful buildings I have ever seen. There are numerous sculptures dotted about on stands and Italian frescoes adorn the walls – it's almost like stepping into a museum. The high, curved ceilings give the impression of entering a vast tunnel. I have just had my ticket stamped at a machine, as is required in many Italian stations, for my onward journey to Varenna. When Adam and I took a train in Naples, we got chatting to a couple who had failed to get their tickets verified and were charged a hundred euros, so I won't be making that mistake.

It's a busy place with various types of passengers bustling around, from those dashing down stone steps to work as they disembark the train, to visitors taking onward journeys to the lake villages, just like myself. A young man in a slightly scruffy-looking blue tracksuit offers to carry my case onto the Varenna train but I grip it firmly and say a polite 'No thank you'. I've been warned about this. They take your case and then disappear with it. There are pickpockets to watch out for too. One of the scams is for a young woman to engage you in conversation, while one of their nearby family members steal from your handbag, so I'm on high alert.

I have half an hour before my train arrives, so I purchase a coffee and a chocolate chip pretzel from a cute little van kiosk and take a seat at a bench to eat. Italian pretzels are sweet and delicious, like a cross between a cake and a cracker.

As I look around, my surroundings feel so unfamiliar yet uplifting. I love my home in the Lake District but I'm excited to be breaking out of my comfort zone.

The station is so big, filled with shops and restaurants, that I feel as though I am inside an airport terminal as I sit and watch the world go by.

A young couple dressed in almost identical blue ripped jeans and zip-up black jackets run along the platform, the girl with long plum-coloured hair laughing loudly. The young man spots the train that is about to leave and scoops a suitcase up in his arms before sprinting towards it where they both step onto it with seconds to spare. I wonder if they've had a weekend together in Milan? I find myself thinking about my first weekend away with Adam. We went to Harrogate and stayed in a hotel that overlooked the glorious flower gardens. We drank tea in floral china cups and ate slabs of cake at Bettys tea rooms as a break from shopping and dined in a

French restaurant in the evening, where I ate frogs' legs for the first (and last) time. It almost feels as if it was a lifetime ago.

I finish my coffee and walk onto platform five, a display board showing the departure time for my train as five minutes away. I send Fabio a quick text telling him I will arrive at the station in Varenna in a little over an hour. When the train arrives, I take my seat and open my glossy magazine and try to distract myself as I realise I am giddy with nervous anticipation…

Chapter Thirty

Fabio walks towards me slowly and my heart does a little flip. He seems taller than I remember somehow and heart-stoppingly handsome He is wearing a black woollen overcoat over an olive green sweater and a pair of dark blue jeans. I suddenly feel a little self-conscious. I refreshed my make-up on the train, so at least I know I look the best I possibly can. My heart is hammering so loudly that I'm sure he must be able to hear it.

'Ciao, Gina,' he says, greeting me with a kiss on both cheeks, before wrapping me in an embrace. He smells divine. 'Welcome to my home town.' He lifts my case and guides me towards the car park. 'How are you? I hope you had a pleasant journey?'

'Fine thanks. The plane was half-empty so I had plenty of leg room.'

'I'm glad you made it through security. No incriminating items in your hand luggage then?' He smiles, remembering the story of the Stanley knife and the glitter.

'Thankfully I remembered to check my bag this time. I found a bottle of sink unblocker that I'd forgotten about.'

Fabio laughs.

'Are you hungry, Gina?'

'I am, I've only had a pretzel at the station.'

'Good.' He smiles. 'I have booked a table at a little restaurant a short drive away.'

I am a little surprised that we aren't driving straight to the villa but decide I could do with some food and a glass of wine.

Fabio lugs my suitcase into his black Alfa Romeo sports car. I knew he would drive a classy model.

'I can't believe you are really here,' he says, stopping to look at me properly. 'You're even prettier than I remember.'

'And you're just as charming.'

Fabio opens the passenger door and we're buckled up, ready to head to the restaurant when a text pings through on my phone. It's from Dad, asking if I have arrived safely. Damn, I meant to text him as I stepped off the plane but I'd been distracted by the Jason Statham lookalike taxi driver. I quickly tap out a reply before placing my phone into my bag and zipping it closed.

Our journey takes us along a breathtaking coastal road, surrounded by lush green mountains and sparkling sea views. The roads bend and twist, passing olive groves and terracotta houses on hills spreading out into the distance, as far as the eye can see. After driving for around fifteen minutes we pull into the stone-coloured gravel driveway of what looks like a house. It has cream painted walls and olive trees in the garden but as soon as I step out of the car, I realise it's actually a restaurant. Fabio walks over to my side, offering his hand to guide me along the winding passageway to the picturesque lunch spot.

'Buongiorno,' says a smiling waiter, greeting us as we step inside. He takes my coat and hangs it on an old-fashioned wooden coat stand near the door. My stomach gives a little growl as I inhale the aromas of garlic and rosemary.

'Buongiorno, *tavolo per due?*' asks Fabio, and we are directed to a table for two near a window that overlooks a courtyard with olive trees and herbs in terracotta pots.

The restaurant is buzzing with life as lunchtime diners enjoy their food, chatting and laughing loudly. Busy waiters weave in and out of the tables with food orders and carafes of wine. The décor of the restaurant is traditional in design with a tiled floor and dark wooden furniture, although there are contemporary touches including eye-catching vases and modern art on the walls. We pass a fridge section crammed with tempting desserts before we take our seats.

'I can't wait to see the villa,' I say as I peruse the menu.

'There's still a lot of work to do. I've had decorators in these last few days, pricing up some jobs. Thankfully the house doesn't need a complete rewiring, just the addition of more sockets. A plumber will hopefully fix the problem in the unused bedrooms, then the decorators will finish things up when that has been done. Maybe you can help me design a website when everything is up and running?'

'I'd be happy to. I can understand why you would want to open the breakfast room as a restaurant. If you could recreate something like this place, you'd be packed out.'

'We Italians love our food. It has to be just right, though. We are also the fiercest critics,' says Fabio as he attracts the attention of a waiter to take our food order.

We place our orders and then a different waiter brings a jug of iced water with lemon to the table and Fabio pours us each a glass. I try not to look at the waiter's impossibly toned backside as he disappears, imagining what Katy would say if she were here.

'Would there be much competition locally if you opened a restaurant in the evenings?' I ask Fabio.

'Not really. Most of the restaurants are near the harbour or a couple of streets away. Most of the villas in the street offer breakfast only. I'm excited by the idea, although taking the villa from a bed and breakfast to an evening venue takes it to a whole new level. I just can't decide if I want that kind of commitment,' he muses.

'I agree it would be a huge commitment. I always have plenty to do back home, even just serving breakfasts. There's the food orders, accounts and housekeeping and so on. Not to mention keeping the garden looking nice. I can't afford to have staff for everything.'

The attractive waiter arrives with our food order of sea bass and salad for me, and a seafood linguine for Fabio. Seeing as I'm on holiday, I also order a large glass of Valpolicella.

'You seem to have some lovely staff at your guesthouse, and of course Hannah. Have you always been close?' Fabio asks as he sips some water.

'I suppose so. She was always the mischief-maker when we were kids. I had to keep her in check a few times when we were younger,' I say, as I remember her penchant for knocking on peoples' doors and running away.

When the food arrives, I tuck into it ravenously, having not realised how hungry I was. It is utterly delicious. The fish has a rich crusted coating of rosemary and tarragon and the wonderful scent had me salivating as soon as it arrived. Fabio's creamy linguine is topped with mussels that are emanating the scent of the ocean.

'This is what I wanted you to sample,' Fabio says, noting my enjoyment of the fragrant sea bass. 'The family have been here for generations making traditional Italian food with the best ingredients.'

I finish my wine, which has gone to my head slightly, and refill my glass of water. Fabio has stuck to drinking coffee and I am torn between finishing off the meal with a cappuccino or a slice of the lemon meringue pie I spotted in the dessert fridge on the way in. I decide to opt for the coffee. Maybe Fabio has plans for dinner this evening, so I will save a dessert until then.

'What have the staff at the villa done during the refurbishments?' I ask.

'Luca and Maria have taken holidays. They took it as an opportunity to visit their son who lives just outside Milan. Their daughter-in-law is pregnant and suffering with terrible morning sickness, so Maria is happy to help look after her. She has only just got over the shock of becoming a grandmother, I think.'

'Really?'

'Yes, she is only forty-eight years old and tells me she is far too young to be a grandmother. I remind her that her son is the same age as she was when she gave birth to him.' He smiles.

We finish our coffees and Fabio settles the bill. The handsome waiters walk us to the front door and shake our hands warmly as we depart, the laughter from the restaurant still ringing in our ears. Outside the afternoon sun is beginning to draw in as dusk gently begins to fall.

'Ciao. Come back and see us soon,' says the waiter with the incredible backside as he waves us off around the corner.

Leaving, we drive past a couple of tiny villages, the dark orange sun of early dusk casting shadows over the green landscape, cats stretched out lazily in gardens and children on bicycles returning home for the evening to the terracotta-roofed houses.

Fifteen minutes later we are pulling in to a cobbled street with a row of pastel-coloured houses. Villa Lucia is at the end of the street. There are two cypress trees standing in the front garden like guards at the doorway. The building is sandstone-coloured with dark green wooden shutters at the windows. It looks glorious and far grander than I imagined, even though the paint is peeling from the walls, giving it a rustic feel. It certainly needs a lick of paint but it has definite appeal.

I already know the hallway is magnificent from our FaceTime conversations, although maybe the rest of the place is a different story. The sun is setting fast and the street is cast in a soft amber glow. As Fabio lifts my case from the boot of his car, I think I may have arrived somewhere very special…

Chapter Thirty-One

We enter the hallway of the villa, which is every bit as pretty as the images I saw on the video call, although a little tired around the edges. I quite like the paintings of the bowls of fruit in the gold frames, although Fabio is still unsure. The wallpaper in the hall looks very faded and I notice the corners peeling away ever so slightly. To the right of the hallway is a dark wooden door which Fabio opens up to reveal a spacious room that seems dark and uninviting, largely due to the dark-coloured drapes at the windows.

'Oh my goodness, it's huge!'

There's a high frescoed ceiling with a rose patterned light fitting at the centre, finished with a gilt edging. Eight wooden tables sit on a striking parquet floor.

'Can you imagine the potential for a room like this? These curtains need to go for a start,' says Fabio as he walks over to the heavy curtains at the windows. 'We need to let the light flood in to such a beautiful space.'

'I absolutely love it. I can see why you would like to have this a restaurant, it would be so romantic in the evenings, with a little work.'

'I would reserve the best table for you,' he says, smiling and fixing me with his blue eyes. 'And I like the optimism of "a little work".'

When we have finished our tour of the house, Fabio guides me to a guest room which is neat and tidy. I am pleased to see that he is taking nothing for granted and is behaving like a perfect gentleman.

I seem to have the best room so I can understand Fabio's desire to update the rest. The basics are all there, though. There are dark wooden Italianate wardrobes and stunning carved wooden headboards on the beds, but the soft furnishings look faded. Tomorrow, I hope I can offer my suggestions to update the bedrooms. Hopefully we can also go into Milan one day and do some shopping, but I try not to run away with myself.

As I'm hanging my clothes in the wardrobe, my mobile phone, which is plugged in to charge up, begins to ring.

'Daphne, hi, how are you?'

'Hi, Gina. I'm not too bad, how are you? Are you busy?'

'Nope. I'm just hanging some clothes in the wardrobe. I'm actually on a little break in Italy.'

'Really? Oh, sorry, Gina, I didn't realise you were going so soon after Christmas.'

'It's OK. Is everything alright?'

'Well, I was ringing to say I'll be moving back home soon. I've left Ben. I'll fill you in when I get home.'

I knew Daphne had been a little homesick but I had no idea her relationship was on the rocks – my heart goes out to her. We chat for a few more minutes, with the promise to meet up when I return home.

I'm about to put my phone away when I receive a text from Hannah.

Well, do you have your own bedroom? xx

I tap out a reply.

Yes. I imagined I would. Fabio is a gentleman.

Suppose so. Don't be 'accidentally' getting into the wrong bed when you've nipped to the loo in the middle if the night x

Won't have to. I have an en suite x

I don't suppose I've ever been one to jump into bed with someone after a couple of dates. I like to get to know someone first.

So what's the hotel like then?

I decide it's probably quicker to give her a quick call.

'Oh, Hannah, the villa is beautiful. It does need some updating but it has so much potential. The location is absolutely stunning, overlooking the lake.'

'Home from home for you, then?'

I don't have the heart to tell her that the views here are even more beautiful than those back home. The lakes are so much bigger and the views more dramatic.

'Sort of. Although thankfully the weather is a little kinder than back home.'

We chat for a few minutes and Hannah tells me about young Ellie, who has uploaded a party make-up tutorial to YouTube.

Apparently, it's already had a couple of thousand hits. She says she's walking on air and dreaming about making a fortune just like Zoella did with her fashion blogs. I really hope she does. She has bags of talent.

'Right, well I'm going now. No doubt we'll speak again. But not in the evening as we may be out.'

'I wouldn't dream of phoning you in the evening. I'd be worried about interrupting something. "When the moon…"'

'Goodbye, Hannah.'

Chapter Thirty-Two

Come the evening, I'm glad I packed a little black dress as Fabio is taking me to dinner tonight. After a shower I walk down the curved staircase to meet with him at the small bar, off the lounge.

Fabio is popping open a bottle of prosecco and stands up to greet me as I walk towards him. I'm wearing my black dress with a lace panel at the top and my red hair is swept up into a chignon. Fabio looks devilishly handsome in a navy suit (which brings out the dark blue of his eyes) over a white open-necked shirt. He is wearing tan-coloured Italian leather loafers and a waft of aftershave which I recognise as Polo by Ralph Lauren drifts towards my nostrils.

'You look beautiful. Just like Christina Hendricks,' he utters, 'but prettier.' He air-kisses each of my cheeks and hands me a glass of prosecco. The touch of his cheek sends electricity coursing through my body.

'So, this evening we are travelling across the lake to a restaurant in Bellagio. The seafood is excellent. The boat leaves at eight o'clock,' says Fabio, taking a glance at his Omega watch. 'Which gives us fifteen minutes, so please sit down.'

I take my time with my prosecco, sipping it gently as anything fizzy goes straight to my head.

I'm glad I've brought my black woollen coat as a cool breeze sweeps along the harbour as we make our way to the boat departure point. Amber-coloured lights are twinkling in the distance on the island of Bellagio and there's a half moon hanging in the navy sky. It's fairly busy along the harbour front with several stalls selling pretzels, pizza slices and hot chocolate. A group of teenagers are sitting on a bench, laughing and drinking. It reminds me of home, where the teenagers hang around the benches near the lakes, often drinking alcohol that they have somehow managed to get hold of. They don't have much to do in the villages, which is probably why so many of them move on.

The boatman guides me onto the boat along with half a dozen other couples as we make the short journey across the lake to Bellagio. I look over to one of the couples sitting across from us holding hands. We strike up a conversation and I learn that they are celebrating their fortieth wedding anniversary. I think it must be wonderful to find such an enduring love and I fleetingly wonder whether Adam and I would have reached such a milestone.

The boat glides along the water as the yellow lights of the restaurants ahead illuminate the harbour, beckoning us towards them. The strains of Dean Martin singing 'Volare' can be heard in the background on the captain's CD player, adding to the romantic feel. It's a little chilly despite a patio heater on deck and I dream of making this journey on a summer evening.

Before long we alight the boat and Fabio tells me it is a short walk to the restaurant. The air feels slightly warmer on the island.

'So have you been to this restaurant before?' I ask.

'Only once but I remember it being outstanding. I brought a client here for lunch. It was a beautiful day in late spring so we sat outside. It's a shame we can't do the same thing this evening, so I have done the next best thing and reserved a table by the window.'

'Is your business going well?' I ask, although judging by the expensive cut of his suit and just about everything he owns I think I already know the answer.

'Yes, very well.' He smiles. 'I save my clients a fortune so they are happy to pay me well.'

'Have you ever had any famous clients?'

'A couple of musicians and film stars.' He shrugs. 'But it's mainly self-employed business people.'

'Film stars? Like who?' I ask, intrigued and slightly star-struck.

'Jason Reynolds.'

'Jason Reynolds, really? What's he like in real life?'

'He's a really nice guy actually. Very laid back, a little shy even. Not a bit like he is when he's playing James Bond.'

We arrive at the waterside restaurant a few minutes later and at once I can see that Fabio has chosen a beautiful place to dine. It's decorated in soft greens and creams with wooden tables. One of the walls displays a huge mural of Lake Como. On the opposite wall, floor length French windows look out over the stunning lake.

'This is just beautiful,' I sigh, taking in the surroundings. There's a huge olive tree in the centre of the floor that the restaurant was built around. It's incredible.

'I am glad you like it,' says Fabio.

A waiter arrives and hands us each a black leather menu. He returns a minute later with some breadsticks and a jug of water.

'I am afraid I will not be able to treat you to dinner like this every evening,' says Fabio, as he peruses the menu. 'There is much work to be done at the villa before reopening in little over a week.'

'It doesn't seem a lot of time,' I suggest.

'The work will be done and we will take bed and breakfast bookings only, until I consider opening for dinner in the evenings. Tomorrow I may have to cook you pizza in the hotel kitchen.'

'Good job I like pizza.'

'You once told me it was no better than cheese on toast,' he reminds me, grinning.

'I didn't say it was no better, I just commented on how everything sounds so wonderful, even the ordinary stuff.'

'You would never describe an Italian pizza as ordinary. You have probably only ever eaten inferior pizza from a food chain,' he teases.

'Errm, excuse me, I've eaten at your uncle Aldo's restaurant, remember. You think I have such little taste as to only eat fast food pizza? Oh, and I've eaten a pizza down a side street in Naples. Have you?'

'I am, I think the phrase is, *winding you up*,' he replies with a huge grin on his face.

I throw him a playful scowl before continuing to peruse the menu.

The food sounds mouth-watering and I can't decide what I should eat. Lemon-topped lobster on a huge white rectangular plate is being delivered to the next table. It looks amazing.

'I can recommend the steak,' offers Fabio, as he notes my inability to select anything.

We finally order some antipasto, and are presented with various meats, cheeses and olives. Fabio orders a bottle of prosecco to drink.

'So where is your own home?' I ask Fabio as I spear an olive with a cocktail stick.

'A twenty-minute drive away,' he says, as he wraps a piece of prosciutto around a green olive and pops it into his mouth. 'So I did the right thing booking us a lakeside table?' he asks as he pours me a glass of prosecco, telling me that the conversation about his home is over. I decide to forget it and relax into my surroundings. It would be impossible not to be charmed by such serene beauty. I glance out of the window and I can see the ferry we arrived in, returning to Varenna on the shimmering moonlit water.

The food is utterly delicious, we order steak for me and veal linguine for Fabio. I learn that Fabio's parents are fairly wealthy and owned several shops for many years, in and around Como. His grandmother had been widowed for many years and had run the villa alone with the help of Luca and Maria. Giorgia would come in and clean the bedrooms as well as run errands to the local market, as his grandmother grew older.

'She worked until the day she took her last breath,' Fabio tells me over coffee. 'I'm so happy I got to see her a week before she died. It was a late-summer afternoon when Maria called to tell me she had found my grandmother in the garden in a wicker chair. She had simply fallen asleep in the sun and never woke up. She was eighty-seven years old.'

'I'm so sorry for your loss. I suppose it must be of some comfort to know that she never suffered with illness. I imagine it must be heartbreaking to watch someone you love waste away,' I say quietly.

A light flashes on Fabio's phone, indicating an incoming call. He excuses himself for a moment as he scoops up his phone and I stare out at across the lake as I finish my coffee. After the most wonderful day, tiredness is now beginning to take over.

Chapter Thirty-Three

As I step into the marble shower the next morning, I think of the previous evening's conversation. When we arrived back at the villa last night we had a brandy as a little nightcap before heading off to bed in our separate bedrooms. Fabio was a little quiet on the return journey to Varenna, almost as if his mood had changed after he received the phone call at the restaurant, or perhaps he was just tired, as I was. In my mind I had expected bedtime to involve a lot of flirtatious anticipation, with me deliberating over whether or not I should spend the night with Fabio, but it hadn't been the case. As the half-moon shone over the lake, I wondered whether I should have knocked on Fabio's bedroom door and asked him if everything was alright. In the end, I decided against it. He was probably just sleepy.

I climb out of the shower and sit down on the edge of my bed. Just as I'm about to give Dad a quick ring, there's a tap on the bedroom door.

'Room service,' says Fabio.

'Wait a minute, I just need to put a dressing gown on,' I shriek, and shuffle to don a waffle gown from the bathroom door.

'Ready!' I shout. In walks Fabio, wearing a maroon jumper that looks like cashmere over a white T-shirt and a pair of smart jeans.

He's carrying a tray with a pot of coffee, pastries, chocolate marble cake and a cherry tart.

'Cake for breakfast? Now this I could get used to.' I take the tray and set it down on the bedside table.

'Tomorrow I will make you smoked salmon and scrambled eggs,' he says, kissing the back of my hand lightly. 'This morning I think you deserve something sweet. I was afraid I had soured the mood a little last night.'

'I noticed you were a little quiet. I thought you were just tired. I was exhausted. Was it something to do with that phone call?'

'Yes, it was just a something of a personal nature. The timing infuriated me a little but I am sorry the mood changed. Today is another day,' he says, smiling broadly, with no trace of the previous evening's air of tension. 'I'm afraid it is going to be a little messy here this week. The electricians are arriving this morning to fit the additional sockets and the plumber will take a look at the spare bedrooms.'

'I can live with that. As long as we get to spend some time together in the evenings.'

'Of course. It's the time of day I will most look forward to.' He smiles. 'The decorators will arrive in a couple of days' time after we have selected some wall coverings.'

'Will that involve a trip to Milan?'

'Yes, I was thinking tomorrow. The best interior design shop is there. You can see it online but I want to see the colours of the wall coverings and feel the textures of the soft furnishings. I am hoping for your input in this area, Gina, I trust your judgement. You have such a beautiful place in England. When everything is finished up, I am all yours for the last few days of your visit.'

Suddenly I'm wishing the next few days away.

He pours the coffee and I select a huge apricot Danish pastry dusted with icing sugar. I'm not sure I can eat anything else so I pour myself another fresh coffee. There's something about Italian coffee that is just so delicious I could quite easily get hooked on it.

Half an hour later we are downstairs and I'm washing the breakfast plates when there is a knock at the door of the villa. I open it and two men are standing in front of me. One is moustachioed and looks around sixty years of age and the other is a younger version. Father and son, clearly. They are both dressed in T-shirts and dungarees and an image of the Mario brothers springs to mind, making me stifle a laugh.

'Buongiorno.' The older man smiles as he steps inside the hallway and plonks a large toolbox onto the floor. The men are here to put additional sockets in all of the bedrooms to cater for modern day devices such as mobile phones and laptops.

'Would you like a coffee?' I ask as Fabio guides them upstairs to the first bedroom.

'Grazie, signorina,' says the smiling older man.

I'm setting the coffee cups onto a tray ready to take upstairs when there's another knock.

I open the door and for a second I am speechless. Standing before me is the hunkiest male specimen I have seen in my entire life. He's well over six foot tall with thick black hair, a handsome chiselled face and the body of an Adonis. He's wearing a tight black T-shirt and a pair of khaki-coloured combat trousers, with a notepad and pen sticking out of a side pocket.

'Ciao. I've come to take a look at the plumbing,' he says, managing to make it sound sexy.

I'm like a flustered teenager as I welcome him inside.

'You couldn't have timed it better. I've just brewed some coffee for the electricians. Would you like some?'

'Thank you. I'll have a quick one. Then I will stick to the water. I have more endurance when my body is fully hydrated,' he says with a sidelong grin.

'Right then, here you are,' I say, thrusting a coffee under his nose before disappearing upstairs with the tray of drinks.

The electricians have worked surprisingly quickly at fitting the additional sockets and a few hours later they are ready to sort the two rooms that have been off limits, but the hunky plumber is still working.

'Why he take so long?' asks the older electrician, shaking his head.

His son, who hasn't said a word up until now, says, 'He's probably too busy admiring himself in the full-length mirror.'

I let out a laugh.

'I think the plumbing is pretty ancient in this house. I imagine it's quite a big job,' Fabio says.

The old man huffs.

'Well, we will take our lunch break now. We'll be back in an hour. Maybe Mr Universe will have finished by then.'

A few minutes later, the hunky plumber walks down the stairs into the hallway. I can feel the testosterone wafting towards me with every step of his muscular thighs.

'Mamma mia, that is a bigger job than I thought,' he says, scratching his head in true tradesman style. 'I have the water flowing in the sink and the shower, but I think there's a blockage in the drainage system between the two bedrooms, which is why the toilet will not flush. I will take some lunch then return with some different tools.'

Once the workmen have left, Fabio and I walk into the kitchen where I prepare a sandwich of salty pastrami and rocket on some fresh focaccia bread.

'I can't wait until they've all upped and left. I'm dying to get on with the shopping trip to Milan.'

'You mean you want to see the back of our plumber? Or should I say, his backside? What is that line from that John Travolta movie, "How I hate to see you go, but I love to watch you leave"?'

'Fabio! How could you say that? I can't say I even really noticed him,' I lie.

We pour some coffee before I wash the cups, setting them on the draining board. I'm perusing the soft furnishing shop online and before I know it the workmen have returned to the villa. This time the plumber has an apprentice in tow.

'I think that toilet problem is more of a two-man job,' says the hunky plumber. The businesswoman in me immediately wonders whether he will try to charge more for the extra pair of hands.

After half an hour I walk in to one of the unused bedrooms to find the young apprentice bending over the toilet with a plunger.

'How we doing here? Would you like a drink?' I ask, as a faint odour of something unpleasant hits my nostrils.

Hunky Plumber is rubbing his chin thoughtfully.

'No thank you, maybe later. I am certain now that we have a blockage in the sewer drain. I think I am going to have to get my big rod out.'

Gulp.

The 'Mario brothers' are hovering on the landing asking how long the plumbers will take, having finished in the other bedrooms.

Hunky Plumber informs us that the only way to clear the drain blockage between the two adjoining bedrooms is to remove the toilets and apply a pressure washer on one side, whilst the apprentice inserts a flushing rod from the adjacent room.

'Beautiful lady. If you could watch the downstairs drain near the back door and let me know if anything appears,' he instructs. 'Usually everything is OK after a good thrusting.'

The windows in the unused rooms are open to ventilate them, so I can hear the plumbers talking to each other.

'OK, I am going to insert the air blaster now. Start poking with the rod.'

'OK,' comes the reply from next door.

Down below I can hear the sound of the pressure hose and the thrusting of the metal rod.

I stand waiting for something to happen, watching the drain like a hawk. Nothing. I stand for a few minutes more as the hosing and thrusting continues upstairs. I'm beginning to think it's a fruitless task, when suddenly I hear a whooshing sound followed by high-pitched screams. Fabio rushes outside as he thinks the screams are coming from me.

When we realise the sound has come from upstairs, we take the stairs two at a time and burst into one of the bedrooms. Hunky Plumber is standing over the space where the toilet has been removed, covered in the source of the blockage.

'Oh my God! Get in here!' I say, quickly switching on the shower and trying not to throw up. I dash to a landing cupboard for some towels.

The electricians have followed us into the bedroom to see what all the commotion is about.

'I see you've unblocked the drain then,' says the older man, trying not to smile. The young plumber emerges from the adjoining bedroom with a serious expression on his face.

'I can't believe thees happen on my first day,' he says in his heavy Italian accent. 'Eet is my first time to try and impress my boss and what do I do? I cover him in *merda!*'

The electricians are making no attempt to hide their feelings now, as they laugh uproariously.

Thankfully after a clean-up and a loan of Fabio's old clothes, the plumbers finish their work and leave, the hunky guy muttering in Italian to the young apprentice as they load their equipment into a white van before speeding off.

I can't believe how different he looked, from the self-assured sex god of this morning to the humiliated-looking bloke who has departed wearing Fabio's clothes.

A couple of hours later the electricians have also left, the older man still shaking his head and smiling at the drainage malfunction.

All the pent-up emotion of trying to keep a straight face during the day's drama comes tumbling out as soon as Fabio and I are alone. We laugh loudly in the hallway, tears streaming down our faces.

'Oh my goodness, that poor man. Talk about ruining your image. I hope he's OK.'

'Well, he did look a little flushed,' laughs Fabio.

'What a day. I feel exhausted even though all I've done today is make coffee and watch outdoor drains for eruptions.'

'Thankfully it didn't erupt over you.'

'I never thought about that! It seems I had a lucky escape.'

'So, we can have a relaxed evening tonight if you wish, then we can set off early in the morning for Milan. How does pasta and a glass of red wine sound?'

'Pasta cooked by a handsome Italian? Sounds absolutely perfect.'

Chapter Thirty-Four

I wake just after seven thirty the next morning and after a quick shower I stroll downstairs to find Fabio in the kitchen. We had a lovely, relaxed evening last night, talking about Fabio's hopes and dreams for the villa and sipping Chianti. We shared a beautiful, long kiss on the sofa but I was so tired I could barely keep my eyes open. I headed up to bed before Fabio, who said he would finish up in the kitchen.

'Ah, good morning. I was going to surprise you with breakfast in bed,' says Fabio as he pours some egg mixture into a pan.

'Two days in a row? You're spoiling me.'

'You deserve it,' he says, beckoning me to him, where he plants a kiss on my lips. 'Please, sit down.'

I watch Fabio effortlessly working in the kitchen and soon enough, I am presented with smoked salmon and scrambled eggs. It's creamy and delicious and I gobble it down.

'Mmm, I could really get used to this. I don't think Hannah is going to wait on me like this when I get home.'

After breakfast I nip upstairs to change into a pair of jeans and a pale blue jumper. I put my black coat on, then add a pink scarf adorned with little black bicycles, which was a gift from Hannah when she visited Copenhagen.

It's a short drive to the station at Varenna and Fabio drops me at the ticket office before parking his car in the station car park. We settle into our journey as the scenery changes from lake views to urbanisation and buildings adorned with graffiti. An American couple are standing up behind our seats as they guard their luggage. The tall black guy with an Afro has a guitar flung over his shoulder.

Two middle-aged women are sitting in the seats opposite us and we strike up a conversation. They tell us that they are meeting their respective daughters in Milan where they are studying art at the university. The dark-haired lady is from the Philippines and the fair-haired lady is English.

'Our daughters have been inseparable for the last two years. We all met up in London last year and have been good friends ever since.'

The Filipina lady notices the American guy with the guitar.

'What can you play?' she asks, smiling.

'What do you like?'

'Do you know any Ed Sheeran? I love Ed Sheeran!'

The American guy slings his guitar over his shoulder and strums a few chords.

'*When your hand…*'

By the time he gets to the chorus, which talks about finding love where we are, Fabio threads his fingers through mine and the six of us have joined in the song, as the rest of the carriage looks on. It's the most magical moment. We disembark the train with handshakes and good wishes to each other to enjoy the remainder of our holidays.

'Maybe there should be buskers inside the trains instead of hanging around outside train stations,' I say, buzzing with excitement.

We round a corner and after walking for ten minutes we head into the centre of Milan, where we stop for a cappuccino at a traditional coffee shop. There are pastries displayed in a glass counter at the front of the shop and I inhale a pungent aroma of coffee. Fabio orders the coffees from the counter and I find a seat at one of the dark wooden tables. As I glance to either side of the café, I take in the walls that are painted blood red and are decorated with framed photographs of movie scenes. There's one of Audrey Hepburn and Gregory Peck riding a scooter in *Roman Holiday*. There's another of a laughing Sophia Loren and Clark Gable on a harbour front in *It Started in Naples*. The pictures make me think of Hannah and her penchant for old movies.

'We'll warm ourselves up with this before we carry on,' says Fabio, placing a large latte for me and an Americano for him down onto the table.

I wrap my hands around my hot drink to warm my fingers, which are still a little cold despite my black leather gloves. I study Fabio's face and his blue eyes with long, thick black eyelashes, considering our contrasting appearances. I have the fair colouring of an English rose in contrast to Fabio's brooding Italian good looks. I wonder if he looks like his mother or his father? He is square-jawed and conventionally handsome so I imagine he must look like his father. Perhaps he has the eyes of his mother, or at least the eyelashes, which are long and lustrous.

'Don't you just love the smell of this coffee shop? Even if you make fresh coffee at home you never get this type of aroma,' I say, inhaling the air around me.

'It's wonderful,' he replies. 'I think it's because they grind the coffee on the premises. You don't get the same aroma with filter coffee.'

'Maybe I'll buy a coffee grinder for the guesthouse back home. I'm sure the guests would find the smell inviting.'

'Unless they don't like coffee.' He grins.

'I never thought of that.'

'Well, you can't please all of the people, all of the time. Being here with you is pleasing me very much right now though,' says Fabio.

Much to my embarrassment I find myself blushing slightly. And I can hardly hide it – it's so visible with pale skin.

'Well, I'm loving being here too. Milan seems exhilarating. So different from back home.'

'You should come here again in the warm weather. Lake Como, I mean. Come and see it in all its glory. I would love to spend the summer here with you,' he says, and my heart soars.

'Right then, come along.' Fabio drains his coffee and gets to his feet. 'We are not going to get anything done today if we get too comfortable here. We can stop for lunch in a couple of hours.'

I recall Fabio once mentioning that his sister lived here in Milan. He told me she was a human rights lawyer, but has hardly spoken of her since.

We fall into step as we walk for a few more minutes, soon entering the main square in Milan. We head into the Duomo piazza and the Gothic grey structure of the cathedral looms into view, its spires reaching towards the sky. Groups of tourists are standing around snapping pictures of the huge building.

'Wow, that's really something. Dark yet beautiful,' I say.

'It took six hundred years until it was actually finished. I think it was finally completed in the 1960s,' Fabio informs me. 'Before you go home we will go inside and take a proper look. But today we must not forget what we came here for. I think we have time for this though.' Taking me by surprise, he pulls me towards him and kisses me. An American tourist with a huge smile asks me if I would like her to take our photograph. We smile for the camera on my phone and I think this is a moment that definitely needs capturing.

We move on. Fabio tells me the store is around a ten-minute walk away. I'm pleased I packed my flat-heeled Chelsea boots which are very comfortable to walk in. The city is crowded and we pass throngs of people of various nationalities. We walk past designer shops and I stare into the windows of a Balenciaga shop and spot a bag which has a price tag of one thousand euros.

'You like the bag?' asks Fabio.

'I really like the colour – it's quite unusual.' The bag is a deep mustard colour with a single black horizontal stripe but it's wildly overpriced.

As we continue walking I take in the stunning buildings, and wish I was here for longer than just a week. We eventually arrive at a huge glass-fronted building that has beautiful sofas draped with stylish cushions in the window. As we step inside I discover that the rooms are all set out with individual designs, showcasing their wallpapers and soft furnishings. Satin wall coverings in every shade are displayed on walls, complemented by sensational lamps, throws and cushions, elegantly displayed around the room. I think it is exactly the right kind of shop to furnish the bedrooms.

'How about this?' I point to a cream-coloured paper with a slight blue two-tone sheen.

To my surprise Fabio pulls a face.

'This one?' I say, pointing at a green waterfall-style pattern.

He cocks his head to one side slightly as he considers it.

'No,' he says finally.

My mind flashes back to how Adam and I would disagree on décor. Adam always came around to my point of view in the end and I hope Fabio won't disagree with me too much. After all, he did invite me here because he admired my eye for interior design.

'If you are having wallpaper in the bedrooms, I think a pastel sheen would be the way to go. I'm thinking soft greens, greys and blues. It would contrast beautifully with the dark furniture. I take it you do want my input?' I say, feeling mildly frustrated.

I show Fabio a photograph on my phone from a country bedroom in a home interiors magazine. It has the same traditional dark furniture, with fresh, light contemporary touches.

'Perfecto!' Fabio smiles.

Thank goodness for that.

Fabio chats to the owner in Italian about some curtains and we are led up a wooden spiral staircase. The curtains are ready made, but of the highest quality and it doesn't take too long before we agree on purchasing some stunning oyster-coloured drapes for the dining room.

Soon enough, the wall coverings for the eight bedrooms are purchased, along with the curtains and some eye-catching chandelier lighting. Sumptuous bedspreads in various shades are bought for the tops of the beds, as well as white, high thread-count cotton sheets. Fabio places the order at the counter for the furnishings to be delivered later that evening by courier.

'Next we need to look for some art prints for the walls,' says Fabio as we step outside into the cool air. We walk along chatting easily, soon taking a turn down a little cobbled side street. On either side there are several artisan shops, selling beautiful ceramics and nestled at the end is a tiny local art gallery.

Fabio clearly knows this area well, as he points out who each of the shop owners are. Finally, we step inside the Mancini gallery, which has large windows with black wooden window frames. An old-fashioned bell tinkles as we enter.

'Buongiorno,' says an elderly man with a grey beard and soft blue eyes as he places his glasses down onto a desk.

We walk along the white walls of the art studio, Fabio tailing my every step. I'm relishing the closeness, enjoying how good it feels to have him by my side. Adam and I would go to galleries at the weekend, but we never got the chance to add the artwork to the walls, before… Well, before it was too late. As we take in the hauntingly beautiful paintings of Lake Como, I remember how the moon cast over the water last night. One painting looks just like the scene the night before; shimmering moonlight with a lone boat gliding across the winter lake.

'What about this one?' I say. 'Doesn't it look like last night?'

'Didn't I say you had good taste, Gina? I could not agree more, it's perfect. We'll take this one,' Fabio says to the delighted gallery owner. 'This one too.' He points to a serene painting of an endless lavender field, peppered with terracotta houses in the background and formidable cypress trees framing the scene.

'That is most of the purchases complete. So now we eat,' says Fabio. 'But first there is something important I need to show you.'

He pulls me around the corner from the cobbled street into a small alcove where he kisses me passionately on the lips, leaving me dizzy.

'I've been wanting to kiss you properly since the night we kissed under the stars,' he breathes. 'I'm surprised I've been able to keep my hands off you but there are so many people around in the city.'

'I take it you're not one for public displays of affection then?' I say, as I finally come up for air. The kiss outside the cathedral had been nothing like this.

'With you it's hard for me to hold back.' He smiles.

He takes my hand and we stroll hand in hand down a road until soon we are opposite one of the main shopping centres in Milan called the Galleria Vittoria. Designer shops including Prada and Gucci nestle alongside elegant clothes shops and interior design stores. They are all housed in a mall with a glittering domed roof that has the same sumptuous style as the train station. Everywhere I look the buildings take my breath away.

I am totally overwhelmed by Milan. I've lived happily in the serenity of the Lake District for so many years but I haven't felt a pulsing excitement like this in a long time. There's just something about Italy that I love. I adored the back streets of Naples on my honeymoon, enchanted by the little market stalls selling everything from Christian statues to bags of colourful dried pasta and bottles of limoncello. I adored the aroma of pizza from the street food stalls, combined with the smell of the Italian leather handbags that created an intoxicating scent. In the air, the sound of scooters roared along the back streets and the laughter of young men on street corners created a happy vibe. Not to mention the culture to be marvelled at, awaiting tourists at each turn. I think this trip to Milan is shaping up to be just as memorable as Naples, much to my delight.

We eventually arrive at a restaurant called Piccolino's and Fabio says he hopes there is a table available.

'Please do you mind if I ask for a table? I've been practising a little Italian,' I ask.

'Be my guest.' Fabio smiles.

'*Hai un tavolo im mangiare per due?*' I say, feeling rather pleased with myself.

The waiter nods and immediately shows us to a table with comfortable high-backed chairs.

'Well that's one way to get the comfy chairs,' laughs Fabio when we are seated.

'What do you mean?'

'Well, you just asked him for a table, because you are eating for two!' He laughs.

'On my God, I never!

'Relax,' says Fabio, as the waiter returns with a jug of water. 'Although don't be surprised if you are advised not to eat soft cheese or raw eggs,' he teases.

I glance around the modern restaurant, its blonde wooden floors and chrome fixtures and fittings in complete contrast to the traditional Italian restaurants we have previously dined in.

I'm just removing my coat when my phone rings and the caller display tells me that it's Hannah. I make an apologetic face to Fabio and nip outside to answer the call.

'Hi, sis, how are you?' I ask.

'I'm good. More to the point, how are you?' Hannah trills.

'Great. I'm In Milan actually. We're just about to have lunch in a swanky restaurant. We've been doing some shopping for the villa.'

'Sounds great. I bet there's some amazing clothes shops.'

'I haven't actually had a chance to look yet, we've been too busy looking at wall coverings and paintings.'

'What's the weather like?' asks Hannah.

'Bright and sunny, although a little chilly.'

'Grey sky and drizzle here, there was even a bit of snow this morning, but mainly just wet and grey.'

Normally any talk of home immediately makes me feel homesick but one glance at the bright blue sky above me and I feel so thankful to be here.

'Listen, Hannah, I'd better go. Fabio's ordered drinks but the waiter will be back shortly to take our food order. I'll ring you when we get back to the villa later.'

'OK, glad you're alright. I'll speak to you later. Enjoy your lunch. Ciao!'

I arrive back at the table to a large glass of Chianti, which Fabio has just poured from a bottle. There is also a basket of focaccia in the middle of the table. I don't know whether to come clean to the waiter about my faux pas, as I don't want him judging me as I enjoy a drink.

'The food here is excellent,' says Fabio as he sips his wine. 'I would recommend the ox cheek tagliatelle, although I know you will probably take no notice of my recommendations at all.' He laughs.

'I'm not deliberately oppositional, you know,' I say with a mock frown. 'It's just that I like to really study a menu and decide what sounds good. There's a bit too much choice here, though.'

I eventually settle on a beef carpaccio starter and a seared sea bream with lime and chicory for the main course. Fabio has chosen a chicken liver starter followed by a lamb and anchovy dish.

When the food arrives, it's stylishly presented and tastes sensational.

'How is Hannah?' asks Fabio between mouthfuls of chicken liver sautéed in chilli, olive oil and balsamic vinegar.

'She's good, thanks. I'm going to ring her back later and have a proper chat.'

'I like how you are so close to your sister.' He smiles.

I want to ask Fabio why he isn't as close to his sister but decide against it. Maybe two sisters are always closer than a brother and sister?

We finish our delicious meals with coffees and soon we are heading back towards the station for our journey back to Varenna.

'Well that was a successful shopping trip. I can't wait to see all the bedrooms once they're completed.'

'Me too. I am looking forward to seeing the villa open once more for guests. We have bookings exactly eight days from now, when Luca and Maria return to work.'

We arrive at the station and once again I'm staring in awe as I glance around the museum-like space. We purchase tickets and are soon seated on the train, Fabio taking the window seat. The train pulls slowly away from the platform when I notice a woman staring at us, before she lifts her arm and gives a wave. She is tall and thin with long, dark curly hair, wearing a camel coat and black knee-length boots. Fabio appears to ignore the woman, so maybe it wasn't him she was waving at.

'Did you notice that woman on the platform?' I ask as the train leaves the city landscape and heads towards the countryside. 'I thought she was waving at you.'

'I never noticed.' Fabio shrugs. 'Are you sure she was waving at me?'

'Well she wasn't waving at me, I don't know anybody in Milan. Maybe I was mistaken.' I smile.

The train rattles along towards Varenna and talk turns to the villa once more but I find myself half listening. I was sure the woman on the platform was staring straight at Fabio, yet he was certain he hadn't noticed her. I don't know why but I feel slightly uneasy. It's a feeling I don't like very much at all…

Chapter Thirty-Five

We are walking along the street towards the villa when a young dark-haired woman across the way waves her arm and smiles. She crosses the road and starts speaking to Fabio in Italian. Fabio doesn't immediately introduce me, so I decide to do it myself.

'Hi, I'm Gina.' I say, smiling.

'Forgive me, Gina, this is Giorgia. She works part time at the villa. Giorgia, this is my friend Gina from England. She is giving me a hand with some interior design.'

Fabio begins to walk up the path of the villa, ending the conversation there.

'I'll be touch,' he says, turning to Giorgia, who seems to be looking me up and down.

As we enter the villa I walk into the kitchen, and a shaft of late afternoon sun streams through the window. I flop down onto a kitchen stool as Fabio flips on the coffee machine.

'I'm exhausted. When I get back home I'm going to start walking the fells with Hannah. I may even start running.'

'Walking is more civilised. Running damages your knees. When you come back here in the fine weather I will take you on a walk up one of the mountains here. The view is so beautiful.'

So Fabio really does want me to come back here in the summer? I imagine it is a special place as it's charming even in the winter. In my mind's eye I see cafés along the waterside filled with tourists just like back home, but with a guarantee of sunshine throughout the summer. We were very lucky with the weather back home this year, but the sunshine never lasts. The rain inevitably arrives, sometimes followed by the floods. Somehow the seasons don't seem as clearly defined as they once were. Dad often talks about the predictability of the seasons when he was a child. Snow and frost in winter. March winds and light showers in the spring followed by long, hot sultry summers. Cool autumns and bejewelled forests would precede winter. He told me that once you had put your winter clothes away, that was it. You had more chance of snow in April (which we regularly have these days) than a heatwave in December.

'So, as the furnishings will arrive later I'm afraid we will be staying home for dinner. I will be more than happy to cook for you,' says Fabio as he hands me a cup of coffee. He's created a delicious cappuccino from an expensive-looking machine in the kitchen that uses ground coffee and a milk frother. Much more authentic than the instant pods we use in our machine back home.

When I think about it, the stylish coffee machine mirrors everything about Fabio, who screams quality, although he is not flashy. I noticed he showed little interest in the designer shops in Milan and favours the Omega watch over the Rolex. His Italian leather shoes are handmade by local tradesman along with his suits.

We finish our coffee and Fabio tells me he is going to nip to a butcher's shop a short drive away to buy some steaks.

'Would you like to come with me? Or maybe you would appreciate a little time to yourself?' he asks good-naturedly.

It's true we haven't spent a second apart these past few days and I would quite like to have a catch-up on the phone with Dad.

'Do you mind if I stay here? I want to scribble a few ideas down about a new website and have a quick chat with my dad.'

'Not at all.' Fabio grabs his keys from the kitchen counter. 'I'll see you later.'

When Fabio has gone I change into a comfortable lounge suit with a thick hooded jacket and step outside onto the balcony. I can see across the lake to Bellagio where we took the boat the evening before. The sky is still a clear blue, although I can feel the chill in the air as it's late afternoon now.

I'm back inside, about to ring Dad when my phone rings. It's him.

'Hi, Dad, wow that's spooky. I was just this second about to ring you. How are you?'

'Absolutely fine, love, how are you?'

'Oh, I'm good thanks. Is everything OK at the B&B?'

'Everything's fine, you've only been gone two days. A middle-aged couple checked in last night for two nights, they seem nice. The woman's a bit of a character.'

'You can say that again,' says a low voice in the background. I recognise the voice at once.

'Dad, is Mum there?' I ask, completely aghast.

'Yes, love. I'm over at my house. We were chatting about a photograph at breakfast this morning. I've just found it in a drawer.'

'She was there for breakfast?'

'No, I mean at the B&B. Your mother came over early this morning to help out. She's driving home later.'

It feels strange knowing my parents are in the same room together.

'Dad,' I say gently. 'You've managed all these years without Mum. Please be careful. I don't want her to hurt you again.'

'There's no need to worry, love. Besides, people can change, you know.'

I'm not so sure, but I let the comment slide.

We chat for a few more minutes before we wrap up the call.

'Oh, just one more thing, Dad. What was the photograph you just mentioned?'

Dad is quiet for a minute before he answers.

'It was a photo of you and Adam outside the B&B the day it was finished. I remember taking that photo.'

I remember it too. It was five years ago and as we smiled for the photograph, we could never have known how short-lived our happiness would be.

As I finish the call, tears are threatening to spill over. I know that I am making new memories here in Italy and that life must go on. But it's so hard to know how the next chapter of my life will turn out...

Chapter Thirty-Six

I'm glancing out of the bedroom window when I notice Fabio has returned to the villa and is getting out of his car. He's carrying a brown paper bag with carrot leaves poking out of the top. His whole demeanour is assured and I feel a sudden rush of something very comforting.

I walk down the stairs and open the front door to greet him.

'Ciao,' he says, planting a kiss on my cheek.

We walk into the kitchen together where Fabio unpacks the bags. He has bought two sirloin steaks and a bottle of Merlot, along with carrots, potatoes, green beans and herbs.

'So tonight, I will cook for you. Steak à la Fabio. It will be the best steak you have ever tasted.'

'Naturally.' I smile. 'Are we eating in the dining room?'

'Where else? Maybe you can even help me cook?'

'We'll see, I might just want to watch your prowess in the kitchen.'

As Fabio heads into the kitchen, I sneak off to lay the table with a heavy cream tablecloth and two bamboo tablemats. I know just the table where we can sit tonight; it's right next to the window overlooking the lake. I place two long-stemmed wine glasses and two water tumblers beside them on the table. Where does he keep the candles, I wonder? I take a red candle from a drawer and manage to drop the whole bunch on the floor.

'What is happening here?' Fabio jokes, bending down beside me to help me pick them up, his closeness stirring my senses.

'I was just laying the table. Do you have a candle holder?'

He goes to a cupboard and retrieves a Chianti bottle with a straw base and I pop the red candle into it. Perfect.

'So who is your favourite chef to watch?' he asks as we move back into the kitchen.

'Gordon Ramsay every time. When he takes the helm in struggling restaurants, and effortlessly cooks up sensational food, it's quite something,' I say, slightly dreamily.

'So you have the hots for Mr Ramsay, huh? Well I bet my steak dinner would give him a run for his money!' he jokes.

It's after six o'clock now, so I tell Fabio I will take a shower and meet him downstairs later for dinner. He tells me he has some paperwork to go over so after a kiss at the foot of the stairs, which sends a shiver down my spine, we go our separate ways.

I'm in my room when a text pings through from Katy.

I've got a job on a cruise ship!! Star of the sea here I come. Woo hoo!! K. xxx

I call her immediately.

'Oh my goodness, congratulations, Katy! I'm so pleased for you.'

'Ah thanks, Gina. Can't chat for long, I'm at work. Not for much longer though, hey?'

'Oh sorry, shall I call you later?'

'I'm OK for a minute, there's no one at reception.'

'So when do you leave?

'Well there's a training session next week then I sail at the end of March. I'm so bloody excited. Anyway, how's things in Italy with the Italian stallion?'

'Fine,' I say, laughing. 'His grandmother's place is really lovely, it just needs some modernising. We've been into Milan today to order some soft furnishings.'

'Sounds fab. Oh, and has Daphne been in touch?'

'She has. I believe she and Ben have separated,' I reply, with a heavy heart for my friend.

'Well I always thought that Ben was a bit of a knob,' says Katy. 'Mr Flash. He was always name-dropping about the soap actors he used to drink with in Leeds.'

'Really? I only met him a few times and he didn't have much to say really.'

'According to Daphne, I don't think he was interested in talking about anything other than himself and how much money he'd made. Anyway, I'm going to have to go now, Gina, some guests have just pulled up in the car park. Catch you later.'

'OK. Congratulations again! Bye.'

I'm thrilled for Katy. I think she will be right at home working the bars on the cruise ships. In fact, she would be perfect as one of the animation team as she has a sparkling personality and a decent singing voice. Whatever she does I'm sure she will shine as people can't fail to notice her.

It seems that this year may be a year of change for everyone.

Chapter Thirty-Seven

It's seven thirty and I'm sitting in the kitchen of the villa wearing a pretty blue and white wrap over dress that is slightly low cut, showing a hint of cleavage. Fabio looks relaxed and effortlessly handsome in a pair of smart chino shorts and a lilac-coloured polo shirt.

I'm sitting at a bar stool at the kitchen island sipping a pre-dinner glass of prosecco that Fabio has poured. The kitchen is surprisingly large and is furnished with cream-coloured wooden units with solid oak worktops. There's a large black eight-burner double oven against an open brick wall. With a few adjustments, I think there would be plenty of space for a professional kitchen, should Fabio decide to open the dining room as a restaurant.

'You may take your table for dinner,' says Fabio as he slices a ball of mozzarella and a huge, juicy beef tomato.

'I quite like staying here watching you work.'

Fabio arranges the slices of tomato and mozzarella on a large blue glazed plate and scatters some torn basil over them, pulled from a plant on the windowsill. He glazes some bruschetta with olive oil and rubs half a garlic clove across it, before searing it in a pan. He removes it from the pan after a minute or two and places it on the other side of the large plate. The kitchen is filled with the scent of garlic and basil, reminding me of the smells emanating from the open kitchen at Aldo's restaurant back home.

A few minutes later we are seated in the dining at the table.

'I am sorry to have to disappear into the kitchen again shortly to cook the steak,' says Fabio as he takes a bite of mozzarella-topped bruschetta. 'Maybe one day I can afford to have Gordon Ramsay come here and cook for you.'

'No need, really. I'm perfectly happy with the chef I have,' I say, chinking my long-stemmed glass of prosecco against his.

The food is absolutely delicious. Even the simplest of ingredients taste great here as the quality of the fresh produce is so good. When Fabio disappears into the kitchen to cook the main course, I follow him, keen to see how he makes the steak dinner.

'Here,' he says, throwing me an onion. 'Get chopping. Onion rings please, rather than slices. There's a chopping block under the counter and knives in the left-hand drawer.'

I slice the onion as Fabio crushes some garlic and thinly slices a couple of potatoes. He rubs the steaks with garlic and drizzles some olive oil before placing a griddle pan over the gas.

'It's better to oil the steak rather than the pan,' he tells me.

He instructs me to chop some carrots and trim some green beans. I am happy to help and I pour us both another drink, enjoying the bubbles. Fabio adds a splash of red wine and some dried chilli flakes to the steak pan as well as a crushed garlic clove. The delicious aroma makes my stomach growl. He then twists in some black pepper from a pepper mill and a pinch of sea salt. In a smaller pan alongside the griddle, he simultaneously sautées the thin slices of potato and onion in foaming butter, his strong tanned arms flipping the pan.

I'm so impressed. It's like watching a professional chef at work. I almost feel like distracting him from his cooking with a lingering kiss but decide to fantasise about doing it later.

When the pan of the water has boiled, I place the thinly sliced carrots in first, before dropping the green beans in for a couple of minutes at the end. A few minutes later Fabio deglazes the pan before adding a teaspoon of French mustard and a swirl of cream. Fabio plates up the food with finesse, still managing to look as cool as a cucumber.

'Oh, my word, you are definitely in the wrong job,' I say, as I devour a mouthful of soft-as-butter steak with the most delicious sauce.

'I'm glad you like it. My grandmother taught me how to make it. I must have cooked it a dozen times before she declared it good enough. She had a little floral notebook with all her favourite recipes written down. The funny thing is, she gave the book to my sister, who doesn't even cook.'

'What, ever?'

'Hardly ever, as I recall. She prefers to dine out. My grandmother would tut and tell Sofia that she would never find herself a husband if she didn't learn to cook. I think maybe only a grandmother could say such a thing to a modern woman.' He laughs.

We finish our delicious food and sip a glass of the Montepulciano that Fabio has opened.

'This was a good year,' says Fabio, raising his glass of red wine and relaxing back into his chair. 'Would you like some dessert?'

'I never noticed you bring any dessert home.'

'Have you tried affogato coffee? It's basically vanilla ice cream with a shot of espresso over the top, it's quite delicious.'

'Mmm, sounds it,' I say, biting my lip.

The truth is I don't want Fabio disappearing into the kitchen just yet and breaking the romance of the moment. The moonlight is streaming through the window, catching the flickering flame of the red candle on the table and I just want to sit here forever. I wonder if Fabio is feeling the magic too?

He reaches across the table and takes my hand.

'You can't imagine how much I am enjoying myself this evening, Gina. I'd forgotten how much fun it is to cook for someone else.'

I can't help feeling puzzled by the fact that women aren't queuing up to have dinner with him. He hasn't spoken of any previous relationships and I find myself wondering how long he has been single.

After a few minutes I follow Fabio into the kitchen and resume my place at the bar stool. He opens the freezer and takes out a tub of vanilla ice cream which he spoons into two glazed dessert bowls. When the coffee machine has finished, he pours a shot of espresso over the ice cream, telling me to take a spoonful quickly.

'What do you think? I find the contrast of the hot and cold is really something. Deeply satisfying.'

A bit like you, I think to myself.

'It's delicious,' I reply, enjoying the mixture of sweetness and bitterness.

Once again, I'm reminded of the passion that seems to go into even the smallest of things. We finish our meal with a dessert wine and I feel wonderfully relaxed.

I notice a photograph on a sideboard of a woman wearing a black dress. She has soft grey hair and smiling eyes.

'Is that your grandmother?' I ask.

'Yes, that is Magdalena. What a wonderful woman. She inspired me so much when I was younger. She came from nothing, being raised in a mountain village, but she always dreamed of running a hotel. She worked very hard to achieve it. Nothing was ever handed to her. She wasn't afraid to give you a slap if she thought you were up to no good.' He laughs, placing his hand on his cheek. 'I can almost feel the sting of her slap to this day.'

'Did you see her much when you were growing up?'

'Yes, every weekend religiously. Every Sunday afternoon my father would drive the family here. I remember Mother always brought her a home-made cherry and almond cake. I caught Grandmother telling her friend on the telephone one day that my mother's cakes were "too dry without a lot of cream". I never did tell my mother about that.' He smiles fondly, reminiscing.

'Where do your parents live now?'

'They live in Lecco, a city on the south-eastern shore of Lake Como. They are semi-retired now. They had several gift shops around Como, but have sold them all apart from a small one near their home at the foot of the mountains. Hopefully, one day you will meet them,' he says, draining his coffee. As he finishes speaking, I get a serious case of the butterflies.

A knock on the front door jolts me out of my dreaming as the van arrives with the furnishings. Fabio inspects the goods before signing the delivery slip and bidding the courier good night.

'So, tomorrow the decorators will be here to finish the rooms. They will be arriving bright and early, so maybe we should finish our drinks and think about going to bed?' He holds my gaze with his dark blue eyes before he takes me by the hand and leads me up the stairs. And I am not surprised when we bypass my room and head straight to Fabio's bedroom…

Chapter Thirty-Eight

The sun is streaming through the windows as I roll over in Fabio's comfortable bed to find he isn't there. A glance at the bedside clock tells me that it's almost half past seven. The decorators will be arriving around eight thirty and Fabio said they like to start early. Should I get up, and go and find him, or stay here? Before I have to decide, Fabio reappears, carrying a breakfast tray of fresh orange juice, coffee and croissants.

'No time for anything cooked, I'm afraid,' he says, setting the tray down and kissing me on the lips.

He's dressed in shorts and an old T-shirt that looks slightly paint-splattered.

'Are you going to be helping with the decorating?' I ask in surprise.

'You mean you are not? I thought you liked to get your hands dirty.'

'I do but I think I'll concentrate on hanging the dining room curtains. That could take a while. And I want to go over that wooden floor with a tea wash.'

'A tea wash?'

'A solution of tea and warm water. It will bring up that old floor up like new. What will you be doing?'

'I think I will be cleaning up mainly. Laying groundsheets, moving a bit of furniture around, that sort of thing. I like to be hands-on and oversee things. Why don't you go and have a wander around the village later today while I am tied up here? Tomorrow I'm afraid I have to go out for a few hours to meet with a client.'

'I suppose I should get up soon,' I say, stretching my arms lazily above my head.

'Well, this is one of the rooms that needs decorating, so you have an hour to shower and leave,' he says, pulling the white duvet off the bed.

I'm suddenly embarrassed by my nakedness as I grab the duvet back and wrap it around me.

'My beautiful Gina,' laughs Fabio. 'Don't be shy. You were not so shy last night,' he teases as he rolls on top of me and kisses my neck.

'Off!' I laugh. 'I need a shower.'

Fabio jumps up and slaps me on the bottom as I grab my robe from the end of the bed and head for the bathroom.

I luxuriate in the hot shower and think about last night. Fabio was a tender and skilful lover. He is the first man I have been with since Adam's death, yet it felt so natural. I never imagined I would open my heart up to someone who came to Lake View, not after all the history Adam and I shared there.

I dress and head downstairs just as the decorators arrive. It's probably better I'm out of their way, so I set about sweeping the floor in the dining room before I wash it using the tea solution. When I've finished I stand back and admire my efforts. As predicted, the striking chestnut shades of the parquet floor are breathed into life, giving the whole room a feeling of grandeur. I grab a bottle of water from the fridge and take a long drink before I press on with hanging the beautiful oyster-coloured curtains. When I'm finally done, I stand back to admire my handiwork as the dining room is flooded with light, the drapes completely transforming the room.

I nip upstairs to find Fabio and one of the workers shifting a wardrobe into the middle of a room, as the other worker mixes some paste.

'I'm going to nip out shortly. Does anyone need anything?'

'We're OK here. I'll head down and make us some coffee shortly. Spend some time relaxing, you've earned it,' smiles Fabio.

'If you're sure. Pop down and see the dining room when you get a minute.'

I'm grabbing my coat from a stand in the hall when Fabio appears at the foot of the stairs.

'I've come to take a look at your handiwork,' he says, turning the handle of the dining room door. He stands in the doorway and is momentarily silent as his eyes scan the room.

'So, what do you think'?

'It looks like a completely different room. It's spectacular. And look at this floor!'

'It's beautiful, isn't it?' I say.

'Just like you, Gina. Beautiful and captivating.'

We say goodbye with a lingering kiss and I set off for a walk towards the harbour. There's a little kiosk near the ferry terminal and I buy myself a coffee, taking a seat at a bench that looks out across the lake. I think about 'my' bench back home overlooking Ullswater. In the months following Adam's death, I found it a very healing place to be. It's on a quiet area of a public pathway, slightly set back and surrounded by heavy trees. I've been known to sit there for an hour or two in low season reading and sometimes I would never see a soul.

After my coffee I take a stroll along the harbour front and the small stony beach, passing lots of pastel-coloured houses in the bay. It's so pretty down here. I pass two old men near a blue and white boat who nod their heads and say 'Buongiorno'. A young couple walking their dog stop at the kiosk I have just left.

The sun is beginning to break through the clouds as I make my way along an uphill path flanked by heather and olive plants.

I notice a timetable near the water's edge that shows the first ferry crossing of the day to Como just before nine o'clock and I consider taking a trip tomorrow, as I've heard it's still quite busy even at this time of year. The air here is so fresh; I take a long, revitalising inhale and press on with my walk.

I follow a path away from the lake and take a sloping road uphill until I find myself in the main piazza, which is dominated by Varenna's principal church, the Chiesa di san Giorgio. A tiny sign has been translated in English which says it was built in the fourteenth century. The church is closed but across the road is a smaller chapel in a similar style. I am able to peer through a window and glimpse a fresco-painted ceiling.

My walk leads me along a circular path that eventually winds back to the ferry terminal, as I recognise the colourful fishermen's cottages coming into view. The clouds have drifted away leaving a bright sun high in a clear blue sky. I pass a young woman with the light brown shoulder-length hair setting up an easel and opening a canvas roll of paints.

'Buongiorno,' I say as I walk past. 'It looks like it's turning into a beautiful day.'

'Buongiorno,' she replies. 'I was hoping it would not be quite so bright actually, I prefer a little shadow when I paint.'

I introduce myself and discover that the lady is called Martina. She displays some of her artwork at the harbourside and as I look closer I realise that the paintings look exactly like the ones we bought from the gallery in Milan.

'Yes, they are my paintings,' she tells me when I mention it. 'The gallery owner is my grandfather. He used to bring me here when I was young to paint the boats. I had a passion for art from a very early age. I also display some of my paintings in a small gallery down a side street just off the piazza. It's called "galleria di sole" which means "gallery of sunshine".'

'What a lovely name. Thanks for letting me know. Are you local?'

'Yes, I live in one of the cottages a short walk away,' she says, pointing towards the colourful houses in the background. 'I take it you are here on holiday?'

'Yes, just for a week. I'm staying with a friend.'

'Not many people visit Varenna in winter, but I think it's just as beautiful, although I suppose I would say that.' She smiles.

I ask her for a business card which she takes from a leather handbag and hands to me.

'Enjoy your holiday,' she says as I depart.

'Thanks. Enjoy your painting.'

I've only been out for a couple of hours but I decide to head back to the villa as I suddenly feel a little tired. Well, I didn't get too much sleep last night, I think to myself with a warm smile, and I've worked pretty hard this morning too. I've decided I will take that trip to Como tomorrow and perhaps buy a souvenir for Hannah.

I send Fabio a text to tell him I will be back at the villa shortly.

Are you missing me already? he asks.

No. I'm just getting a little cold x I reply, laughing to myself.

Music is playing from a radio as I enter the villa twenty minutes later, reminding me of Dad, who always has his radio blaring when he does any painting and decorating. I find Fabio in the kitchen making coffee for the workmen.

'Look at you. Quite the domestic, aren't you? Looking after the workers.'

'Look after your workers and you get better results,' says Fabio, lifting a panettone from a cupboard, unwrapping it from its yellow wax paper.

'Can I do anything to help?' I offer

'Relax,' he says, planting a kiss on my cheek. 'The weather is bright enough to sit outside if you wish. I'll bring you some coffee.'

'I'm not really one for sitting around. Are you sure I can't do anything to help?'

'You need to learn how to relax,' says Fabio. 'Besides, you have done enough. Choosing the wall coverings and lighting has been a huge help to me. And I wouldn't have known where to start hanging those curtains, not to mention all your hard work on the floor…'

'I suppose so. I wouldn't do it if I didn't enjoy it though.'

'I would feel guilty if you did any more. You are here for a break, I want you to enjoy yourself,' he says.

'OK, if you insist. I've got a book in my suitcase. I'll just nip upstairs and get it.'

Seated outside, I check my Facebook page, noticing that Hannah has posted a new picture of herself and Greg near Ullswater. They're wearing bobble hats and thick jackets and the picture reminds me of the photo of me and Adam on my dressing table. Katy has also updated her status announcing her new job on the cruise ship, with a GIF of the queen waving on the deck of the royal yacht. Dozens of people have wished her well, and I feel really happy for her.

A few minutes later Fabio appears with my coffee and a slice of the panettone.

'The decorators will only take a short lunch and then they will carry on until around five o'clock. No siesta in the winter months. When they leave, I am all yours.'

He pulls me to my feet, dragging me closer and kissing me deeply on the lips. He smells of paint, coffee and a hint of aftershave and it feels so comforting.

I open up my book and settle down to read, taking a bite of the deliciously sweet panettone. Heavenly as it is, I wish the decorators would hurry up and leave for the day.

Chapter Thirty-Nine

The decorators leave late afternoon, having decorated four rooms, and they will return tomorrow morning to finish the rest There are two decorators which means that they have finished two bedrooms each today. I think of Dad and how he can wallpaper an entire room in a few hours, even now in his sixties. He's recently been sprucing up his house with a lick of paint and some wallpaper and I can't help wondering whether that's for Mum's benefit.

I'm looking forward to the rooms here being finished so that we can add the finishing touches of bedspreads, lighting and cushions. It's all going to look absolutely beautiful.

After a shower, I am downstairs with Fabio, looking at some chandelier lighting on the Internet that I think would look perfect in the dining room.

'I'm not sure about a crystal chandelier,' says Fabio, chewing the end of a pen thoughtfully.

'And I'm not sure about a black one. Hang on, yes I am. Definitely not black.'

Fabio scrolls down the page.

'How about this?' He points to a humongous, purple, glittery monstrosity.

'Are you serious?'

'Of course not,' he laughs.

He eventually agrees with my choice of a stunning glass 'waterfall' light as a centrepiece for the ceiling that would sit equally well in a breakfast room or an evening restaurant.

'So,' says Fabio, 'I am feeling a little hungry. I hope you are not expecting a repeat performance of my culinary genius last night.'

'Well, we have to eat. What do you have in mind?'

'Tonight, I will make pizza.'

'Pizza?'

'Well of course, you are in Italy. You must try an Italian pizza.'

We make our way to the kitchen where Fabio switches the oven on before he makes a start on the pizza dough. He stretches, pulls and twists the pizza base in such an expert fashion that once again I forget that he is not a professional chef.

I am set to work chopping and simmering tomatoes in a saucepan for the sauce and slicing a ball of creamy mozzarella and some salami. The tomato base is cooled and spread across the pizza before the salami and mozzarella is added. Fabio adds a generous topping of roughly torn basil, filling the kitchen with its heady scent, before sliding it into a hot oven.

'I think we will have beer with the pizza. Are you OK with that?' asks Fabio, taking two bottles of Moretti from the fridge.

'Sure. I think it's a beer and pizza kind of evening.' I smile.

Fabio removes the pizza several minutes later and it looks and smells amazing.

'Oh my goodness, this is unbelievable,' I say as a gooey strand of salty mozzarella stretches out from my mouth. 'It's so tasty.'

'Quality ingredients. That is all you need,' replies Fabio.

We finish our meal and Fabio drains his beer bottle, stifling a yawn.

'Am I keeping you awake?' I ask.

'There is no one I would rather stay awake with.' He smiles as he slides off the bar stool and lifts me from mine. 'Although I think it's time we both had an early night.'

Chapter Forty

The next morning Fabio and I are having a breakfast of cereal, yoghurt and fresh fruit juice in the kitchen. For some reason, I feel as though there is an air of tension about Fabio, although I say nothing. We spent another wonderful evening together last night, so I wonder what could be on his mind. I tell myself perhaps he was thinking about the meeting with his client.

The decorators arrive just as Fabio is heading out to his meeting. I offer them a coffee and tell them to help themselves later on. I feel quite at home in this kitchen, I realise.

Fabio is dressed in a light grey suit which he throws a black overcoat over as he prepares to leave. He kisses me on the cheek and tells me he will call me later.

The decorators drink their coffee then disappear upstairs to finish the remaining bedrooms. I notice a radio which I switch on and at once the air is filled with classic Italian music, reminding me that I really must learn a little more of the language as I can't understand much apart from '*ti amo*' – so I presume it's a love song.

I decide to hang around the kitchen a little longer and pour myself another glass of orange juice, which I take to a table in the dining room. It's a perfect place to sit, giving a view of stunning greenery and the shimmering lake beyond. It feels so warm and comfortable with the sun streaming through the window that I consider staying here until Fabio returns. It's so wonderful having sunshine at this time of year and I think about how cold it must be back home. January often brings frost and snow so the B&B is usually quiet apart from during the February half term week, when parents arrive with children who they drag outside for winter walks to 'blow the cobwebs away'.

After I've read a few chapters of my book I decide to walk down to the harbour as Fabio told me there is a market today. I think I might surprise him by cooking dinner tonight. I'm not even going to attempt cooking a steak, though, as mine couldn't compete with Fabio's, so I am hoping to find some inspiration at the market. Maybe I will find a nice piece of fish.

I'm just grabbing my coat when I hear a knock on the front door. Maybe Fabio has forgotten his key? I walk across the tiled hall floor to open the door.

A slender woman with long, dark wavy hair steps inside without being invited to.

'Is Fabio here?' she asks in a thick Italian accent, looking around the hallway.

'No, he's gone out on business,' I say, a little shocked. 'I'm sorry, who are you?'

'I see he has got rid of that disgusting patterned carpet,' she says, glancing down at the blue tiled floor. 'Fancy covering this up.' She taps the tiles with the pointy toe of her black boot. 'Grandmother always had a thing about carpets. She said tiled floors were too noisy.'

So this must Fabio's sister Sofia.

'You ask who I am, but who, may I ask, are you?' she says, without a hint of warmth in her voice.

'My name is Gina, I'm a friend of Fabio's. I take it you are Sofia?'

I wonder why I introduce myself as a friend. Is that what I am?

There's something familiar about the woman standing in front of me but I can't think why.

'Fabio has talked about me?' Sofia asks.

'He just mentioned he had a sister, so when you said your grandmother—'

'Gina, huh?' She cuts in. 'You know that is an Italian name, but I don't see anything Italian about you,' she says, eyeing me up and down.

She walks across the hall and opens the door to the dining room, a slow smile spreading across her face.

'Now this looks very tasteful. And I'm pleased to see that the dreadful carpet has been removed from this room too. So how do you know my brother?' she asks as she shrugs off her coat and switches on the coffee machine, making herself very much at home.

'He stayed at my guesthouse in England when he came to visit Aldo.'

'You want some coffee?' she asks, lifting two white mugs from a cupboard.

I nod and take a seat at one of the kitchen bar stools.

'So you have your own hotel?'

'Yes, in the Lake District. Not too dissimilar to this place really. Overlooking a lake too.'

I'm not going to tell Sofia that this place is like a grand palace compared to mine even though it only has two more rooms.

When the coffee is made, filling the room with the lovely aroma, she places a mug in front of me before sitting opposite on one of the stools.

'So why are you here?' she asks, matter-of-factly.

'Fabio was impressed with the décor in my hotel. He invited me over to give him some input over the décor here, as he's been modernising things. And I needed a little break too.'

She says nothing as she gets to her feet and brings some small packets of biscuits to the counter.

'Would you like some?' she asks, pushing a packet towards me.

'No thanks.'

She opens a packet, takes a small biscotto and snaps it in half with her fingers. Her nails are long and painted red.

'So I am just wondering why my brother would have a woman staying here when he is trying to get things back on track with the love of his life.'

The walls in the kitchen suddenly feel as though they are closing in on me. All of a sudden, I'm struggling to breathe.

'The love of his life?' I repeat, the words sounding strangled in my throat

'Yes, Lucina. It broke my brother's heart when she broke things off with him. He always believed they would marry. I am sorry to be the one to tell you this.'

I have to get out of the room. I have to get out of the hotel. Sofia is staring at me with an expressionless look on her face, almost as if she's enjoying delivering this news to me. I suddenly recall where I have seen her before. She was the woman at the railway station in Milan who waved at Fabio. The woman Fabio pretended he didn't see. Now it all makes sense.

'What do you mean, trying to get things back on track?' I ask in a whisper.

Sofia sighs deeply.

'Well, I know that they have been in contact with each other lately. I think things have been going well between them. That is, until you came into his life and complicated everything. Where do you suppose Fabio is now?'

'Visiting a client,' I say feebly.

'So that is what he told you.' She almost smirks. 'I saw them walking into Roberto's restaurant near the station when I disembarked the train.'

I don't need to listen to any more. I have to leave. I race upstairs to the bedroom that still smells of fresh paint and wallpaper paste and breathlessly throw my clothes into a suitcase.

I try to keep my composure as I go downstairs, walking across the floor to the front door. Sofia is standing in the hall, her arms folded across her chest.

'It was nice to meet you. I'm sorry you had to find out this way,' she says, not seeming sorry at all.

I think you enjoyed every minute of it, I think to myself as I head for the door. I realise I am shaking as I make my way down the hill towards the harbour. Glancing back at the villa, I see Sofia standing in the doorway with her arms crossed, smoking a cigarette.

The train station is around a fifteen-minute walk but as my suitcase is so heavy I take a taxi from near the ferry port.

Five minutes later the driver deposits me at Varenna train station and I pay him before quickly walking inside, desperate to get out of here.

The love of his life. I say it over and over in my head but I can barely take it in. For a brief moment I wonder whether I should turn back and wait for Fabio to return so I can listen to his side of the story. But what explanation could there be? Whatever the situation, Fabio never told me about any unfinished business with an ex. And I slept with him. Something I don't do easily. I'm filled with a rage that won't subside as I buy my ticket, realising that I will have to wait half an hour before the next train arrives. Then I remember the name of the restaurant Sofia mentioned. Roberto's. I walk out of the station and glance across the road to a row of eateries. Roberto's is almost directly opposite. I trundle my case across the road, my heart racing as I wonder what I am about to find. There are several chrome tables outside the restaurant but only one is occupied, by a gentleman having coffee and reading a newspaper. I'm about to cross the road when I see them emerge from the restaurant. They are smiling, their body language totally at ease with each other. Lucina is slim and petite, her glossy brown hair cut into a stylish bob. I wait, my breath catching in my throat. A moment later they are in each other's arms, hugging tightly. I feel weak at the knees. I turn on my heel and walk back into the station.

I check plane times to England on my phone and discover the next plane from Milan to Manchester is at 11 p.m. this evening. The last thing I want is to arrive back home in the middle of the night so I decide to spend the night in Milan to gather my thoughts.

As I hold back the tears, I wonder whether I should have stayed at home and never come to Italy in the first place. Maybe all I experienced was a simple holiday fling that should have been left at that. Maybe I was just a pleasant dalliance for Fabio whilst he sorted things out with his ex-girlfriend? Maybe he was just using me all along?

I need to distract myself so I plug my earphones in to my phone and listen to a compilation playlist on Spotify. An Ed Sheeran song plays, which immediately reminds me of the train journey here several days ago. How things have suddenly changed since then.

I unplug my headphones and decide to go for a little walk to clear my head. The train station is fairly small so it isn't long before I'm sitting at a bench again, having bought a coffee from a kiosk. I take my book from my handbag and begin to read, but my brain can't process a single word.

Eventually the train glides into view and I take a window seat. I glance out of the window mindlessly as we pass the open landscape until we finally arrive at Milano Centrale station.

I depart quickly and walk through the station, barely noticing its beauty as I had done on my arrival. I head across the road to an unremarkable-looking hotel and walk through the sliding glass doors and into the reception area, which is filled with red leather tub chairs and several large potted plants. Thankfully they have a single room available on the third floor and I quickly check in. The room is clean and functional.

Fabio will not be back at the villa yet and I wonder if his sister will still be there when he returns. I'm wondering why Sofia was there in the first place, as Fabio told me that she had no interest in their grandmother's villa. Then I realise that she probably saw me with him on the train and came to find out who I was. It was probably her plan after all.

I head into the Santo Spirito shopping district, passing the Balenciaga shop where I once again notice the mustard-coloured handbag in the window. I go inside and after running my hands over its smooth hide, I decide to purchase it. It almost feels like an act of defiance against Fabio and his dislike of the designer shops. As the assistant is wrapping the bag in tissue paper before placing it into a store bag, I hear a text ping through on my phone. It's from Fabio.

I'll be home around four. Hope you've enjoyed your day. X

I stuff my phone back into my bag, take my purchase and head off towards the main shopping area, my heart hammering in my chest. Sofia has obviously not been in touch with him. I can't believe I have been taken for such a fool.

Over the next few hours I manage to distract myself from my feelings slightly by browsing the shops. I purchase a green leather purse from Prada for Hannah, who would probably faint at the price but she deserves it, and I buy some Italian biscuits and limoncello for Dad.

It's almost four o'clock now and despite my lack of appetite, my stomach reminds me that I haven't eaten since breakfast, so I look for a place to eat. I decide on a small trattoria down a side street and order spaghetti bolognese and a glass of Chianti. I haven't eaten spaghetti while I've been here and the dish, when it arrives, is delicious, although I find myself unable to eat very much. I drink a glass of water then settle the bill, heading back towards the Duomo square area.

Once again, I am in awe of the Gothic granite cathedral that looms before me as I head into the square. This could be the last time I visit Milan, so I decide to explore the interior, opening the heavy bronze entrance doors and slipping inside.

Sue Roberts

The arches and the beautiful stained-glass art on the windows make me gasp. In here the space is cool and soothing, and as I walk around I notice that there are three altars adorned with various marble sculptures. I light a candle and take a seat on one of the highly polished dark wooden pews. There are several people seated in the church, some of them women who are wearing black lace headscarves. I think most of the people are tourists like myself who are moving around slowly, admiring the stunning architecture. I say a silent prayer and suddenly think of Adam, who would have never hurt me like that. Have I been a fool, allowing myself to be seduced by a handsome Italian who came to stay at the B&B? I think of how his mood changed when he received that phone call during dinner with me in Bellagio. It all makes sense now.

As I head back towards the hotel I'm suddenly overcome with exhaustion. I was up early and have walked the streets of Milan in a rage, in and out of shops trying to distract myself from the pain and humiliation I was feeling. I feel the need to lay down and process my thoughts.

Back at the hotel, I order a large whisky from the bar, which is on the first floor. Once I'm in my bedroom I have another from the small mini bar and lie on my bed. I'm tired but suddenly regretting not taking the 11 p.m. flight this evening. What difference would it make if I arrived home in the middle of the night? Suddenly I'm on the telephone cancelling my flight for tomorrow morning and booking the flight for later this evening, thankful that there are still some available seats. I need to get out of this place. I need to go home.

Chapter Forty-One

I step into the black taxi just after eight o'clock, having decided against ringing the driver who brought me here. The last thing I need is to engage in any conversation about my holiday. Right now, I just want to disappear inside the airport anonymously.

Fabio has sent three texts asking where I am, the third one more desperate than the other two.

Gina where are you? I need to talk to you? Please call me x

Fabio will have noticed that my things have gone from the wardrobe so must have realised I won't be returning. I hope he doesn't turn up at the airport. Right at this moment I just want to get on the plane and go home. I'm still angry and in no mood to speak to him right now, although a part of me feels like a coward just running away. But there's no way I could face him like this.

Anxiously I await my flight in a busy departure lounge before the call comes for boarding. An immense sense of relief floods over me when I take my place on the aeroplane and thankfully the seat next to me is vacant. My phone is now in flight mode so I will be unable to see any more messages from Fabio for the next couple of hours. When the drinks trolley passes I order a large whisky in the hope that it will make me sleep for a little while. I can barely wait for the flight to be over and to be on the final leg of my journey home. I just need to be as far away from him as possible.

I text Hannah when I arrive at Manchester airport as I don't want her being alarmed when I arrive home in the early hours of the morning.

Hannah is on the phone the second she receives my text.

'Gina? Is everything alright? Why are you coming back so early?'

'It's a long story. I'm going to call a cab. I'll be with you in a couple of hours, I'll fill you in then.'

'A cab? You're joking, aren't you? That will cost you a bloody fortune, it's over a hundred miles. Stay right where you are. I'm coming to get you.'

Tears are threatening to spill over.

'Oh, Hannah, really, you don't have to, it's late,' I say, trying to keep the emotion from my voice.

'Too late, on my way,' she says. 'Get yourself a coffee. I'll text you when I'm closer. Love you, sis.'

'Love you too,' I say, swallowing a lump in my throat.

I walk to the food area and buy myself a coffee and a toasted teacake as I feel a little peckish. It's just after 12.45 a.m. and I stifle a yawn. Immediately I regret checking my mobile, noticing three missed calls from Fabio, but I put the phone away – I don't want to hear his voice.

The next hour or so is spent in a fuggy haze, and I pass the time drinking coffee and glancing through a newspaper until I receive a text from Hannah telling me that she's about ten minutes away. I finish my coffee and head to the pick-up area to begin my onward journey home. Finally.

Chapter Forty-Two

Hannah holds out her arms and I fall into them as soon as she gets out of her car. It's all I can do to negotiate my case in to the car boot and settle into the front seat. Then I burst into tears.

'Oh, Gina, what's happened?' asks Hannah, hugging me tightly.

'Hannah, do you need a rest?' I sniff. 'It's a four-hour round trip.'

'I'm fine. We'll stop at some services later on. I'm more concerned about you, are you alright?'

'I will be, just drive. I'll fill you in later.'

We take the exit road from the airport and soon we are on the motorway. Hannah squeezes my hand every now and then and after a while I struggle to keep my eyes open as tiredness takes over. Hannah must have let me sleep a little, as soon enough we are pulling in to a Starbucks just off the motorway.

We order drinks from the bored-looking young woman at the counter then find a seat at a table in a corner.

'I don't think I can face any more coffee after all,' I say, as Hannah places an Americano in front of me.

'So why have you come home early?'

'An ex who Fabio still happens to be friendly with. I think I've been taken for a complete fool.' I stare out of the window into the darkness.

'What do you mean "an ex"? And what's the problem if it's an ex?'

'The problem is that maybe the flames of passion are being fanned again. I learned from his sister that Fabio's ex, Lucina, has recently broken up with the guy she left him for. She told me that Lucina was the love of Fabio's life and broke his heart. They've had several meetings together, according to Sofia. She thought my presence was just getting in the way of their reunion and I don't want to be responsible for that.'

'Oh my God, Gina, are you sure? Well, I suppose you must be. Did he tell you this himself?' she asks, a look of doubt on her face.

'No. He didn't have to. I saw them together.'

'Oh no, Gina, I'm so sorry. What did you see?' she asks tentatively.

I tell Hannah about them hugging outside of the restaurant.

'I know it must have looked bad, but hugging isn't exactly locking lips, is it? So you haven't actually spoken to Fabio himself about this? There might be some perfectly simple explanation.'

She's looking at me as though I'm a petulant teenager who's run off in a strop. I suppose it must seem strange that I didn't wait for Fabio to return and have it out with him but I felt so hurt. And if it had been so innocent, why didn't he tell me who he was meeting with?

I'm almost annoyed with myself for growing so close to Fabio. Maybe even fallen in love. I'm certain Sofia would never have lied. And his voicemail never denied it either. It just said 'we need to talk'. How could he have said nothing about meeting with an old flame? Even if there was a simple explanation, he should have told me.

My phone rings, the harsh trill breaking the stillness of the quiet café. It's Fabio. I ignore it.

'Aren't you going to answer that?' asks Hannah, a note of irritation in her voice.

'No,' I say, switching off my phone and placing it in my bag. 'Look, Hannah, I know you think I should speak to Fabio, but I'm in absolutely no mood to do that right now. I'm exhausted. I just want to go home.'

And those are the last words we exchange before we pull up outside Lake View. I've never been so happy to be anywhere in my whole life.

Chapter Forty-Three

Hannah places a tray of tea and toast at my bedside table. I glance over at the clock, which tells me it's just after half past ten in the morning. I let out a yawn as I stretch my arms out and sit up.

'Thanks, sis. Sorry for sleeping through breakfast. You must be shattered too,' I say, taking a sip of strong Yorkshire tea, a welcome change from all the coffee I've been drinking lately.

'It's OK,' she says, sitting on the edge of my bed. 'Greg's still here and Dad's been over. He's calling back to see you later, actually, he was worried about you.'

'What did you tell him?'

'Not much. I thought that was up to you. Anyway, no rush to get up. I really think you should talk to Fabio though. You can't avoid him forever.'

'I know, I will,' I say, wondering when I will be able to face doing so.

I climb out of bed and go over to the window, staring out at the familiar sight of the fells. Less than twenty-four hours ago I was glimpsing Lake Como as the morning sunshine danced on the water. I can't help thinking to myself what a difference a day makes.

I walk downstairs just as Ellie is arriving and I realise it's Saturday.

'Gina, hi, how are you?' She beams. 'Ooh, you look a bit tired. Can I do your make-up?' She's wearing a full face of make-up with a slight silver sparkle in her super-long eyelashes.

'Maybe later?' I say, forcing a smile.

Dominika is just walking down the stairs with a basket of sheets that need laundering from the bedrooms.

'Hello, Gina, how are you?' she asks.

'Not too bad thanks, how are you?'

'I'm good. Happy in my own skin, which doesn't need pampering, plucking or enough make-up applied to it to make me resemble a drag queen on a Blackpool stage,' she says, turning to Ellie with a forced smile.

'Snotty cow,' says Ellie when she is out of earshot. I can't help wondering whether Ellie has driven Dominika mad with requests to give her a makeover. 'I only said she might look nice with a bit of colour on her cheeks. She's so pale.'

'She has a natural beauty. Sometimes less is more,' I say as I look at Ellie's heavy eyebrows and theatrical eyelashes. Maybe a good make-up course would teach her this.

'Oh well, whatever. I still think she should wear a little bit of make-up though. She's got lovely blue eyes.'

Ellie scoots off to do some cleaning in the kitchen and I smile at her enthusiasm.

I nip upstairs into one of the empty guest bedrooms and glance around at the décor and the modern, light wood bed frames, in complete contrast to the heavy wooden frames at the villa in Varenna. Instinctively I straighten a cushion as Dominika walks through the door.

'So you are not happy with my housekeeping?' she jokes.

'You know I am, Dominika, I suppose I'm just busying myself. Is someone checking into this room today?'

I realise I haven't even looked at the booking register.

'Yes, a couple attending an evening wedding reception at the hotel across the road. How did you like Italy? I see that you have come back early.'

'It's complicated. Maybe things didn't turn out exactly as I imagined they would. Italy was beautiful though.'

I don't want to say too much to anyone other than Hannah as I'm not even sure what's going on myself, and Dominika doesn't press me. I'm back downstairs crossing the hallway when Dad arrives.

'Hello, love,' he says, giving me a hug. The smell of his aftershave is familiar and comforting.

'Aren't you working today?' I ask, noticing that it's only just after one o'clock.

'Just having a break for lunch. I wanted to see how you were,' he says, a concerned look on his face. 'Shall we go for a little walk?'

'Yeah that will be nice, Dad, thanks. I'll just grab my coat.'

As we step outside, I realise just how cold it is in January as a freezing wind whips around my face.

'I don't know how you stand being out on the water in this weather all day,' I say, thrusting my hands deeper into my pockets.

'You get used to it after all these years. I barely feel the cold any more.' He shrugs.

We walk along the path that leads to the bench overlooking Lake Ullswater and sit down.

'Hannah told me a little of what happened. Have you really not spoken to Fabio about what his sister said about him meeting with his ex-girlfriend?'

'What is there to say? I spent all that time with him and he never once mentioned a meeting with an ex-girlfriend. Whatever the situation, how can I ever trust a man that is so secretive?'

'But how do you what the truth is if you haven't even spoken to him about it? This is not like you, Gina. You don't usually make a judgement about someone without giving them a fair trial.'

I sigh deeply. 'I know you're right, Dad. I'll talk to him later. That is if he wants to talk to me. I've ignored every single one of his texts and phone calls.'

'Of course he will talk to you, love. He's probably just giving you some time, he's not going to let a cracker like you slip through his fingers.'

We sit and chat for several more minutes before we go our separate ways, me heading back towards the guesthouse as Dad heads towards the steamer jetty to resume working on the lake. I'm just turning a corner when a white van pulls up and Paul Barlow pops his head out of the driver's window.

'Alright, Gina, how's things?'

I'm surprised to see Daphne in the passenger seat.

'Hi, Paul, oh hello, Daphne. I see you got your van then, Paul, I thought you were saving up for one?'

'Would you believe I had a decent win on the Irish lottery? Four numbers came in, giving me enough to buy this beauty. I'm on my way to a factory in Penrith to collect three doors that need delivering to Bradford.'

Daphne leans across Paul to speak to me.

'Hi, Gina. I'm going along for the ride as I've heard there's a brilliant fabric shop in one of the old mills. I've been getting on with a bit of dressmaking lately. I'd forgotten just how much I enjoy it.'

'That's brilliant, Daphne. And I'm really pleased you got your van, Paul.'

Making small talk is the last thing I feel like doing right now and I'm pleased when they announce their departure.

'Anyway, must be off, Gina, see you later.'

'See you soon for a catch-up, Gina,' says Daphne, before they disappear around a corner.

I'm just about back at the guesthouse when a blue Peugeot pulls up outside and out steps Mum. It seems everyone's making an appearance today.

'Hello, Gina, how are you?' she asks, as she walks towards me.

'Hi, Mum, I'm OK, thanks. What are you doing here?'

'I've just come over to see if I can help. And to see if you're OK, actually. Hannah told me that you'd cut your visit to Italy short. Do you want to talk about it? We could go for a drive?'

To my surprise I accept, thinking it would be nice to go for a drive, maybe up into the fells. I don't feel like going back to the guesthouse just yet.

'Sure,' I say. 'Why not?'

We drive along a winding road until we are at the foot of a beautiful spot called Aira Force. It's a short climb to the top and the walk feels exhilarating, passing stunning waterfalls and scenic woodland. My mum's pretty fit for her age, still slim and strong-limbed. She used to walk miles with me and Hannah when we were kids, making dens and fire pits in the forest. She was such fun that I suppose it made things even harder when she disappeared from our lives. We were adults though, as she's pointed out to me before, but it still left a great big hulking hole in our lives.

'Quite a view from here, isn't it?' says Mum as we view the valley below.

'Beautiful but cold,' I reply, pulling my coat tightly around me.

'It's good for you. Fresh mountain air. Nothing better. So what's happened to the Italian bloke?' she asks matter-of-factly as she lights up a cigarette. I can't help thinking it's wrong somehow, polluting the fresh mountain air with cigarette smoke.

'Well, it seems he has been having meetings with an ex-girlfriend,' I say, still barely able to believe the words that are coming from my mouth.

'And what's he had to say about this?'

'I don't know because I haven't spoken to him. And before you give me a lecture, I needed to get my head around it. I know it's the truth though because I saw them together. Plus his sister basically told me I was getting in the way of their reunion.'

'Did she now?' says Mum, taking a long drag of her cigarette. 'Have you thought that maybe she wasn't giving you the full story?'

'And why would she do that?'

'Maybe she wanted to get you out of the picture. Hannah told me that Fabio was modernising a hotel. Maybe she thought you were muscling in on her inheritance or something. Perhaps she was really good friends with the ex. Who knows? You'll never really find out unless you speak to him, will you?'

' I don't know, Mum. All I know is what I saw with my own eyes.'

'And remind me what that was again.'

'They were smiling together. Then they departed with a big hug.'

'Well, whatever the case you'll never know unless you actually speak to Fabio, will you?'

'I'll speak to him later. Although I've probably completely messed things up by coming home,' I sigh.

'Things will work out if they're meant to,' she says, coming towards me and unexpectedly embracing me. 'I know I haven't been there for you in recent years, Gina, but I'm here now. If you want me to be.'

I cling onto Mum for several minutes as I begin to cry gently.

'Come on now, Gina, you're made of stronger stuff than this. I know you've been hurt but at least you were prepared to open your heart to someone again. That takes real bravery.'

There's no wisdom like a mother's wisdom, I think to myself as we make our way down the stony footpath. She's made me see things in a different light. I never thought that Sofia might see me as some kind of threat. I need to find out the truth about all this, I realise, and there's only one way. I must talk to Fabio.

Chapter Forty-Four

It's seven o'clock in the evening and Greg and Hannah are off out for a meal at the Black Bull.

'Fancy joining us, Gina?' asks Hannah.

'No thanks, I've got a few things to do. And someone I need to talk to.'

She walks over and crushes me in a lingering hug. 'Good luck.'

'Thanks. See you later.'

I lie on my bed wondering what the hell I am going to say before I dial Fabio's number. My outrage has dissipated, my state of mind having transformed from feeling numb with shock when I fled the villa, to now feeling like a bit of a drama queen. I take a deep breath and dial his number but the call goes to voicemail.

'Hi, it's Gina. I'm sorry I didn't return your calls. I needed to think things through. Please get in touch whenever you can.'

All I can do now is wait, so I flick the television on and the first thing that appears on the screen is a travel programme about Italy. I switch channels and find Alan Titchmarsh doing a garden makeover. Perfect.

I feel exhausted even though I had a lie-in this morning and soon I am struggling to keep my eyes open, lulled to sleep by the comforting drone of the television. It's just after ten o'clock when I am awoken by the sound of banging on the front door.

I make my way to the front door anxiously and peer through the small window.

As I open the door, I'm stunned to be face to face with Fabio.

'Fabio! What are you doing here?'

He has the look of a man who has barely slept and there are dark shadows underneath his blue eyes.

'Why do you think I am here? I must explain things to you, Gina.'

I sigh deeply before inviting him in and taking a bottle of whisky from a kitchen cupboard. I think we're going to need it.

'Drink?'

He nods and we make our way to the large sofa, where I pour us each a drink.

'So go on. I'm listening,' I say, taking a long gulp of the soothing liquid, enjoying its burn.

'I barely know where to start,' says Fabio, running his fingers through his dark hair.

'You could start by telling me if it's true. Have you been meeting up with an ex-girlfriend?' I ask, meeting his gaze.

'Technically, yes,' he says in a low voice.

'What the hell is that supposed to mean?' I ask, my heart sinking to the floor.

'It's true I have recently met with Lucina.'

Her name is like a stab to my heart.

'I look after her financial affairs,' he continues. 'She runs a large shop in Como and I do her accounts. I have done for years, even after we split.'

'She was the one you were having a business meeting with?'

'Yes. I believe I told you I was meeting someone concerning business. I'm sorry, Gina, I didn't want you reading anything in to it, that's all.'

'But I saw you outside the restaurant,' I sniff. 'You looked very cosy, embracing each other, as I recall.'

'I arranged to meet to tell her that it would be better if I handed her account over to someone else. I told her all about you. She is happy that I have fallen in love again,' he says, looking searchingly into my eyes.

Did he really just tell me that he has fallen in love?

'She has recently become engaged herself. What you saw was nothing more than a friendly farewell hug. We'll probably never see each other again.'

'Probably?'

'Yes, unless we happen to pass in the street and exchange a casual hello. But I doubt it. She lives across the water in Mennagio.'

I've never been a jealous person, so I'm surprised to find a feeling of envy coursing through my body when I think of them together.

'But your sister said she had broken up with someone and had designs on you again. She said I was, and I quote, "getting in the way" of you two being back together.'

'Gina, it's not true. You have to believe me. It's you I see my future with, no one else.'

I breathe deeply in an attempt to expel the negative feelings from my body as I realise what Fabio has just said.

'You told her you had fallen in love?' I ask, meeting his gaze.

He takes a large glug of his whisky and puts down his glass.

'Of course I did. I love you, Gina. I had expected to tell you this in a far more romantic setting, but now it doesn't matter,' he says, gripping my hands and looking into my eyes.

My heart flutters as he says the words, but there's still more I need to know. 'So why did your sister want me off the scene?'

'She was trying to protect me. Yes, I was hurt when Lucina broke things off with me but that was over two years ago. I don't think Sofia wanted me to go through that heartache again. Also, maybe she thought you were a gold digger taking an interest in the hotel.'

Two years ago. It seems that Fabio was going through his own heartbreak at the same time that I was experiencing mine.

'She's assumed a hell of a lot.'

'I know, and she's sorry she messed up. You have to believe me. My feelings for Lucina have been over for a long time. Do you think I could have fallen for you so quickly if that were not true? You took my breath away the moment I laid eyes on you.'

I suddenly feel so sorry for him. Yes, he was a fool not to tell me about Lucina but perhaps I overreacted. And hasn't he just told me that he loves me?

I wrap my arms around him and he squeezes me tightly.

'Gina,' he breathes. 'Please forgive me. I am so sorry, I thought I had lost you forever.'

'Let's take things one day at a time,' I say, clinging onto him like I never want to let him go.

Greg will be staying with Hannah in the annexe so I take Fabio to the main house where there is a vacant bedroom. I text Hannah, telling her Fabio has arrived and we need somewhere to talk privately.

She texts me back immediately.

Are you OK?

I tell her I'm fine and she tells me to message her if I need anything. In some ways it feels like Hannah is the older sister lately as she's always watching out for me.

Fabio and I stay up into the small hours, talking everything through, before we finally climb into bed and wrap our arms around each other. We fall asleep in each other's arms with thoughts of forgiveness and new beginnings.

Chapter Forty-Five

The next morning, I wake around nine o'clock and go downstairs to find breakfast in full swing. I had forgotten to set my alarm and am slightly cross with myself.

'Morning, Gina,' says Hannah. 'Everything alright with you?'

'Yes, and I am so sorry I missed the early breakfast service. I'm here now if anything needs doing.'

'Relax, Dad's here as well as Greg and Ellie. There's more than enough people to look after four bedrooms. Well, five actually including you and Fabio, but you can get your own breakfast.' She winks. 'Ooh, and Gina, will you be around at twelve o'clock? Mum will be here too.'

'Sounds intriguing. What's up?'

'Well, you'll just have to be here to find out.' She grins.

I take a tray of coffee, croissants and orange juice to the room as Fabio is stepping out of the shower. He looks refreshed after a good night's sleep.

I place the tray on the table near the window that overlooks the fells and pour us each a coffee.

'Thank you, Gina.' He smiles, taking a sip of his coffee.

'So what now then?' I ask.

'Now the decorating at the villa is finished, I will head back to Milan in a day or two. I have a client to meet with and then I must oversee the set-up of the hotel ready for the reopening.'

'Is your sister still at the villa?'

'No, she disappeared not long after I returned the day you left, back to her Milan apartment. We had a blazing row. We've made our peace as I think deep down she had my best interests at heart.'

I lean across the small table, grasping Fabio's hand.

'We have to meet downstairs at twelve as Hannah has something to say to us. We could go for a little walk, or you could hang around here and read the newspaper until then?'

'A walk sounds good. No fell walking though, I don't have the appropriate footwear.' He smiles, glancing down at his suede loafers.

'Don't worry, it's a bit too cold to be climbing and we won't be out too long.'

It's just after eleven as we take the road away from the village, passing the church and carrying on down a winding path that leads to a glade. We pass two hikers, dressed in thick jackets and woollen hats, who say 'Good morning'. They each have a large rucksack on their back and wear cheerful expressions, seemingly unperturbed by the cold weather.

After completing a short circular walk, we are soon passing the Hotel on the Water as Katy is walking down the driveway.

'Gina!' she says, hurrying over and embracing me in a hug. 'Hi, Fabio. Erm – aren't you two supposed to be walking around Lake Como instead of Ullswater?' she asks, looking a little perplexed.

'It's a long story. I needed to come home for a few days,' I say, not really feeling it's the time to go into details. 'I was going to call and see you at some point today, actually. Well done on your cruise ship job. I bet you're really excited.'

'Oh, I absolutely can't wait. I think I'm really ready for a change. Anyway, catch you guys later. I'm just nipping to the shop for a packet of cigarettes from Val's. Filthy habit I know but I'm on a bit of an alcohol detox. I'm not giving up both or I'll be taking holy orders next,' she says, throwing her head back and laughing.

I'll miss Katy when she goes off sailing around the Mediterranean Sea, or whichever ocean she takes to. I enjoy our little chats and catch-ups at the cabin café and love listening to her amusing stories, of which there are plenty. I'm sure she'll be sorely missed at the Hotel on the Water too.

We're just back at the B&B when I spot Jean from the Traveller's Inn opposite placing a recycling bin outside. She raises her hand and waves.

'Hi, love, how are you?'

'Fine, Jean, how are you?'

'Not bad, love. I'm just thinking about a menu for a Spanish tapas evening here next week, what do you think? Ted thinks I'm out of control, wondering what I'm going to come up with next. It's only during the school holidays, though, when the tourists are here,' she laughs.

'Maybe Fabio can give you one or two ideas about that,' I say, turning to Fabio. 'Although I'm sure he would say Italian antipasto is better.'

'I like Spanish tapas. The idea for tapas originated in Italy anyway.'

'You've just made that up, haven't you?'

'Maybe.' He smiles.

'We might pop over and have a drink this evening, Jean,' I say, before we walk up the path to the bed and breakfast.

We walk across the hall and enter the lounge to find a group of family and friends including Mum and Dad gathered in the lounge. There are several bottles of champagne and some glass flutes on the coffee table.

Greg clears his throat and begins to speak. 'Welcome everyone, and thanks for being here. I just thought as you're back home, Gina, this would be a nice time to share some good news. Well, I hope it's good news anyway.' Greg drops down onto one knee in front of Hannah and opens a small blue velvet box, revealing a sparkling solitaire ring. 'Hannah, I know I've only known you for a few months but I know I want to spend the rest of my life with you. Will you marry me?'

Hannah's hand flies over her mouth. 'What? I thought this was to celebrate your job promotion! Greg's been made general manager of the factory, everyone!'

'Well, we can celebrate that too, I suppose,' he laughs. 'Sooo, are you going to give me an answer then?'

'Yes, yes of course I'll marry you!' says Hannah as she jumps up and wraps her jean-clad legs around Greg's waist.

Everyone whoops and cheers and I unexpectedly feel a tear roll down my cheek.

'Congratulations!' I say, crushing Greg and Hannah in an embrace. 'I am so, so happy for you both.'

Fabio steps forward and shakes Greg by the hand and kisses Hannah on both cheeks.

Dad proposes a toast as everyone is handed a glass of champagne.

'I would like to wish Greg and Hannah a lifetime of happiness together. In the short time I have known Greg I can see that he is a fine young man. But more importantly, his love for Hannah shines out of him. It's something really special when you find the love of your life,' he says, and I notice him cast a sideways glance at Mum, whose eyes have misted over.

'To Greg and Hannah,' says Dad.

'To Greg and Hannah!' choruses everyone in the room.

People mingle and chat and Ellie approaches Hannah as she is about to go into the kitchen.

'Hannah, can I ask you something?' she says, a little nervously.

'Yes of course, Ellie, what is it?'

'Well, I was just wondering. Can I do your wedding make-up?'

Chapter Forty-Six

Katy collars me as she is about to leave the impromptu engagement party.

'We must have a leaving do before I start work on the ship,' she says. 'I start a week's training in Manchester on Monday and then I'll find out where my maiden voyage will be. I was thinking a girls' night out at La Trattoria might be in order? I know the hotel will be doing a little farewell party but I want something more intimate too for my closest friends.'

'I think that's perfect.' I squeeze her arm gently. 'I can't think of a better place to give you a send-off. Actually, will you back for the weekend? Jean's organising a Spanish night at the Traveller's, she's hiring a bucking bronco and everything.'

'Really? Well I can't say I've ridden anything as wild as that but I've probably come close,' she laughs. 'Yeah, I'll be back on Friday night. Sounds like fun. See you later, Gina. I'm so thrilled for Hannah and Greg,' she says as she departs.

Mum comes over and fills my empty glass with more champagne before offering a glass to Fabio. Even though I haven't forgotten the pain she's inflicted on Dad, if everyone else has forgiven her then I'd better start too.

'Mum, this is Fabio,' I say, introducing her.

'Nice to meet you,' she says, smiling. 'I hope you're treating my daughter well.'

'I intend to make it my mission in life,' he responds, casting a loving glance at me. There go those butterflies again.

'Well, I'm pleased to hear it. You won't get anyone on this earth who's as good a catch as our Gina.' She plants a kiss lightly on my cheek. 'She's the best daughter any mother could wish for.'

I'm flabbergasted; I can't recall Mum ever being one for open displays of affection. Clearly she's softened with age. I spot Dad in the corner walking towards us and smiling affectionately.

'Now then, I was just saying to Greg, we should all go for dinner to the Black Bull tonight. My treat. Might be nice to get to know you a little better, young man,' he says, to Fabio, shaking his hand.

'I think that's a lovely idea, Don,' says Mum with a huge smile on her face.

Greg's parents, a grey-haired couple in their late sixties, are among the guests and are staying in one of the guest rooms overnight. Dad has also invited them to join us for a meal.

Daphne's amongst the gathering and has brought Paul Barlow along with her. She's positively glowing, which I suspect has something to do with her blossoming 'friendship' with Paul.

'Hi, guys,' says Daphne as she and Paul are about to leave. 'We're just going to have a little drive into Penrith to pick up a gift and an engagement card for Hannah. Do you need anything while we're there?'

'No thanks, Daphne. Thanks for coming over. You look really well. I love your dress,' I say, admiring the vintage-style black dress with a striking floral pattern.

'Homemade,' she says, giving a little twirl.

'She's good, isn't she?' says Paul proudly.

'Very. I know where to come now when I want a one-off dress.'

'Oh, Gina, I'd love to do that.'

'I'm so pleased for you, Daphne. Watch out Stella McCartney, hey?'

I spot Val walking towards us with a glass of champagne in her hand.

'Hey, Val. I think you left some of that cherry brandy last time you were here. It's in one of the kitchen cupboards.'

'No thanks, I'll stick with champagne. I'm off that cherry brandy for a bit. I had a right headache the following morning after spending the evening here. I barely got up in time to open the shop,' she chuckles.

As I laugh, looking around the room at all my friends, I feel a fizz of excitement. And I can't believe Fabio has just met my mother!

Chapter Forty-Seven

Fabio and I pop into the Traveller's Inn for an hour before we head for the engagement meal at the Black Bull.

'So are you sure about Spanish tapas?' Fabio asks Jean, who is wearing a blue velvet tracksuit and her blonde hair in a topknot.

'Why not? Everyone loves a bit of Spain, don't they? I'm thinking sangria at the bar too. Maybe even a bucking bronco outside. A bit of a wager, for whoever stays on the longest. The money could go to charity.'

'I take it you won't be putting your name down for that?' I ask Fabio.

'Oh no. What a dreadful shame, I won't be here!' says Fabio, tapping his forehead with the palm of his hand and winking at Jean. 'I would have loved to have had a go at that.'

'Yeah right,' I laugh.

'Maybe after a few glasses of sangria, I would have. It's a shame we'll never know.' He grins.

'Exactly! We'll get the sangria flowing, people will be queueing up for a go. It's nice to let your hair down once in a while, isn't it?' says Jean. 'Anyway, I'm thinking paella for the food, along with olives, meatballs, that type of thing. I had the nicest chorizo and white bean stew on holiday in Malaga once, I might have a go at making that.'

'Sound wonderful. I don't think you need any input from us, Jean, you seem to have everything under control,' I say.

'Brilliant. I just wanted to know what you thought. Right then. Have a great night at the Black Bull and pass on our congratulations to Hannah. I'll pop a card over tomorrow.'

We make our way to the pub, where everyone else has already arrived and are in ebullient mood, laughing and drinking. Dad waves us over to the table.

It seems strange approaching the table with Fabio, as on every other family occasion I have been alone or had Adam in tow.

Dad is on his feet first and embraces me in a hug, before doing the same to Fabio and patting him on the back.

'Right, let's order some more drinks,' says Dad, taking charge. It's so lovely seeing the old sparkle return to his eyes and for a second I feel a little overcome with emotion.

Fabio and I sit down and have a look at the menu, which has recently changed. The restaurant has had a bit of a makeover too and now has plain green curtains and seat covers rather than the old tartan pattern. The stag's head over the fireplace has been replaced with a huge mirror with an intricately patterned gilt frame. I think I preferred the stag's head if I'm honest.

When more drinks have arrived and everyone has placed their food orders, I tell people about Jean's plans for a Spanish evening the following weekend.

'That sounds like a lot of fun,' says Greg. 'I love a bit of Spanish tapas. I had a go on a bucking bronco once on a stag do in Newcastle. I did pretty well too. The groom didn't fare so well though. He fell off and lost both of his front teeth two days before the wedding. The bride very nearly called the whole thing off.'

Everyone laughs.

'That's it then. You're going nowhere near any bloody bucking bronco,' says Hannah, who's looking beautiful this evening in a slinky blood-red dress with lipstick to match.

'Spoilsport!' laughs Greg.

'Right then,' says Dad. 'Can I have everyone's attention? As it's a day of celebrating happy news, I would just like to announce some news of my own. These past few weeks me and Julia have become quite friendly again. And, well, the thing is,' he says, almost struggling to find the right words, 'we're going to try and make another go of it.'

Hannah jumps up and claps her hands together, as Dad looks over in my direction, not knowing how I will react. Despite myself, the corners of my mouth turn up and a small grin appears on my face.

I'm on my feet at once going over to give Mum and Dad a hug. Hannah joins us and for a few minutes there is no one else in the room as our family reunites again. I hear the sound of people cheering and clinking their glasses together and I close my eyes, savouring every moment of this wonderful evening. Sometimes you just have to let things happen naturally, I think to myself as I glance over at Fabio, who is smiling at me lovingly.

Chapter Forty-Eight

It's the next morning and Fabio has booked a flight for ten o'clock in the evening so today will be our last day together for a little while. I don't want him to leave but he needs to start overseeing the set-up of the hotel and have a chat with a couple of potential chefs.

Whilst I was doing some online shopping after breakfast, I came across a Mac make-up tutorial course on Groupon that issues a certificate at the end of it, so I've bought it for Ellie. It's a five-hour masterclass that includes a set of make-up brushes. At fifty pounds that's a saving of over seventy-five per cent, or so they claim. I can't wait to tell Ellie and text her to call over when she gets a minute.

After we've finished up the breakfast service and Ellie has popped in and been told of her make-up course (which included much *whoop-whoop*ing and crushing embraces), I ask Fabio if we could take a drive later to Forest Side in Grasmere. It's a romantic Victorian mansion with an award-winning restaurant. What he doesn't know is that I have telephoned ahead and booked a lunch reservation for one o'clock.

I want to show Fabio how the hotel and restaurant have been so sympathetically restored. The reception rooms with their original fireplaces have been redecorated and refurnished beautifully, but the star of the show is the dining room. A stone terrace forms an extension full of light, which is perfect for summer evenings.

We drive along the meandering country roads until we pull up outside the imposing grey stone building that is Forest Side.

As we enter the building from the cold, I immediately feel the warming effects of the roaring fire in the entrance hall. A smiling young woman welcomes us into the dining room. The furnishings in the room are honey-coloured wood, the tables made from the building's original floorboards. Light is flooding in through the picture window frames that reveal the fells in the background, dotted with Herdwick sheep. Contemporary bronze lighting is suspended from the ceiling, creating a cosy, rustic feel.

'Wow. I hope the food is as good as the décor,' says Fabio as he shrugs off his coat and places it over the back of the chair at a table near the window.

'I'm sure it will be. There's an award-winning chef at the helm.'

'It's not Gordon Ramsay, is it?' Fabio smiles.

'No, but I imagine he's every bit as good.'

We order some drinks, water for me and a Lakeland beer for Fabio, who really does enjoy a pint of locally brewed ale. We both dine on the finest fell-bred lamb, juicy and tender, with home-grown vegetables and creamy, rich dauphinoise potatoes. Then we finish off with a delectable crème brûlée for me and a cheeseboard of local cheeses for Fabio.

'Well, that was excellent,' says Fabio, leaning back in his chair and exhaling. 'I think I have consumed enough food to keep me going until I arrive home tomorrow.'

'Well, maybe we should go for a little walk outside. I have something to show you.'

We settle our bill and, with prior permission given, walk outside to have a look around the Victorian walled garden.

There are neat footpaths flanked by fruit trees and trimmed box hedges. Raised beds grow a variety of herbs and vegetables that are all used in the restaurant kitchen.

'This is amazing,' says Fabio as we wander through the garden, inhaling the scent of the garden herbs, including rosemary and mint.

Fabio pulls a basil leaf from a plant and runs it between his fingers before smelling it.

'It reminds me of home.' He smiles.

'I don't think you're meant to handle the plants. There's probably CCTV out here,' I gently warn him. 'Can you imagine if you did open a restaurant at the villa? You have enough room in the garden to create the same type of thing.'

'Now there's an idea. The climate in Italy produces the finest vegetables in the world.'

'Naturally,' I respond with a smile.

'My grandmother grew tomatoes and basil and we have the olive trees, but this…' says Fabio, surveying the garden, 'this is incredible.'

'Something to think about,' I suggest.

'You always give me something to think about, Gina,' says Fabio as he pulls me closer and plants a lingering kiss on my lips. 'You occupy my thoughts constantly.'

We head back towards Glenridding just after three thirty so that we can spend a couple of hours together before Fabio has to leave for the airport.

I know I'm going to miss him when he leaves and I wonder how long it will be before we are reunited. We have a full house at the B&B next week and Fabio has bookings at the villa, although I suppose he has staff who can take care of them.

A watery sun breaks through the clouds as we drive home and by the time we arrive back at Lake View there is an unseasonably clear blue sky and a bright sun.

'The weather has gone a bit crazy in the UK. This sun is actually quite warm,' I tell Fabio as I open the door to the annexe. I make us a coffee to take outside and sit in the small garden. 'Might as well make the most of this sunshine.'

'I can think of a better way to spend my last couple of hours with you,' says Fabio, pulling me close and running his fingers up and down my back. 'The coffee will keep.' He leads me into my bedroom.

Sun is streaming through the skylight keeping the room bright even as I draw the curtains at the French windows. There is something urgent and exciting about our lovemaking, as neither of us know exactly when we will see each other again.

Afterwards, Fabio leans up on one arm, staring at me and smiling.

'I wish I didn't have to go home but the sooner I get things sorted at the villa the better. We need to get on with the rest of our lives,' he says, kissing me on the forehead before jumping up to shower. 'I love you.'

My eyes follow his backside to the shower and I repeat those three words in my head, feeling gloriously content.

I try to overcome a slightly anxious feeling when I think about Fabio leaving for Italy, but I know I must trust him. I don't give my heart away easily but now I know for sure. I love Fabio. And I know he loves me too.

Chapter Forty-Nine

Later in the evening I drop Fabio at Manchester airport departures with a lingering kiss before I head home. He has promised to call me as soon as he arrives.

It's almost midnight when I arrive back at the guesthouse and I am surprised to find Hannah still up, watching a black and white film. She looks as if she's been crying.

'Hi, sis. Hope you're OK. Did Fabio get off alright?'

'Yes, fine,' I say, slumping next to Hannah on the sofa, stifling a yawn. 'You're up late.'

'I know. I'll probably regret it in the morning. I shouldn't have started watching this really, I always have to see a film right through to the end.'

I realise she's watching *Brief Encounter* as it's the final scene where Alec leaves Laura at the train station. He places his hand on her shoulder, expressing tenderness, longing and regret. Hannah grabs a tissue as she stifles a little sob.

'You're so soppy,' I laugh.

'Oh, Gina, I just love this film. I think it might be my all-time favourite. I feel so sorry for Laura, snatching a few moments of happiness, knowing she will never leave her husband.'

'I know. The way times have changed, though. It makes you wonder whether she would be off like a shot these days if she was so unhappy.'

We chat for a few more minutes before we head off to our rooms. As I lay in bed I wonder how many people in the world are living in unhappy relationships, and if so why do they stay? Isn't life too short to expect anything other than happiness? And could my own second chance at happiness be just around the corner?

Chapter Fifty

The following morning, despite having had a late night the evening before, I busy myself with the breakfast service.

Surprisingly, the previous day's good weather looks set to continue today, to the delight of the fell walkers who are just finishing their breakfasts. Perhaps I may go for a little walk myself later? I'm determined to get fit this year. Fabio suggested we visit the mountains in Italy over the summer, so I would have to be in pretty good shape…

I finish up in the kitchen with Dominika, grab my coat and head off towards the road leading away from the village. As I pass the Hotel on the Water, I wonder how Katy is doing on her training course for the cruise ship. I'm sure she'll have made instant friends and I think about how much I'll miss her when she leaves.

As I head along a path beside the lake I pass a family with two little girls. One of them has ginger curly hair, the other is blonde. They remind me of Hannah and myself when we were children and to my surprise a lump forms in my throat. The little girls are dressed in jeans and matching green parkas. They are both wearing wellingtons; the older girl's are pink, the younger child wears green ones, the feet in the shape of a frog. Dad is skimming stones in the water and the girls jump up and down excitedly as their father manages several jumps along the water with the stone.

I remember Dad skimming stones when we were little. Mum would be walking along smoking a cigarette, her hair tied back in a headscarf and looking like a movie star. I can't believe how quickly the years have rolled by. And now things seem to have come full circle as they prepare to give things another go and spend their retirement years together. Getting my head around the idea hasn't been easy, but seeing them so happy together is better than I could ever have wished for. It's time I stopped being concerned about other people's welfare, I decide. Everyone has their own path to follow. It's time I thought about my own direction in life.

I've been walking for over an hour, stopping occasionally to admire the view of the lake and surrounding fells when a text comes through on my phone from Fabio.

Missing you already. Call you soon x

I glance at my watch, and as it's just after eleven o'clock I decide to call in at Emmy's café in the village for a coffee and maybe even a cake.

As I enter the shop, I find Emmy's shoulder-length hair a vibrant shade of mauve. She's wearing dungarees and a pair of mismatched socks; one is black and white striped, and the other pea green.

'Hello, Gina, haven't seen you in here for a little while. Take a seat, I'll be with you in a minute.'

I glance around the café. There are six tables, made from recycled railway buffers, with vintage style mismatched chairs. Three of the tables are occupied by a group of tourists who are eating cake and sandwiches and drinking tea from floral china cups. I take a seat in a corner near the window.

'Coffee, is it?' she asks as she reappears. 'And today's cake is passion fruit and ginger.'

'Oooh that sounds rather nice. Go on then, I'll have a slice of that.'

My cake, when it arrives, is a huge slice glazed with icing and I devour it hungrily, trying to lick my fingers without anyone noticing. I'm just finishing my coffee when my mobile rings. I scoop my phone up and take the call outside.

'Fabio. How are you?'

'Ciao, Gina, I'm OK. I slept in a little later than I would have liked this morning. I wish you were here. This place seems so empty without you.'

'Oh, are you at the villa already?'

'Yes, I'm going to stay here this evening. My two chefs arrive tomorrow so I want to make an early start and go over some menus. We have bookings in exactly three days' time. Wait until you see the dining room. It looks even more spectacular with the new lighting, I hope you approve.'

'Ooh, will you send me a photo?'

'Hmm, maybe you should fly over immediately and see it in person for the full effect,' he teases.

I wish I was there with him to celebrate the reopening of the villa, but I have my own work to do here and I don't want Hannah to think I'm taking advantage. I've planned to visit in a couple of weeks anyway, when Mum is coming over to look after things. I've suggested Hannah takes a holiday to Amsterdam in the spring with Greg.

We chat for a few minutes more before we end the call.

'Ti amo Gina.'

'Bye, Fabio. I love you too.'

As I say the words, I still can't quite believe I've fallen in love again. Yet I have a strong feeling that Adam would approve of Fabio. All that would matter to him would be that I was happy. And I feel happier than I have done in a very long time.

Chapter Fifty-One

The week has flown by and soon enough it's the Saturday of the Spanish evening at the Traveller's Inn.

Greg drove over to be with Hannah last night as soon as he finished work. He travels over every Friday now for the whole weekend and is finding it harder to depart on a Sunday evening. Sometimes he will also stay through the week, setting off early to travel the hour and twenty minutes to work.

I'm watering the hanging baskets outside the B&B when Hannah and Greg appear from the annexe, asking if they can have a word with me.

'Sure, what's up?' I say, taking my gardening gloves off and stepping into the lounge. 'It's not another announcement, is it?'

'More of a proposal,' says Hannah, glancing at Greg.

Greg takes up the conversation. 'The thing is, you know how hard it is for me and Hannah to be separated; well, I've been looking for something in the village to buy. I don't have to tell you how expensive property around here is, even with my pay rise.'

'Yes…' I say, not certain where this is going.

'Well, we were wondering, and of course you are going to need time to think about it, but would you consider letting us buy into the B&B?'

'Buy into it?'

'Yes, live here and own fifty per cent of the property. That way if you were ever to move, for example to live in Italy, you would always have a share in a home back here. I know it may be a bit small in the annexe for three of us, but maybe in time we could extend some more.'

'Give it some thought, Gina,' says Hannah. 'Things are changing for everyone and we just have your best interests at heart. Mum and Dad are back together and me and Greg are going to be planning our wedding soon. Katy will soon be gone and Daphne and Paul seem to be getting more serious. It's time to think about your own future.'

'Are you trying to get rid of me?' I ask, raising an eyebrow and smiling.

She comes over and wraps me in a hug.

'Not a chance. Just giving you options. Think about yourself now, Gina. Everyone here is OK.'

As I return to my gardening I think about what Hannah has just said. *Everyone here is OK.* I say it to myself over and over. Maybe I have spent a lot of time worrying about other people's lives. I've also put my heart and soul into the business to ensure everyone has the best time at Lake View. It's been the focus of my existence for the last few years, especially following Adam's death. I remember being in the same situation as Hannah all those years ago, being unable to afford a property in the village. We were lucky to acquire the old house from Iris at a discounted price. There's nothing to think about here really. My mind's made up. Hannah has always been there for me unconditionally. It's time for me to be there for her.

Chapter Fifty-Two

The tapas night has arrived. Jean has somehow managed to get hold of some posters of a bullfight which are plastered around the bar area. There are also Spanish fans depicting dancing señoritas on the walls. Jugs of sangria with an alarming amount of fruit poking out are lined up behind the bar alongside a tired-looking wicker donkey. Jean and Ted are wearing huge sombreros and 'Y Viva España' is blaring out from a CD. It feels like a seventies party in Torremolinos.

'Hola!' says Jean as Hannah, Greg and I enter the pub. There is only one other couple sitting at the end of the bar, although it's only seven o'clock.

Jean places some little terracotta tapas bowls on the bar containing olives, patatas bravas and sardines. There's also a huge platter of jamón, Manchego cheese and a huge basket of bread.

'Plenty more where that came from. I've made a huge chorizo and bean stew for later on. The bucking bronco should be here any time now,' says Jean, glancing at her watch.

'I'd advise people to eat the food *after* they've had a go on the bull,' laughs Greg.

'Remember you're not going on it. I like you with teeth.' Hannah smiles.

Jean looks puzzled so Greg tells her about the groom-to-be who lost two front teeth.

'Well, they must have set it up on hard ground, which they're not supposed to. No, this one has a soft base underneath, like a bouncy castle. They've already delivered that bit. Ted's inflating it outside while the bloke's gone off to collect the bucking bronco from an afternoon party in Penrith.'

'I might just have a go then,' says Greg, casting a sideways glance at Hannah.

The pub quickly fills over the next hour and soon the Spanish evening is in full swing, with the sangria flowing and Jean in and out of the kitchen topping up the tapas. The little dishes of chorizo, Padrón peppers and Manchego cheese are delicious.

Outside Ted has set up a trestle table where Jean will serve up the Spanish stew later on.

It's just after eight thirty and I'm chatting to Val at the bar when the door opens and in walks Katy.

'Katy, you're back! How did the training go?'

'It was an absolute blast,' she says, grabbing a tall glass of sangria from the bar and passing some money to Ted. 'It's going to be hard work though by the sounds of it, although I'm not afraid of that. I met some great people. We find out where and when our first sailing will be next week.'

Katy takes a sip of her sangria and pulls a face. 'Ugh! This could strip the enamel off my teeth. I think I'll have a gin next.'

There's a small gathering of people at the bar who are having a little wager as to how long they can stay on the bucking bronco. It's five pounds a ticket and the winner takes all. Jean has suggested that if any of the hoteliers win, they donate the money to the air ambulance, which is entirely self-funded. Everyone agrees.

Fifteen minutes later Jean is announcing that the competition will shortly begin outside and for people to get their names down if they want to have a go.

First up is a young local lad who is being cheered on by his mates. The bull starts up and he is flung off in ten seconds, to the sound of much laughing and jeering.

Next up is Paul Barlow, who rides the machine with confidence as the bull thrusts and twists him through the air, slowly at first but gradually gaining speed. He nods and smiles at Daphne, who is practically swooning in admiration. He looks self-assured for a short while, but when the speed is increased again his black hair is flailing around like a windsock as he holds on for dear life. He manages a very respectable time of one minute forty seconds before he is finally flung off.

A succession of people step up to have a go on the mechanical beast, all enjoying themselves and having fun before quickly being evacuated from the saddle.

It's almost time for the Spanish stew to be served, so Jean asks if there is anyone else who would like to have a go.

'Aye, go on then,' says Ted, heading towards the bull. Jean looks stunned.

'Ted! What do you think you're doing?'

'I broke in a couple of wild horses when I was young. I used to work at some stables. It can't be much worse than that.'

'But Ted, that was over forty years ago. I'm not sure your heart could stand it,' says Jean anxiously.

'I'm as strong as an ox, me, and I've never had a problem with my ticker.'

Mum and Dad have just entered the pub garden, each carrying a glass of red wine.

'Just in time for the entertainment,' I say. 'Ted's going to have a go on the bucking bronco.'

'Oh good lord,' says Mum. 'I hope he'll be alright. Jean will probably murder him herself if he ends up in hospital.'

A crowd has gathered outside as Ted makes his way to the innocent-looking beast. He mounts the bull quite niftily for a man of his age and starts it up slowly. He's holding on really well as Jean stands a short distance away with her hand over her mouth. Seconds tick by.

'Faster!' shouts someone in the audience. Jean throws them a withering look.

The whirring machine quickens pace as Ted duly obliges, throwing the speed up a notch. Over one minute. Over two minutes.

It's quite extraordinary. Ted is riding the bull like a twenty-five-year-old ranch hand and Jean is watching him with her mouth gaping open.

'Are you sure you're alright?' she asks him.

'Nearly three minutes!' someone from the audience shouts. 'Go on, Ted!'

'I think so. But I think my false teeth might be coming a little loose,' Ted says, putting his hand to his mouth.

It's coming up for three minutes and someone starts a countdown. Ten, nine, eight…

Ted is unsuccessfully trying to push his false teeth back into his mouth as the countdown continues.

Five, four, three, two, ONE…

Everyone cheers at the exact moment Ted's false teeth shoot out of his mouth and plop into Katy's large gin glass.

'Eeeww!! What the hell?' says a startled Katy, chucking her drink onto some nearby grass. The huge gnashers lie motionless alongside the empty glass.

The crowd is hysterical. Jean is mortified.

Laughter is ringing around the pub garden as a patio door opens and someone is walking towards me.

'Sounds like I've been missing all the fun,' says the tall, dark, handsome man.

'Fabio!' I stammer. 'What are you doing here?'

'It's the weekend. What better way is there to celebrate it than with my love? Don't tell me I've missed the bucking bronco.'

The entertainment has finished and most of the guests have filtered inside or gone home. We're sitting contentedly at a long table in an alcove, drinking the remains of some wine and chatting. Hannah is yawning and Mum and Dad are drinking coffee and laughing at something that Katy has just said.

'What a wonderful evening. I can't remember having such fun in a long time,' says Hannah. 'I think these themed nights are exactly what the village needs. I've always loved living here but I love it even more now.' She snuggles in to Greg, who wraps his arms around her shoulders.

I glance over at Mum and Dad, who are laughing again. They look so happy. I wonder whether Mum might have stayed if there had have been a little more excitement in the village all those years ago.

Paul, Daphne and Val come over to join us, followed shortly afterwards by Katy. Jean gave Katy a large gin free of charge after the teeth incident, which still makes me howl every time I think about it. Dad asks for everyone's attention before they head off home and asks us all to raise a glass.

'What are we celebrating?' I ask.

'Us.' He smiles.

'To us!' everyone repeats as they raise their glasses.

'And happy endings,' says Katy, as she glances in my direction.

'Happy endings,' I repeat, smiling at Fabio. 'I'll certainly drink to that…'

Chapter Fifty-Three

A few days later, Fabio has returned to Como and Daphne, Katy, Hannah and I are dining at La Trattoria to say bon voyage to Katy, who is setting off on a cruise.

'What a week it's been,' says Katy in between mouthfuls of fragrant penne arrabiatta. 'I can't believe I'm off sailing the Canary Islands in a couple of days. Just as you're coming back here, eh, Daphne?'

'I know,' says Daphne, taking a sip of white wine. 'I think deep down I knew I'd always return to the village. It turns out I had nothing in common with Ben. I'm really enjoying getting back into my dressmaking again. Actually, I've got some news. Someone has commissioned me to make their wedding dress.'

'Woo hoo! This calls for a celebration!' Katy beckons a waiter over and orders a bottle of champagne.

'Champagne in an Italian restaurant? Aldo won't let you back in,' says Hannah.

'I think he will. The champagne is twice the price,' laughs Katy.

'Would you believe that the bride-to-be has also agreed to let Ellie do her make-up?'

'I'm not surprised. She's brilliant, Ellie, she's really come a long way. She's been posting photos on social media of her models. They look amazing,' says Hannah.

'And it all started with a Mac make-up course from Groupon,' I say. 'Though thinking about it, I'm not sure that's true. She was already crazy about make-up but let's just say having some training has refined her style a little.'

'Well, I'd definitely let her do my wedding make-up,' says Katy. We all turn to look at her.

'I know what you're all thinking, I'm not the marrying kind. But I will settle down one day. I just haven't met the man of my dreams yet, that's all,' she says, topping up her glass. 'How are you getting on with your wedding plans, Hannah?'

'OK, thanks. We don't want anything too fancy as we're hoping to get married next spring. We haven't quite decided where to tie the knot but we'll probably have the reception back at the B&B.'

'A spring wedding? How lovely, the village will be full of daffodils.'

It makes perfect sense for Hannah and Greg to marry in St Patrick's Church, but I know she is aware of the memories it holds for me.

'Anyway, Daphne, this time next year you might be making your own wedding dress. I've seen the way Paul Barlow looks at you,' I say.

To my surprise Daphne looks a little embarrassed.

'It's true we've been getting to know each other lately. He's lovely, you know, not at all what you'd expect. He can't do enough for me.' She smiles with a slightly dreamy look in her eyes.

'Not to mention being pretty easy on the eye, hey?' Katy winks. She's incorrigible.

'Ah, how nice is this?' I say as the waiter arrives with our champagne and four flutes. 'All the gang together. I propose a toast.'

Our waiter pops the cork and places the champagne in a silver ice bucket before disappearing to tend to another table.

I fill everyone's glasses and we raise them in the air.

'I hope we all find what we're looking for this year. And wherever we may be, let's toast our friendship. May it last forever.'

'To friendship,' we say as we chink our long-stemmed glasses together.

'Ah, we're just like the three musketeers,' sighs Daphne.

'I know. There were four of those too as I recall, just like us. I've never really understood why they were called the three musketeers when there were actually four of them,' I reply.

'Anyway, Daphne, I for one am glad you're back in the village, what with these two buggering off around the globe,' says Hannah, nodding her head in my and Katy's direction.

'You know I always come back though. I'm like a homing pigeon.' I laugh, yet wonder if the Lakes really will be my permanent home. I'm flying out in two weeks' time to see Fabio and I'm counting down the days. I don't exactly know what the future holds but I do know that everything has changed. There was a time when I thought nothing was forever. But friendship? Well, true friendship never really ends, does it? Sometimes it just finds a different direction, with all roads eventually leading us back to our lifelong friends.

Chapter Fifty-Four

Sun is streaming through the stained-glass windows of St Patrick's Church and the bells are ringing out in celebration as we prepare to witness the marriage of Hannah and Greg, in the first week of May.

Winter has gently turned to spring again in the Lakes and there's a profusion of daffodils dotted along the lakeside and in the church graveyard. It's a perfect day for a wedding as the previous day's clouds have lifted, replaced by blue skies and glorious sunshine.

'Are you sure you feel OK me being married here? I hope it doesn't bring back painful memories?' Hannah asks, squeezing my hand gently.

'Of course not. Your home is here. Where else would you get married? And Adam's here with us, isn't he? I feel as if he is a part of it all. I'm sure he would have looked at you and said, "you scrub up well".'

And he'd be right. Hannah looks absolutely beautiful. Daphne has excelled herself making Hannah the most exquisite cream wedding dress, gently swathed across the middle and encrusted with sparkling crystals. Ellie arrived a couple of hours ago with her huge box of make-up, bursting with excitement.

'You are going to be the most beautiful bride ever,' she said confidently as she laid out her Mac and Illamasqua products. 'I'll do your make-up too, Gina.'

By the time she's finished with Hannah, I have my own make-up refreshed as tears stream down my face. My sister is without doubt the most beautiful bride I have ever seen. Ellie has enhanced Hannah's natural beauty with a soft heather palette for her eyes and delicate apricot lips but there is also an inner happiness radiating from her.

Mum and Dad arrive as Ellie is putting her make-up kit away. Ellie offers to do Mum's make-up, although it has obviously already been applied.

'I've always done my own make-up, even at my own wedding,' she says, casting a glance at Dad. 'Thanks very much though. Hannah looks beautiful. So does Gina.'

'Now then, look at you. You look absolutely stunning,' says Dad, kissing Hannah lightly on the cheek. 'Greg's a lucky man. Have we got time for a small glass of champagne?' Dad looks so handsome in a dark grey pinstripe suit with a silver-grey waistcoat underneath.

'Just a small one,' replies Hannah. 'I don't want to be squiffy walking down the aisle. How's Greg?'

'Excited. Maybe a little nervous, but that's perfectly normal. He's scrubbed up pretty well too.' He smiles.

Greg stayed at Dad's house the night before and had been joined by his parents this morning. Fabio had also popped in this morning to congratulate him and no doubt indulge in a small whisky.

'Well, love, I think it's time,' suggests Dad, glancing out of the window at the ribboned car that will make the short journey to the church.

'Before we go, I just want to say I'm so happy to be here today,' says Mum, who looks striking in a cornflower blue dress with a matching hat. 'Ellie, would you mind taking a picture of us all?'

'Mum, the photographer will get lots of photos of us all together later,' Hannah reminds her.

'But this one's special. Just the four of us. Before you get married and become a part of someone else.'

'Oh, Mum. I'll always be me. And I'm happy that you're here today too.'

'I'll never be too far away again, I promise. One thing I've learned in life is that nothing is more important than family.'

Tears are threatening to spill over and ruin my make-up again.

Ellie shouts, 'Say cheese!' and as the four of us smile for the camera I think to myself that this is definitely a photograph of a happy moment.

Shortly afterwards, we follow the line of guests filtering into the chapel and Fabio and I take our place in the front pew. Hannah, a vision of loveliness, glides down the aisle to a thumbs-up from Katy and warm smiles from Daphne and Val. As Hannah and Greg exchange their vows at the wooden altar in the whitewash-walled church, Fabio curls his fingers around mine and squeezes my hand. Mum and Dad are watching proudly and Val is gently sniffing into her handkerchief. I can feel Adam's presence here with us too. And rather unexpectedly, it feels quietly reassuring.

Chapter Fifty-Five

I'm lying on a sun lounger with Fabio, who's on the adjacent sun lounger holding my hand. We've taken the boat across to Como and are enjoying a day at Lido di Bellano, a popular beach area with a good selection of bars and restaurants.

I've had several visits to Como in the last few months. I've been busy helping Fabio set up a website for the villa and advertising its new restaurant on social media. And it's been a long time coming but I'm finally having a beach holiday in Italy!

It's early August in Lake Como and the strong sun is beating down so I have a huge umbrella covering me as I read my novel. I'm currently sporting a gentle golden glow but I have to be careful with my fair skin, as I can turn red in an instant.

I glance at Fabio, who's wearing stylish sunglasses and navy swimming shorts, his oiled, bronze skin soaking up the sun. I'm listening to the lapping of the waves at the water's edge and wish I could stay here forever.

Fabio sits up to take a sip of his bottled water.

'Are you ready for some lunch?'

'I'd love some. But can I finish this chapter of my book first? I'm at a good bit.' I smile.

'Of course. You can do whatever pleases you, you're on holiday!'

'I'm just enjoying the relaxation today. I think my leg muscles are still protesting over that walk to the castle yesterday.'

Yesterday we set off after breakfast and walked up a mossy path to the castle of Vezio. It took around half an hour and the view of the lake from the tower was breathtaking. Luca and Maria at the villa have been wonderful hosts and waved us off yesterday morning with a packed lunch, Maria fussing over me like a concerned mother. She made sure I was wearing a hat and applying factor fifty to my fair skin. She kept pointing at my shoulders, shaking her head and saying '*Non bruciare*', which Fabio told me translates to 'Don't burn'.

Fabio wipes his face with a towel before reaching over and kissing me softly on the lips.

'It's enjoyable though, yes? Como in the summer is a little different to the winter.'

'It's just wonderful,' I say as I stretch my toes out along the sunbed, immediately feeling the searing heat as they are exposed to the sun.

Fabio notices this and unscrews the top of the sun lotion. He rubs the lotion into his hands before gently massaging it into my feet. It feels heavenly. Not for the first time, I can't believe my luck.

'Let me see your neck, it looks a little red,' he says, coming closer.

'But I've been in the shade, I…'

Then he's covering my neck in gentle kisses and suddenly the temperature is off the scale.

'I thought you hated public displays of affection,' I remind him, recalling the day in Milan when he ushered me into an empty shop doorway to kiss me.

'We are covered by the umbrella, and maybe these days I don't care. I am crazy in love,' he laughs.

I can't believe how beautiful it is here in Lake Como in the summer. There's a profusion of pink blossom everywhere and the pastel shades of the houses take on a vibrant hue under the bright sun. There are lots of man-made bathing areas with swimming pools overlooking the lake called 'lidos', with occasional stretches of beautiful public beach areas like this one.

I stand to slip my linen dress over my bikini when a passing hunk lowers his sunglasses and eyes me up and down. I'm glad Fabio doesn't notice.

We dress and head away from the beach in search of somewhere to eat and after a five-minute walk we ascend some steps to Meridiana restaurant. The restaurant is busy but we are lucky enough to find a table on an outside terrace with a view to die for. We are surrounded by the greenery of weeping willows and the sweet smell of apricots from a nearby tree. The landscape beyond the shimmering lake is varied, with wild mountain slopes and rows of cypress trees interspersed with small villages.

Fabio attracts the attention of a busy waitress, who despatches a menu before taking our drinks order.

'I'm having such a wonderful time here. It's just so beautiful,' I say, taking in my surroundings.

'You deserve it. I have had you working on your previous visits. It's about time you relaxed and enjoyed some sunshine.'

'This is exactly how I imagined a holiday in Italy would be. You're so lucky to live here,' I say, flicking through the menu.

'I suppose so. Although you become accustomed to it. There is nowhere in the world I would rather live, though.'

I've learned from Fabio that he has travelled extensively in Europe and also went to America as a child, when his family visited Disney World. His sister adored it but Fabio preferred the Florida beaches to the pleasure park. I wonder if I would yearn for the Lake District if I lived here in Italy? With every passing second I spend here, I'm less sure that I would. And it's only a two-and-a-half-hour flight to Manchester after all.

'A penny for your thoughts? If that is the right expression?'

'I'm just imaging how I'd feel if I moved away from the Lakes. I do love it though. I just wish we had a little more sunshine.'

'I agree. You live in a beautiful place but I couldn't live through those winters.'

I recall Fabio wearing a scarf tucked inside a thick woollen coat on an evening that I wouldn't even have considered particularly cold back home.

'I think you're right. I don't think you could cope with the freezing winters in England.'

A jug of iced water with lemon slices arrives, along with two cold bottles of Moretti beer. I order a risotto and Fabio orders a lobster salad and the smiling waitress disappears to the kitchen with the order.

'What do you want to do after lunch? The boats are every hour, so we can have a wander around the shops if you like?'

'Wow. A man that doesn't mind wandering around shops. I think I've found my soulmate!'

'I hope so,' says Fabio quietly. 'Actually, I could do with some new leather loafers. There's a little shop just off the main street that sells the finest quality.'

A passing waiter is carrying two pizzas in baskets, arms aloft and leaving a scent of oregano in his wake, making my stomach rumble.

'Sounds good. Maybe I'll have a look for some sandals. I haven't bought anything made from Italian leather. Some of the handbags look lovely too.'

Our food arrives and the scent of fresh garlic assaults my senses as a bowl of creamy risotto topped with parmesan shavings is placed in front of me. Fabio's lobster dish looks equally delicious and we tuck in to our food hungrily.

Just over an hour later, Fabio generously tips the smiling waitress as we leave the restaurant.

'That really was excellent. We must remember this restaurant next time we come here,' says Fabio, grasping my hand as we stroll contentedly towards the narrow streets full of shops and cafés.

As we walk, we pass bakeries displaying cakes and pastries in glass cabinets, souvenier shops, art galleries and gelatarias all jostling for space. We walk past shops selling hand-painted ceramic bowls and olive oils, with bunches of dried chillies and garlic hanging in their doorways. After scaling some steps, we turn into a narrow cobbled side street until the unmistakeable smell of leather guides us to a shop entrance.

We are greeted with a smile and 'buongiorno' from a middle-aged man wearing a white short-sleeved shirt as we enter the shop. The air-conditioned interior is a welcome respite from the searing heat outdoors.

Fabio disappears to the back of the shop to look at the leather shoes, whilst I browse the gorgeous leather handbags. My eye falls on a soft over-the-shoulder bag in a warm apricot shade. I run my hands over the smooth leather which the owner tells me is 'the finest calf leather'. There and then, I decide to buy it.

Fabio finds some footwear and soon we are paying for our purchases, much to the delight of the shop owner, before meandering through the streets once more.

An hour later we manage to find a seat outside a gelataria where Fabio buys me an ice cream. I'm glad I didn't have a dessert at the restaurant as the hazelnut ice cream, or *nocciola gelato*, is utterly delicious – sweet, nutty and creamy.

On the boat journey back to Varenna, I find myself struggling to keep my eyes open, sated by the wonderful food and the heat of the day. I lean contentedly into Fabio as he wraps his arms around my shoulders, almost feeling my eyes closing. Soon enough the harbour at Varenna comes into view and I untwine myself from his arms and pick up my bags.

As we arrive at the harbour, busy with tourists, a queue already forming for the next trip to Como, I glance up at the coloured houses on the slopes. And in that moment I feel something. I feel as though I have come home.

EPILOGUE

Lake Como....
Three years later

I'm standing in the sun-drenched garden of the villa in Varenna picking some basil for a salad, which I place into a basket. Matteo and Salvatore, our two chefs, are gathering vegetables for tonight's meal in the restaurant, arguing over whether or not to use chicory in a new lamb dish.

'It will overpower the lamb,' says Matteo, shaking his head.

'No, it won't,' says Salvatore, in his heavily accented vowels. 'Chicory has been paired with lamb for centuries.'

'Exactly. So let's try something different,' persists Matteo.

As I stand looking across the bejewelled lake, Fabio walks into the garden and takes me by the hand inside.

'You should be resting. Not listening to those two divas.' He laughs as he strokes his hand gently over my burgeoning tummy bump. He's become very protective as I enter my final trimester of pregnancy.

'Sit down, have some lemonade,' he says, placing a glass in front of me.

'I'm fine,' I say, shushing him. 'I'm hardly exerting myself picking a few herbs.'

'I want to look after you, Gina. And our little bambino. I cannot wait for his arrival.'

The Italian Garden restaurant and hotel opened its doors just over two years ago and has been fully booked since day one. Thankfully it's had wonderful reviews on TripAdvisor and seems to be going from strength to strength. The income, along with Fabio's inheritance, has provided the money to convert the spacious basement into living quarters for Fabio and me. It has floor length windows that glimpse the lake, almost mirroring the guesthouse back home.

Everything seemed to fall into place for everyone in England so I decided to follow my heart and live my life here in Italy. It's a decision I have never regretted. I love the climate, the food and the people and I have been lucky enough to make some nice friends, including Martina who I met at the seafront and who owns the Galleria de Sole art gallery.

Back home Ellie and Daphne have combined their skills and set up Lakeland Brides, offering a bespoke dress and make-up service, to excellent reviews from customers. I'm so happy for them. Daphne's relationship with Paul is still going strong.

Greg and Hannah are now living together at Lake View as man and wife and I couldn't be happier for them.

Katy is having a whale of a time on the high seas. She surprised us with a visit recently when her ship sailed into Como, and she had a bloke called Neil in tow. I asked her if Neil was 'the one' but she just laughed and said she was having far too much of a good time to settle down.

And Mum and Dad? Well, despite my reservations, they seem to be having the time of their lives, heading off for frequent weekends away and giving Jean ideas for the next themed night at the pub. In many ways I don't feel as though I've set up home in a different country, as I still feel very connected to the people I love and my family are even flying over here to spend Christmas with us. Our new arrival will be two months old by then.

There's one thing that my family and I can't seem to agree on though and that's where Fabio and I should have our wedding. Hannah feels there can only be one place and that is back home in Glenridding, possibly at the B&B. It's a possibility but the garden here in Varenna would more likely mean a guarantee of sunshine. The wedding will hopefully take place next year, so there's plenty of time for more disagreements!

In the meantime, I can't wait for my new son to meet his family. Italy is my home now but a little part of me will always belong to the Lake District. It's as if I have split my heart in two. And home is where the heart is…

A Letter from Sue Roberts

I want to say a huge thank you for choosing to read *My Very Italian Holiday* – I hope you enjoyed it. I had a great time writing about Gina's journey to happiness, with the support of her sister Hannah and friends Katy and Daphne. It was nice to see things getting back on track with her mum too!

If you want to keep up-to-date with all my latest releases, just sign up at the following link. Your email address will never be shared and you can unsubscribe at any time.

www.bookouture.com/sue-roberts

I hope you loved *My Very Italian Holiday* and if you did, I would be very grateful if you could write a review. I'd love to hear what you think, and it makes such a difference helping new readers to discover one of my books for the first time.

This is my second novel, the first being *My Big Greek Summer* which is available online now.

I love hearing from my readers – you can get in touch on my Facebook page or through Twitter.

Thanks,
Sue

suerobertsauthor

@SueRobertsautho

Acknowledgments

With many thanks to:

My publishers, Bookouture, and my editor, Christina Demosthenous, who took over the reins for my second book and made the transition seamless. To Natasha Harding for her continued support and encouragement.

To the design team for their fabulous book cover and to Kim Nash and Noelle Holton for their tireless publicity and promotion.

To my long-term partner, Derek, for quietly keeping things ticking over at home when I'm writing and for all of his support.

To my sister Rebecca, who always manages to make me laugh and for her belief in my writing.

Lastly, to all my grandchildren and Olivia Foley for her weekly visits and insight into the teenage world.